Persephone's Song

by

Mary M. Schmidt

 Los Hombres Press

Persephone's Song

All rights reserved. No part of this book may be reproduced or transmitted in any manner whatsoever without written permission except in the case of brief passages quoted in reviews. For further information, write Los Hombres Press, Box 632729, San Diego, CA 92163-2729.

Cover by Lue Sinclair

Library of Congress Cataloging in Publication Data
Persephone's Song
ISBN 1-879603-02-0

Printed in the United States of America

Copyright ©1992 by Mary M. Schmidt

First Edition

1 2 3 4 5 6 7 8 9 10

Los Hombres Press
Box 632729
San Diego, CA 92163-2729

ACKNOWLEDGEMENTS

Many thanks to Jacqueline Lichtenberg
and Charles Butler III, for believing in me.

To Heinz Heger, for invaluable information
on the pink triangle.

And to the staff of the Lambda Rising book store,
Dupont Circle, Washington DC,
for innumerable kindnesses.

DEDICATION

to R. H.

Chapter 1

CONSIDER THIS BOWL OF TANGERINES ON THE KITCHEN COUNTER, the sort of thing you might see in a still life painting. It was the first thing I noticed the minute we got in. I picked up the one on top and gave it a squeeze. It was so firm and fresh. I remember....

"Longianna." I heard Phillipe speak my name.

"I bought these this morning," I said. "Aren't they fine? I was thinking that maybe I could interest Rory in eating a few. He always did like them."

"Yes. They're splendid tangerines. But look at you, you're soaking wet."

"I am?"

I saw myself reflected in the sliding glass door that leads to the back yard pool. Outside, an angry rain coursed down; the night was so black it seemed the Earth had swallowed us up.

How absurd I looked. I wore the outfit for my Minnie the Moocher number at Mighty Joe Young's Safari Lounge. My hair hung in wet strands; my make-up was disintegrating.

"Longianna, if you don't get out of that dress...."

"Are you afraid I'll *catch* something?"

"Yes," Phillipe said. "I am. And we can't afford to have you sick too. Not now."

I pulled a strand of hair out of my face. "Have you heard about Minnie the Moocher?" I asked. "She sure could kick the gong around."

"Yes, Gianna, I have."

"It was Rory who got me the job at Joe Young's. Singing, dancing, mooching. He was always so good to me, always there when I needed him." I began to shake. "And then this had to happen."

For an instant I thought I was going to fall apart. *I cannot do this*, I thought. *I'm the only well person in this house. I have to be strong.*

I was still holding on to the tangerine.

"Gianna," Phillipe said.

"No, no, I'll be all right. This tangerine. I gave Rory one, once."

"Rory told me you did. And of how much he appreciated that first tangerine."

"Did he now?"

"More than you know."

"Phillipe, I'm wondering if we did the right thing tonight. I mean, putting Rory in that stupid hospital." I sniffled. "If we did nothing, he'd be dead by now. But I couldn't let him die like *that*, fighting it. The doctor said he had a temperature of 107. I don't know how much more he can take. Or, how much more I can either."

"You stayed with Rory," Phillipe said. "You stayed on, even after his so-called lover George abandoned him."

"George, that creep!" I said. "He was out of here so fast. I couldn't leave even though Rory wanted me to. I remember the time Rory first told me, 'Gianna, I have AIDS.' I said I'd stay. That he shouldn't be alone in this big house at night. 'No, you can't,' he said. 'You don't know what I'm going to look like. You don't know what I'm going to *smell* like. You're a nice straight girl, Gianna. Go find a nice straight guy. I can't be a ball and chain to you.'"

"You stayed anyway."

Again, I sniffled. "I wish I knew why. My family is furious with me. My grandmother's the only one who thinks I'm doing the right thing, but she's thousands of miles away. I miss her so much. My parents think I'm insane. My sister Donna talks to me on the phone but won't come near me. If you want to know the truth, I think Donna soaks her phone in boiling Lysol after each of our little chats. She wants me to have every drop of my blood tested before I'm allowed near her spoiled-rotten kid."

"It sounds as if you and Donna get along as well as my mother and her sister Rosie. They've been at each other's throats for nearly eighty years."

I giggled. Phillipe could always do that to me.

"At any rate, before I became a lawyer, I was a priest, used to dealing in absolutes. And I must tell you that what you did tonight, in getting Rory to the hospital, was *absolutely right.*"

"If you really think so...."

"I know so. And now there's one other thing. You must absolutely change into something warm and dry."

"All right. But I'm too wired to sleep. If it's not too much trouble, will you please make some of that perked coffee?"

"It's not what you need at this time of night, but I will, for us both. And you'll tell me about that first tangerine you gave him."

I went halfway down the stairs to my room, realized I still had the tangerine in my hand, and went back to the kitchen to return it to the bowl.

The coffee smelled terrific. The rain hadn't let up, but I felt safe from it.

I hurried to change into something dry. When I came back up, Phillipe asked about the tangerine I'd given Rory. "Was it the first day you met him?"

"Oh, no. But I'll never forget the first day. Boy, was I scared. It's funny how it seems like a thousand years ago. I was taking the elevator up to the sixth floor with this really dippy woman. She told me her name was Madge."

"What's yours?" she asked.

"Longianna," I repeated. "Longianna Raimondi."

"I've never heard one like that before."

"I was named after my grandmother in Monreale."

"Monreale? Where's that?"

"In Sicily," I said, hoping I wouldn't hear a Mafia joke.

"Here's where you'll be. Some of the people you'll be taking calls for have offices on this floor—Harry Morrison, Suzanne White, Rory McCormick."

Not wanting to start off on the wrong foot, I didn't say that Morrison's tropical plants made his office look like the set of a Tarzan movie, nor that White's was a nightmare in French Provincial. McCormick's, though, was different. It reminded me of the Villa of the Mysteries in Pompeii.

Whoever this Rory McCormick is, I thought, *he's the only one of the pack with any taste.*

"Here's your phone with all the numbers. The names are right on it. Now, say, if thirty-six rings, you say, 'Luxor Studios, Mr. McCormick's office, may I help you?'"

"No problem."

"Any questions?" Madge asked.

"Just one for now. This is a studio, right?"

"Of course."

"So why do people call the lower level the produce section?"

"You've never heard that expression before?" Her voice dropped to a whisper. "The men there are fruits. You know what I mean?"

"Yes," I said, sorry I'd been so naive. I'd never cared for that sort of comment, but, I desperately needed this job and couldn't afford to antagonize anyone.

"You're not that way yourself, are you? I mean, you're married?"

"No. I'm not 'that way.' But with luck I won't be married for much longer. Raimondi is my maiden name. My divorce is in the works."

"Oh, I'm...sorry."

"Don't be. Getting rid of Renzo is the smartest thing I ever did." I hoped that changed the subject. It didn't.

"Let me explain something to you while I have the chance," Madge went on. "It's not just the lower level. This whole place is overrun with *them*."

Them. It gave me a taste of what I'd gotten myself into.

"The powers that be on the top floor don't like it. You know Luxor and Grimalkyn Records and Tapes are owned by Snappy Cereal. Snappy has an *image* to protect. I'm sure you've seen those Snappy commercials."

"I have. Glorified heterosexuality, first thing in the morning."

"So around here, most of *them* stay in their closets or they don't get anywhere. Or, they're careful. Some of our straightest-looking stars, would you believe...? If there's any bad publicity, it's studio policy to deny it."

"Is that so," I said.

"But there's something I'd better warn you about. If it's another husband you're after, you'd better forget Rory McCormick."

That surprised me. "If the powers on the top floor don't let gay people get too far...."

"What's Rory McCormick doing on Six? They tolerate him, all right. They do more than tolerate him because he won an Oscar. He's the one who composed the score for our LYNX science fiction epic. So they give him what he wants. And behind his back, they rip him to shreds. Pity about him. So good looking. He doesn't act queer, but is he ever. I have it on the best authority. You need anything, I'm down the hall."

I studied the Luxor health and retirement plans and tried not to worry. This job had to work out. Going back to Renzo was out of the question. Renzo. What did I ever see in him?

"You've got a great voice. You'll go far," Renzo had predicted. "I've got connections. In no time I'll have you cut an album."

Renzo's pitch was the old "stick-with-me-I'll-make-you-a-star" line. He had me convinced he knew what he was talking about. He really did have connections in the music business, people who knew people who turned out to be emptying wastebaskets at Grimalkyn.

My parents were fooled by Renzo's charm and wept for joy when I married him. They thought I was finally going to settle down and be like my sister Donna.

What I'd failed to comprehend was that Renzo's horn wasn't the only thing he was tooting. At least I had sense enough not to get pregnant.

We lived in a filthy apartment in a Hollywood slum. Renzo didn't care where he was as long as he could stay high. He used to steal money from my purse for cocaine. We had our phone and electricity cut off before I decided, *enough*, and left him.

How different this was from Donna's life. She and her husband are both executives for a major computer company. Donna "has it all"—husband, a glamorous career, and a baby. My parents never cease to remind me.

Of course Donna never wanted to sing. And at that point in my life, neither did I. My career in music had only been a series of sad mistakes.

I never should have tried.

Extension thirty-six rang, breaking into my thoughts.

"Luxor Studios, Mr. McC—"

"Is he there? *Is he there?* Rory has got to be there!"

"I'm sorry, Sir, Mr. McCormick hasn't arrived yet. Would you care to leave—"

"Is he in the building? Can someone go look for him?"

What could I do? I couldn't leave my place. And I didn't even know what Rory McCormick looked like.

"This is a terrible emergency! I must get hold of him right away!"

"Sir, if I could have Mr. McCormick call you—"

"You tell him to call me the instant he gets in! He knows who I am! He'd better." So saying, the caller hung up.

"Wait, I don't know who you are. Oh, don't tell me I've screwed up my very first call!"

I stepped over to the water cooler and took a Valium. I'd been taking them since I filed for divorce. Rory McCormick would be furious over my loss of an emergency call.

He could get me canned for this, I thought, which would look great on my résumé. The Valium wasn't helping. Maybe I needed another.

At that moment, the elevator door opened.

"Are you the new receptionist? I'm Rory McCormick."

"My name is, ah, Mr. McCormick, Sir, I—" He must have heard my knees knocking. Thirty-six rang again.

"L-l-luxor Studios. Mr. McCormick's office. May I...."

"He's got to be there! I've called every other place he could possibly be! I've tried his car phone! If he's not there, I'll just die!"

"Just a moment, Sir." I said. "Mr. McCormick, it's for you. He called earlier but didn't give his name. He says it's an emergency."

"It is, is it? I think I know who this is. Do you mind if I take it out here? I won't be long."

"No, go ahead."

"George?" he said. "I thought so. I'm on the hall phone so I can't talk long. What's the problem this time? All right, it can't be that bad. Take a deep breath and tell me what happened."

From the one-sided conversation, I learned that: 1) George had put a souffle in the oven; 2) George went out to check the chlorine in the pool; 3) George went back to find black smoke billowing out of the oven; 4) George tried to rescue the souffle, but it was beyond human help; 5) Gobs of goo had baked onto the oven walls and the whole kitchen stank.

A look of despair crossed Rory's face. "George, as my Ma used to say, 'Glory be to Saint Patrick.' Are you sure that's all? No volcanos, floods or earthquakes? No, I'm not mad. Here's what I want you to do. Are you listening? Good. Open the window. Turn on the fan. Then, look on the third shelf of the pantry. You'll see the Squeeky Kleen. Use it according to the directions on the label. Do you think you can manage that?"

A torrent of words came through the phone.

"No, George. I won't be home till late. I told you why. Yes, because I have to take Carlos to the clinic for his appointment."

More frantic words.

"You're being ridiculous. What am I supposed to do? Wear a space suit with a life support system? Will that make you happy? Let's not discuss this now. I'm not going to tie up this phone any longer. I'll see you tonight. Yes, I love you too. Goodbye, George."

Rory hung up. "George has got to get his act together. Don't let him get the better of you."

"I'll try not to. Tell me, does he call here often? Just so I'll know what to expect."

"Often enough." Then Rory added, "I suppose you've guessed. He's my lover."

"No problem with me, Mr. McCormick."

"Please. 'Mr. McCormick' reminds me of Sister Martha in the eighth grade. She was always leaving 'Mr. McCormick' in charge of the class while marching 'Rocky' to the principal's office. I'm just Rory, all right? Rory Michael if you get fed up with me."

"I'm Gianna, except when I mess up, and I probably will."

"Don't *worry* about it and you'll do fine. Now, here's the payoff. Will you run me ten copies of this draft?"

"I'd be delighted."

So it was that I made my first friend at work. The next day I learned what a good friend he was. I had a massive order to run through our largest copier. I was singing "Volare" as it ran, not aware of my audience of one.

"Say, you're good," Rory said.

"Ooops. I'm not disturbing you, am I?"

"Have you ever sung professionally?"

"Yes. But I'm sorry I did." I told him about Renzo. "It's just led to one big mess. So I think it's best not to try any more."

"Yeah, but just because you messed up once.... And if Renzo's such a jerk, you can't let him go on running your life."

"It was a mistake I've learned from. No more singing for me."

"You won't change your mind?"

"I'm sure I won't."

"If you do, I want to be the first to know. I'm part owner of a place called Mighty Joe Young's Safari Lounge. I doubt you've heard of it; it's a gay bar."

"In fact, I have." Many big names had passed through there.

"We welcome new talent. And we could use someone like you who can sing soprano. I can't promise anything but you could try."

"But...but...Joe Young's is big time, isn't it?"

"I'd like to think so. Actually, it's a good place to practice in front of a live audience. Will you think about it?"

I shook my head no. "I'd better not. I don't feel up to it yet. It was kind of you to offer, though."

"If you change your mind, I'm right across the hall. Seriously, Gianna, I know a good voice when I hear it."

"*That good?*" I asked with skepticism.

"I know *good.* I hear enough *bad.* And I often hear *ghastly.*"

It was inevitable. One day I told Rory, "Yes, give me an audition." That was after I learned how easy it was to talk to him about my marriage. I told him about Donna and why my parents thought she was perfect.

"I have a twin sister, and she's perfect too," Rory told me.

"How? Is she a highly-paid executive?"

"No. Believe it or not, she's a nun."

"You're kidding."

"I swear. At least, to the best of my knowledge. When I came out, twenty years ago, Pat was determined to enter the convent. I guess she did."

"You weren't around to see it?"

"I couldn't stay. My family refused to accept my being gay. In fact, they had a plot to marry me off to Benedict Cardinal Corby's niece."

"Awesome!"

"My sweet fiancée. I couldn't stand her. I let her keep the ring, just to be rid of her. And besides, I was in love with someone else."

"Oh," I said, wondering who that someone was but not ready to ask. "And, your twin? What sort of nun is she? Which order?"

"Divine Compassion."

"You must be kidding. Donna and I both went to Divine Compassion High."

"Then you must both be good, proper Catholic girls."

"Donna sopped that up better than I did. Besides, I'm not in the Church any longer."

"Neither am I."

"For twenty years?"

"I've survived."

"But you haven't seen your family in all that time?"

"It's impossible, Gianna. My father was your friendly neighborhood queerbasher. He couldn't live with the fact that his only-begotten son, with whom he wasn't the least bit pleased, was one of *them*. My twin was in his camp. And my mother worried about what the neighbors would think. No, they're all better off without me."

I found such coldness incredible. If my kid won an Oscar, I'd want to know. How could anyone be ashamed of such a decent person?

Rory told me other things he felt bad about too, particularly the way George acted. He told me his lover's ranting and raving had caused the former receptionist to leave for lunch one day and never come back.

"Is George insecure?" I asked. "Is that why he invents all of these disasters?"

"Maybe," Rory said. "but not like I was when I came out. I was so insecure it was pathetic. No, it's more that George is scared."

"Of what?" I asked.

"These days, there's a lot to be scared of," Rory said. "But I can't protect George from the thing he fears most—"

My phone rang. It had a way of doing that at the worst of times.

And then, out of the depths of my ignorance, I offered him the tangerine.

"Would you like this?"

Rory looked up from the script he was studying. "Sure, Gianna. Don't you want it?"

"I want it, all right. But all I can have is the rind."

"Did you lose a bet?"

"No. But I'm on this new diet. You eat all you want, except every other day, when you eat only tangerine rinds."

"I see. And where did you find out about this great new diet? From *Nightfall*, or one of the other finer tabloids?"

"You know Carlos on the lower level? He told me all about it. He's been on it for a while and the amount of weight he's lost is incredible. In fact, I think he's lost too much. So I asked him how he did it, and he said...."

"Jesus, Mary and Joseph. Shut the door. There's something I'd better explain."

"Did I do something wrong?"

"No. But there's something Carlos wants to keep quiet. So promise me you won't tell anyone else."

"Of course."

"All right. Carlos is very ill. His weight loss has nothing to do with egg shells, plum peelings or tangerine rinds."

"I'm sorry, I didn't know." I looked down at the pattern in the carpet for a moment, then I whispered, "Carlos has AIDS, doesn't he?"

"Yes. Gianna, he does. And there are other problems. Mind-game playing on the top floor; they're trying to cut off his health insurance. His landlord wants to be rid of him. So I do what I can for Carlos. Then I have to go home to George."

"This is what George is so scared of."

"George used to be a licensed vocational nurse. He became a flight attendant because he couldn't stand to see what this sickness does. He won't have the word AIDS spoken in his presence. If it's mentioned on TV, he changes the channel."

"And you have to put up with that?"

"He's so scared he'll get AIDS. Or that he already has it. So he cooks up these disasters as background noise. I can't protect him. There's too much I simply can't do. I'm sorry, Gianna, you don't need to hear all of this."

"Maybe I do. I hear things, I read things, but I'm straight."

"So many have died, and it just goes on and on. People you see here at Luxor every day. They're like Carlos; they lose too much weight, and they're gone."

"Would you like my tangerine?" I asked him.

"It's yours," he said.

"I insist," I told him.

Rory had to leave early that day. The next day, Madge called in with a migraine and I had to stay late to keep up. I didn't like being alone; I kept imagining a grim reaper making his way up the corridor. I nearly jumped when the elevator door opened.

It was Rory, and he looked like hell. He was dressed in jeans, a LYNX shirt and running shoes. "Gianna," he said. "I'm glad you're here. Will you please make two copies of this and bring it to my office? I have to make some calls."

"Yeah, sure."

I couldn't help but notice that the paper Rory gave me to copy was from a funeral home. He was on the phone and not speaking English. I learned later that the language was Alsatian French. Then I saw the notes on his legal pad.

Carlos had died at six that morning.

"Jesus. I'm so sorry," I said when Rory hung up.

He leaned back in his swivel chair. "I told you I know *good* when I hear it. Well, Carlos had a voice that could span four octaves. Four, can you believe it? He was twenty-two years old. What do I do with him now? Put him in the ground is what. Forgive me, Gianna, I've been up all night. All night long! What a fight that kid put up."

"It's not fair," I said. "It's not right." Rory's eyes were red and swollen.

"You can do me a favor," he said. "Tell people I won't be back till Wednesday. After the funeral I'm going to San Francisco. I need to be with my Number One for a while."

"Sure," I said. "Is he the one with the beautiful French accent?"

"Phillipe François Leveque."

"It's a joy to take his messages."

"I'll tell him you said so. He was my *first*. And he's the only one who can handle me when I don't feel quite rational."

Rory stuffed papers into his attaché case. "You're darn right it's not fair. Phillipe's got it, too."

"Oh, no."

"He's got ARC, AIDS-related complex. He's on AZT. Which works fine for him. But for how long? Well, at least George has to work. He'll be in Tahiti, so I won't have to put up with *that*."

"Rory, would you like a Valium? I've got some with me."

"You're taking that stuff?"

"Well, yeah. It helps to deal with Renzo's crap."

"I thought it was helping me once. I got addicted to it. Don't fool with it."

During the telling of this story, I'd gone through two cups of coffee. There was no way I'd be able to sleep that night.

"And that's how you found out about me," Phillipe said.

"His Number One," I said. "He tossed aside the Cardinal's niece, in favor of you."

"Thank God he did."

"Rory did so many kind things for me. He got me that second job, singing at Mighty Joe Young's. And he got me off the Valium. When he took me home and saw the dump I was living in, he had me move into his spare room downstairs. 'It's a maid's room,' he said. 'Adoración just quit, thanks to George. But you won't be the maid. You can have it at a nominal rate till you're back on your feet. I'll make it clear to George that you're off-limits for all his disasters.'"

"At least, living here, you were able to stay when he got sick. But let me ask you, Gianna. Why did you do that? You were free to go at any time."

"He wanted me to go. I don't know. Part of it was gratitude for all he'd done. And the other part? I guess I felt sorry for him. He'd wake up at night, soaking wet all over, looking like a lost sea-creature washed up on the beach. Who would change the sheets, if not me? I hate to admit it. I just plain felt sorry."

"You still do?"

"I don't know. I don't think it's possible to feel only pity for someone like Rory. He lives with so much pain, and he won't let it destroy him. As for what I do feel...Phillipe, I just don't know."

"All right," he said. "All right."

I sensed what he was thinking. *Do you love him?* Did I love the most unavailable man I have ever met? There was no way I could answer a question like that.

"May I ask you something?" I said.

"Of course."

"I told you about my family. At least they're still speaking to me. What about the McCormicks? Has there really been no contact since 1968?"

"None at all. We did learn that Rory's father died on Christmas day in 1981. A friend back East sent me a copy of the obituary. It didn't list a son among the survivors."

"They really are that bad."

"No, Gianna. Just frightened and trapped in their own little world. A world that Rory and I don't fit into."

I poured myself a third cup of coffee. "Do you know what I was thinking?" I asked. "If there were some way I could make contact with the McCormicks. Even if they hang up on me. Something like this, and he still has a mother and a twin. They ought to be told."

"It would be a great kindness. Certainly, it would be more merciful than letting them learn it through the papers. And they wouldn't want to hear it from me. But be warned that their first impulse may be to reject any attempt you make."

"I wouldn't feel right if I didn't try. Rory told me that his twin became a Divine Compassion nun. I could start there."

"Go carefully if you do, and don't expect a miracle."

"You knew Pat. What was she like in 1968?"

"Nothing like Rory," Phillipe began. "You'd never even know they were twins. They were opposites in every way."

We talked for awhile, then Phillipe went to bed. I sat alone in the kitchen, thinking of what he had nearly asked me.

Did I love Rory?

I honestly don't know.

Chapter 2

SISTER AGNES HAD BEEN DREAMING. She was making her way up the aisle of Mary Queen of Martyrs Cathedral. A choir of monks sang *Veni Creator Spiritus*. Seated on a throne in front of the altar, Pope Paul VI waited for her. Beside him stood Benedict Cardinal Corby holding a gold crown to be placed on her head. In the crowd Sister Agnes saw her parents and smiled at them. Her mother shed tears of joy, her father gave her a thumbs-up.

"I knew our little girl could do it, Gertrude." he said.

"Oh, Edward. This makes up for everything."

Somewhere a telephone was ringing.

"Wait...no...this is wrong," she said, suddenly confused. "Pope Paul is dead. Cardinal Corby is dead. My father is dead. My mother's confined to a nursing home. Why am I here? What have I done, that they should honor me?"

She woke up. The shining hands on her alarm clock said five minutes of three. The phone on the table outside her cell was ringing. Sister Agnes pulled herself out of her single bed.

At this unholy hour, she thought, *all the calls would be drunks or wrong numbers*. She stormed out of her cell and picked up the receiver. "What is it that you want!" she snapped.

A woman's voice in a long-distance mist said, "Is this the Divine Compassion Convent on Wheeler Avenue?"

"Yes, and it's three o'clock in the morning."

"Oh, no." the caller said. "Forgive me, I wasn't thinking. I forgot you're three hours ahead. Stupid of me."

"What seems to be the trouble?" Sister Agnes said, as if to a recalcitrant student.

"I'm trying to reach a Sister of Divine Compassion whose name was Patricia Marie McCormick."

Sweet Jesus. It's me this one is looking for.

"I'm sorry that I don't know the name she took, but do you know where I might find her?"

"*Why* do you need to find her?"

"Sister, she has a twin. Rory Michael McCormick."

Blessed Mother. It's been twenty years. What's Rory done this time? Wasn't it bad enough when he and that radical Father Leveque went queer on each other and left town? Stay where you are, Rory. Stay in the past, buried in time. Don't come back and disturb us now.

"No such person is here," Sister Agnes said quickly. "My name in the world was McCormick. I would know if we had another Sister by that name. And I never knew a Rory Michael."

There. It was done. Saint Peter was famous for saying, "I know not the man." But I have no choice.

"Oh. I apologize for waking you for nothing."

"Why is it that you need to contact this Patricia Marie McCormick?" Sister Agnes asked. *Surely it's late where you are too. What is so important that it couldn't wait till morning? At least let me know what trouble Rory's in now.*

"I wanted to get in touch with his family and let them know Rory's sick."

"How sick?"

"He almost died tonight."

He did what!

How dare he!

"What's the matter with him?" she asked in spite of herself.

"He has AIDS, Sister."

"He has what?" Oh, surely not that. Not with Aloysius Sweeney, president of the Traditionalist League, coming to the honors assembly. Sweeney was demanding a quarantine for all persons who tested positive. Sweeney wanted them isolated from so-called Decent People.

"He has Acquired Immune Deficiency Syndrome," said the caller, close to tears.

"I understand," Sister Agnes said.

"I really think his family ought to know. So I'm trying to find his sister. That is, if she's still in the Divine Compassion Order. If I have to, I'll call the motherhouse in Rome. It's all right, I speak Italian."

Oh, no. Whatever you do, don't do that. "Ms...ah...."

"Raimondi. Longianna Raimondi."

"Ms. Raimondi. I'm Sister Agnes. I understand...in dealing with Mr. McCormick's sickness...you're under a great deal of stress."

"I guess it shows. I mean, forgetting I'm three hours behind is pretty—"

"You're under too much pressure. I'll see what I can do. Give me your telephone number."

Longianna gave her the number with a Los Angeles area code and spelled her name.

"I'll see if Patricia Marie McCormick is still in the Divine Compassion Order."

"You *will?*"

"I didn't say that I'll find her. The Church has undergone radical changes, and many Sisters have left. But I'll do what I can and call you tomorrow night, one way or the other."

"That would be *terrific.* Let me give you some information that might help you find her."

Sister Agnes heard bits of her own life played back in fast-forward. "She and Rory were born June twenty-first, 1946. Her father was Edward Vincent McCormick. Her mother's maiden name was Gertrude Mary Mulligan. Edward McCormick was the president of McCormick Ford on Wheeler Avenue, not far from where you are now."

"That certainly is a coincidence."

"Rory told me that during the late Sixties, McCormick Ford was the largest-volume dealership in the state."

That, it was, she remembered, *until my father was driven to drink and ruin. By Rory.*

"Patricia would have entered the convent in late 1968 or early 1969."

"That will be most useful," Sister Agnes said. "And now, Ms. Raimondi, I suggest you go get some rest. You must have had a difficult day."

"Yes. But you've given me new hope, Sister Agnes. It would mean a lot to Rory, if he could see Pat one more time before it's too late. They had problems. Rory has told me many times he wished he could have worked them out."

Longianna knows me as well as I know myself, Sister Agnes thought.

"I'll do my best, Ms. Raimondi. Now good-night."

"Good-night, Sister Agnes. Good luck."

Sweet Jesus. Sweet, suffering Jesus on the cross. My twin has AIDS.

She staggered back into her cell, collapsed into her bed and pulled up the covers. *Well, Twin*, she thought, *you always did have everything.*

Sister Agnes stuffed her head under her pillow and worked out her plan. It was simple. Tomorrow night, she'd call Longianna and say that Pat McCormick had left the Divine Compassion Order in 1975 to get married. Further, that she'd taken her husband's name, but no one recalled what that *was*.

"There's no more McCormick Ford," she'd conclude. "The dealership at Fifth and Wheeler is now Sunshine Toyota."

"Problems," Sister Agnes mumbled to herself. "Rory told this Longianna that there were problems, did he? If there were, he was the cause of all of them. We were a *happy* family. We had a lovely home on Lemon Tree Lane, right down the street from Saint Catherine's Church. My mother *stayed in her home*, my father worked hard to build up McCormick Ford and provide us with the best. And then Rory had to go and spoil everything."

She imagined her psychology professor saying, "You sound quite angry with Rory."

"I am not," she defended herself. "I forgave him long ago as is my duty. But I can't let him back into my life. Consider what he *does.*"

"What does Rory do that's so terrible?" the professor would ask.

Sister Agnes rolled over, hoping for a few hours sleep before the bell rang for Mass.

"What does he do?" she argued. "Dad worried himself to death because of him. And it's Rory's fault that Ma's had three strokes."

Again, she rolled over. *What does Rory do that's so terrible?*
He makes love to other men!
And now, Sister Agnes, he's going to die very soon.

She remembered herself as a child. She'd been Daddy's girl, the image of Eddie McCormick. Big, her hair pulled back into a tight pony tail and her wide body covered in the uniform of Saint

Catherine's School. She had Mulligan eyes. Green like spring, her only good feature.

Rory, however, was different. He looked like his mother who'd resembled Alice Faye.

Patricia herself had grown too fast, been too clumsy. Rory was slender and blonde and beautiful. When Ma took them shopping, old ladies stopped and made a fuss over Rory.

Patricia didn't like it; neither did Eddie.

"Gertrude, he's not going to be a little boy forever!" Eddie would rant. "He's going to be a man. Men have to learn to defend themselves. They have to learn how to fight."

"My son is not going to engage in fights, Edward," Ma replied.

At age nine, Rory came home with his lip swollen and a rip in his jacket. He'd been attacked by Tommy, a great mountain of a twelve-year-old.

"My poor little baby," said Ma. "What happened?"

"Nothing, Ma," Rory said.

"Patricia, did you see this?"

"Yes, Ma."

"Well?"

"Tommy went up to Rory and used that word you said we weren't supposed to say. The one that means odd or peculiar. Rory tried to keep on walking."

"*What* word?" her father asked.

"Queer."

"Aw, for Christ's sake," Eddie muttered. "I won't let anyone call my son *that.*" He turned to Rory. "That's a very bad word Tommy called you. If anyone says it again, even in fun, you let him have it, you hear?"

"Edward!" Ma said.

As it turned out, Eddie was right about one thing: the twins weren't little forever.

Pat was the first to change. She loathed what was happening to her body. A stubborn case of acne set in and stayed with her into her thirties. Rory, however, had flawless skin and perfect bones. On him, the green Mulligan eyes were like precious gems. Where was the fairness in that?

Sister Agnes looked at the clock. Four-thirty.

When they were fifteen, she thought the world was going to end. Eddie caught Rory in his car with Jimmy Starke.

The next day the left side of Rory's face looked like raw meat.

His eye was black and swollen shut. Gertrude tried to pretend there was nothing wrong. She told Rory to go to school as usual, to tell Father Benoit he'd fallen down the stairs. Rory wouldn't get out of bed. "I prefer not to be seen in public like this," he said.

Eddie came out of the bathroom, freshly shaven, a wrist held limply. *"I pwefer not to be theen in public like thith."* he said. "Jee-zuz Christ!"

What's going on? was the question she dared not ask. "Patricia, it's off to school with you this instant," Ma insisted.

Rory stayed in bed all day. At dinnertime Gertrude took him a tray of food.

"Gertrude, if he's hungry, let him come to the table," Eddie said. "You baby him. That's ninety-nine per cent of the problem."

"Is Rory sick or something?" Patricia asked.

"Yes, Honey, he is," Eddie told her. "But it's not like mumps or the time you both had polio. This is something inside his head. It's bad, Patricia. So don't discuss it with anyone else. That means don't talk to Eileen Daley, even if she is your best friend."

"Yes, Dad. But can Rory get well?"

"I'm going to have to find out. Some people are coming over to try and help me find a cure."

"Who?"

"One of them's Dave Wolfe."

Dad had called his lawyer. Rory was in more trouble than she could imagine.

"And the other's our pastor."

When Ma took her place at the table, he didn't acknowledge her presence.

"Christ, if my old man had lived to see *this*. His grandson. His namesake."

"Oh, Edward, *please.*" Ma said.

"I'll tell you this. He doesn't take after *my* side of the family."

At seven, Gertrude was exiled to the kitchen. Patricia retreated to her room, planting herself by the heat register where she could hear every word from the living room.

Mr. Wolfe was the first to arrive. "First, about the Starkes," he said.

"I should have killed him," said Eddie. "Every time I think about his hands on my son—"

"It's a good thing you didn't hurt him," Wolfe said.

"What jury would convict me?"

"You don't want to go through that, Eddie. I had a long talk today with Mr. and Mrs. Starke. If you drop charges, they'll move away."

Eddie considered. "Yeah, well, I guess that's fair," he agreed. "Provided they take their sicko kid with them."

Pat heard the doorbell ring. "Monsignor, how are you?" her father said. "I believe you know my attorney, Dave Wolfe?"

The three men spoke in low voices, which Pat strained to hear.

"I know you're upset," Monsignor Hayes said. "But you've had some time to cool off. Now tell me exactly what happened."

"I caught my son having sex with another boy."

"Ah," said Hayes. "Now, are you *sure*? Boys often indulge in harmless horseplay."

"I know what I saw. I've been worried about Rory for a good long time. He's growing so fast. But he's not interested in girls. And that's not right."

Pat smelled cigarette smoke. "So I made it my business to keep an eye on him. And everything was Jimmy, Rory and Jimmy. Always together. I couldn't even make a call, Rory was on the phone with Jimmy. Then last night I found out for sure...."

A long silence followed. Then Pat heard a high keen of grief and understood why she'd been barred from the meeting.

Dad's crying. Men cry! That's their secret.

"Rory's my only son! He means the world to me. Monsignor, did you ever ask yourself why Gertrude and I had only two kids? There were twelve in her family, seventeen in mine. That's the kind of family we wanted. But God sent us only two.

"Gertrude got as big as a battleship, in labor three days. It ripped up her insides so bad— But I figured I had a son to carry on my name, give me grandchildren. But if he's— if he's—"

"Maybe Rory was only under the temporary influence of this Jimmy."

"No, Monsignor, my son's a faggot."

Pat felt the blood drain from her face. So that was it. Rory, queer.

Hayes cleared his throat. "Eddie, the thing that concerns me most is the state of Rory's immortal soul. *If this keeps up*— Rory is now how old?"

"Sixteen next month."

"Good. Then I know we can save him."

"I'll try anything."

"I have a friend who specializes in cases like this. He's a medical doctor. A psychiatrist."

"You mean...a headshrinker?"

"Some would call Dr. Engel that, yes."

"You want Rory to go see him?"

"He has a remarkable rate of success in his work with teenagers. He uses what he calls aversion therapy. The patient is forced to confront how revolting these unnatural acts are, resulting in nausea at the very thought of—"

"A headshrinker. How much do those guys get? Twenty-five bucks an hour or so?"

"I think Dr. Engel may be a bit higher."

"Eddie, you have family health insurance at the dealership, don't you?" Wolfe asked.

"I can't let the people who work for me know this. Or at the insurance company. What do I tell them? My son's a queer? No, thanks. You may think I'm rich. I'm not as rich as a lot of people think. But Gertrude and I, we'll scrape up the dough. We've faced tough times before. That is, Monsignor, if you think this will work."

"Look, Eddie, suppose something else were wrong with Rory. A bent spine. Would you let that go?"

"No."

"It's the same principle. And here's the important thing: *you got to it in time*. While Rory is still young enough to be cured."

"All right, Monsignor. Give me Engel's number. I'll call him in the morning, set up an appointment."

"I'll say a special prayer for you."

"Twenty-five dollars an hour. I'll have to sell a lot more cars."

Monsignor Hayes said, "God will provide. And, Eddie, consider this like being in Confession. Not *one word* of what you have said will ever pass beyond these walls."

"That's right," said Dave Wolfe.

My twin is queer, Pat McCormick thought then. Now, *My twin has AIDS*.

She remembered her parents talking on that night. "Rory's a teenager, Edward," her mother said. "He's going through a stage."

"Oh, yeah? I was his age once, and believe me, that's one stage I never went through." Pat heard her father pacing. "If he steals, if he kills, I could learn to live with it.

"Why?" her father shouted, his words carrying out into the mild Spring night. "Because he's 'your baby?' Don't you see how much you're to blame for this, Gertrude? Fussing over him, treating him like goddam visiting royalty? Letting him take music lessons, music lessons." Eddie stormed down the stairs. "Aw, this family's nuts. If it weren't for my sweet Patricia, I'd flush them down the toilet."

He slammed the front door. The car lurched into reverse and sped down Lemon Tree Lane.

The bell for Mass called Sister Agnes away.

Sister Agnes Mary, O. D. C., (also known as Sister Agnes Agony of the Jungle), principal of Benedict Cardinal Corby High School for Girls, walked briskly up the stairs to the main entrance.

A no-nonsense expression bolted to her face, she wore a dark blue business suit with a veil and crucifix. In her right hand, she carried her attaché case, her raincoat slung over her left arm. It was a late summer day: cool and clear.

She passed before a woodcut of Saint Kristen, foundress of the Order of Divine Compassion. According to legend, Saint Kristen lived in Norway. The widow of a wealthy merchant, she led a life of luxury till the outbreak of the Black Plague. Moved by the suffering of its victims, she founded an order of nursing sisters with which she worked in one of the pest houses till she, too, died of the plague.

It was said that on the day she died, white roses fell from the sky instead of snow.

Across the lobby from Saint Kristen hung a large oil portrait of Benedict Cardinal Corby, 1900-1979, looking splendid in his red regalia, *capa magna* and gold pectoral cross.

"You'll never guess what happened to me at three o'clock this morning, Benny Old Boyo!" Sister Agnes muttered. Then she strode on to the privacy of her office.

Now, as she sat at her desk, she reached into her pocket and touched the scrap of paper on which she'd written the number with a 213 area code.

To Sister Agnes, death was a symbol of Divine favor because

God had called you. She thought of the last time she had seen her father, at the end of 1981.

His embalmed body, like a wax doll, was dressed in his best blue suit. A flag draped the bottom half of his casket; a rosary was entwined in his fingers. Flowers surrounded him; a vigil light burned. One person was missing, one whose name was not to be spoken. Eddie's dying wish was granted. "I will not have any queers around my casket," he had wheezed.

Dressed entirely in black, Gertrude kept watch beside Eddie. She was speaking with Biddy O'Toole, the housekeeper at Saint Catherine's during the late Sixties.

During Father Leveque's brief stay.

Sister Agnes was surprised to see Biddy. She thought she'd have died long ago. She had to be in her nineties.

After all that happened, Biddy had one hell of a nerve showing up. We did as we always did, we pretended nothing was wrong.

"Eddie was a wonderful man," the visitors told Gertrude. "Surely he's gone to a great reward."

Divine favor, indeed. Rory could not be buried in the Church. Not after what he had done.

"Unless he tells God he's sorry. I wonder...has he? Will he?" she asked herself.

Sister Agnes' fingers felt again for the paper in her pocket. *I'll have to ask Ms. Raimondi*, she thought. That was the very least she could do. Longianna. What an unusual name, like an Italian princess who sells beauty products on TV.

Chapter 3

On the way to the hospital I told Phillipe about my telephone call.

"I knew there was a Divine Compassion Convent on Wheeler Avenue," I told him. "So I got the number from Directory Assistance. I forgot it was three in the morning there."

"That got you into a little trouble, *n'est-ce pas?*"

"Sister Agnes was plain *pissed off*. When I told her why I needed Pat McCormick, she softened up. I'd thought that maybe, since the convent was right in that city, I'd find Pat. She wasn't there, but Sister Agnes is going to see if she's still in the Order. She's going to call me back tonight."

"That's very kind of her. Perhaps she's an exception. However, I don't think we should tell Rory about this."

"Not till we know for sure."

Looking back on that first call, maybe I should have been suspicious. It all seemed so easy. But there was too much else on my mind.

Phillipe and I took the elevator to the AIDS unit. Rory's temperature was down to an even hundred, a nurse told me, but still I feared what might have happened to his mind.

He appeared to be sleeping, but I didn't think he was.

"Rory?"

He opened his eyes. "Ja-na."

What a relief. "Look who I have with me."

"Pretzel." That's his name for Phillipe. "Pretzel. Stay? *I don't dare show how much I'm hurting inside.*

"I stay, *mon amour*," Phillipe said, giving Rory a kiss. "Is there anything you require?"

"My leg hurts."

Rory rarely complained, so I knew it was bad. It was his right leg, the one most affected by polio.

"He's just had a pain killer," the nurse said. "It hasn't had time to take effect."

"We will draw the pain out."

I remembered the Sunday afternoon about a year ago when I first suspected something was wrong with Rory. Tony, the first man I'd been serious about since Renzo, had called. His TV was on the fritz; could he please watch the Redskins-Cowboys game on mine?

It was Tony's first visit. "Nice place," he said.

"Glad you like it."

"Are the guys upstairs...are they—"

"Yes," I said.

"Doesn't that bother you?"

"Not in the least. They're neat, they're quiet, and so am I. We get along fine."

"How did you get a place like this, anyhow?"

"Let's just say I offered Rory a tangerine."

"Oh, yeah? If I gave him a five pound bag of oranges, would he—"

"I don't think so."

"To each his own."

During the third quarter, we heard a VA-ROOM going into the garage. "Is that a Porsche?" Tony asked.

"It's Rory's. So's this house."

"He's got it made."

"He's done well."

I heard Rory come into the house, go to the kitchen and open the fridge. Then I heard a loud crash. I dashed upstairs.

He sat on the kitchen floor, holding his right knee, going "dammit, dammit, dammit."

"Are you all right?"

"I'm...fine. Fool thing just gave out on me."

"Let me see. You went down pretty hard."

"No, it's nothing. It does this sometimes."

"Look, Mr. Modesty. All you have to do is roll up your pants leg. Your knee might swell."

"No, there's nothing wrong."

"Can you get up?"

"Certainly I can get up."

"Men," I said. "So stubborn."

After the game Tony wanted to fool around on the couch. I tried, but I know he had a better time than I did. I was still worried about Rory.

Something is off-center, I thought. *Something is here in this house that doesn't belong.*

I watched Phillipe draw the pain out of Rory's damaged leg. Like a battle between good and evil: Phillipe's gentle hands against the sickness.

"This is better, no? You rest for a while; Gianna and I, we stay with you."

"I'm sorry I'm such a mess."

"No. Not a mess. You are beautiful always." Phillipe covered him. Soon he fell asleep.

"We won't disturb him, will we?" I asked.

"Rory would sleep through a nuclear war. When we were living in Washington, we bought a house on Capitol Hill, a little side street. Very quiet, I thought. On our first night, the sidewalk under our bedroom window got ripped up with jackhammers. This one? Slept through it all."

"Bothered you, I think."

"A bit. Gianna," Phillipe said, becoming very serious, "you must remember that Rory does have a family and always will. You and I, we are his family."

I knew what he meant. *In case Sister Agnes can't produce Pat.* In case it didn't work out.

Phillipe wore a gold medal on a chain around his neck. "May I see this?" I asked.

"Of course. You were a Divine Compassion student. I don't have to tell you what it means."

On one side were the words "Sancta Kristen Ora Pro Nobis;" on the other the image of a white rose. "My mother was educated by the Sisters of Divine Compassion in France. This was an award for distinguished scholarship in chemistry. She put that knowledge to good use."

"Rory told me she was a Resistance fighter."

"A demolitions expert. The Nazis never suspected her. They thought her a harmless widow and never thought to check her baby carriage. When they least expected it, ka-BOOM! Yes, *Maman* had a useful knowledge of chemistry."

"She sounds like quite a woman."

He smiled. "This Saint Kristen medal has quite a story behind it. It was not always mine. It was given to me by my cousin, Jean-Pierre."

I studied the gold medal, sparkling in the sunlight.

"He was the son of my mother's sister, Rosie. My mother gave this to him. When things got too hot at Rosie's house, Jean-Pierre came to live with us. My mother insisted. *Maman* loved him as if he were her own. So she gave him this. The ironic thing is that *Maman* was not at all religious. But she was willing to try anything.

"She wanted Jean-Pierre to go to America. To get out of Alsace, out of France, while there was still time. This was to protect him on his long journey."

"Which he didn't take?"

"He didn't think the danger that great. 'Come on, Aunt Sophie, quit worrying.' he used to say. 'You've been listening to silly rumors. Hitler is bad, but he's not *that* bad. Nothing is going to happen to me.'"

***

I do not remember my father at all. I have searched my mind for a man I called Papa, and I never found him.

Papa was a railroad worker in Alsace. He was killed in an accident when Maman *was pregnant with Anne.* Maman *never re-married. She said, "I had the love of a good man once, I'll never see the like of him again."*

Her sister Rosie tried to play matchmaker. Finally, Maman *said, "No more, Rosie. Every one you send wants a cook, a housekeeper, a slave." "You never did appreciate a thing I did for you," said Rosie And the fight was on.*

But never was there such a display of temper, as on the day Rosie put her own son out of her house.

"I am in trouble now, Kid," Jean-Pierre told Phillipe. "I am in *so much trouble*, I don't even want to think about how much trouble I'm in."

I was five then, my sister Anne only two. "What did you do, Jean-Pierre? Why is your mother mad at you?"

"You wouldn't understand."

"I would to. Tell me."

"Kid, at your age, there's a lot you don't know."

"I know plenty. I can count, and I know a lot of big words."

"I am twenty-one and I know more words. There are some words you'd better not repeat. And what I am, is one of them."

Jean-Pierre lit a cigarette and drew deeply. In the parlor, Sophie Leveque dialed the number of her sister Rosie's house.

"What is going on?" she demanded. "Jean-Pierre is here—"

"In your home? With Phillipe and Anne?" said Rosie. "Bah! Better he should have gone to the bottom of the river with a rock around his neck. I would have done that on the day he was born if I had *known*."

Jean-Pierre took another puff that left ash at the end of the cigarette. "I don't think I'll ever be in *this* much trouble again," he said. Phillipe took the carton of cigarettes and studied it. He drew one out.

"Rosie, what is wrong with you? How can you say that about your own son?"

"Ah, what he did. Unspeakable."

"You seem to have no difficulty speaking of it."

"I will tell you. I went to Mass this morning. Of course, Jean-Pierre stayed home. He's too intellectual for that sort of thing. When mass was over..."

Phillipe placed a cigarette in his mouth and lit it. He blew a few puffs as Jean-Pierre watched his Aunt Sophie grow more livid. Then Phillipe inhaled, and had a fit of coughing.

"This is terrible."

"Hey, Kid. What are you trying to do? Give me that. You'll burn the house down."

Phillipe turned red. Jean-Pierre confiscated his cigarettes and book of matches.

"Why did you do it?" he asked.

"I want to be like you."

"Listen. You do not want to be like me."

"You're smart, and you're nice to me and Anne, and my mother likes you."

"And my own mother can't stand the sight of me. No, Kid, you don't."

"Yes, I do!"

"If you grow up like me, I'm going to be worried about you."

"I won't make you worry."

"Yes, Kid. You will...."

"When you got home from Mass, what did you find?" Phillipe's mother asked. "Tell me, my sister, without singing the whole opera."

"Jean-Pierre and that so-called friend of his, Henri. In my bed."

"Doing what? Cutting each other up with knives?"

"No." Rosie gasped. "Behaving as if they were man and wife. Ah, how it shames me to say it."

"And that is all?"

"My sister, how can you make light of this?"

"How can you be such an idiot? So your son loves another man. Is that the end of the world? Isn't Herr Hitler spreading enough hate around?"

"Suppose it were your Phillipe?"

"He'd still be my son."

"And you call me an idiot."

"You are an idiot, ten thousand times over. You are the one who threw Jean-Pierre out. One day, you will regret it, throwing him out. But Jean-Pierre isn't alone. He's my nephew, my godson, and always welcome in my home."

"Never have I been so insulted. Sophie, you are insane."

"Unless you accept Jean-Pierre as he is, I'll not speak to you again."

Both phones slammed down. "That settles it," Sophie Leveque said. "Jean-Pierre, you are staying here."

Phillipe took a joyful leap off the couch. "Now you can teach me everything you know," he said.

"Not *everything,* Kid," Jean-Pierre said.

I remember that time so well, Gianna. Jean-Pierre taught me how to read, how to write, how to do sums and subtract. Everything of value I learned in the university and seminary is only an extension of what I learned from him.

I worshipped him. What could be worse than a five-year-old with a crush? But he was patient with me. We'd go shopping together, and when I got tired, he'd carry me piggy-back. He took me to the movies, horse operas with subtitles. We'd memorize the English dialogue. "Smile when you say that, Pardner. Head 'em off at the pass."

A stalemate existed between my mother and Rosie. The ironic thing is that we began going regularly to Mass, just so Maman and Rosie could make faces at each other during the service. They'd phone each other simply to say, "I am not speaking to you." All of that changed, Gianna. All of it, the morning I woke up and saw a giant swastika outside my window.

A strange man strode into the living room. His French was terrible. He had a heavy German accent and SS insignia on his uniform.

"You are the Widow Leveque?" he asked.

"Yes, sir," Sophie replied. "With me here are my son Phillipe, my daughter Anne, and my nephew, Jean-Pierre Ferrant."

"Ah, your nephew. Why is he living here?"

"He's a student at the university. He has to finish his law degree."

"Very good. You will have plenty to study, Ferrant, many laws are changing. And for the better. For your own sake, make yourself aware of them *all*. You're a good-looking kid. You must have all the girls in the neighborhood after you."

Phillipe told the man, in English, to get out of town by sundown.

"Clever little fellow," he said, not understanding a word. To Sophie's great relief, he left.

"Oh, mercy me." Sophie's knees gave out and she fell onto the couch.

"He wasn't that bad, Aunt Sophie," Jean-Pierre said. "Pull yourself together."

"The way he looked at you. I don't like it, Jean-Pierre. I think you should go to America as quickly as you can. Take Saint Kristen with you."

"Aunt Sophie, that's easier said than done."

"We'll think of some reason. Some way to get you out—you and Henri. When he spoke of laws, do you know what he meant? This one. This Paragraph 175."

Her voice dropped to a whisper. "Whether you love Henri or not is immaterial. What you two are doing is *against this law*. If you're caught, you'll be sent to jail."

"We have no intention of being caught."

"A lot of difference that makes. I have heard things. They will not send you to jail, Jean-Pierre. Oh, they might, at first. But then, you'll be transferred to a *different* place." Sophie's eyes grew wet. "One of those camps. We must think of a way to get you out. Until then, I beg you, *be careful.* I don't even want you and Henri to walk on the same side of the street."

"Stop being a worrywart. And, please, don't listen to rumors."

"Jean-Pierre?" Phillipe asked. "If you go to America, can I come see you?"

"It's very far away."

"How far?"

"Across an ocean."

"And how big is the ocean?"

"Deeper and wider than you will ever know, Kid."

Things changed, Gianna. I'd been warned not to speak to any of the Germans. If they spoke to me, I was to answer politely, but if they asked me anything about what went on in my mother's house, I was to say I didn't know.

"Be careful," Maman kept telling Jean-Pierre. "There are collaborators, even among our neighbors."

Someone was watching Jean-Pierre. To this day I don't know who. I was sitting by our window one day and I saw Jean-Pierre and Henri together. They lit their cigarettes off the same match. In another house, a curtain moved. Someone was spying, and didn't like what he saw. And then, one winter night....

Several cars screeched to a halt. Their lights stayed on and their engines kept running. Phillipe took a quick look out the window.

"Get away from there," his mother snapped. Then, "Who is it?"

"Those SS men."

"Oh, my God! Jean-Pierre—"

"Aunt Sophie, they're out back, too."

"Then we'll have to hide you."

"No," he said. "If it's me they want, they'll find me. And if I'm hidden, it will be worse for you."

"Open up in there!" One of them pounded on the door.

"Jean-Pierre, why do they want you?" Phillipe asked. "Are they going to take you away?"

"Open this door. We know you're in there." The pounding got more insistent.

"I want you to have this," he said, handing me the medal.
"This is your Saint Kristen."
"It's yours now. You must be brave. I ask you to grow up fast."
"No, Jean-Pierre, please don't go away."
"I should have listened to Aunt Sophie, but now there's no more time."
"I'll come with you."
"You can't, Kid. Please, don't cry." Jean-Pierre picked Phillipe up and held him close.

Sophie screamed as the door flew open. "We got here just in time, Herr Kommandant," one of them said. "That queer has his hands on a child."

Phillipe was tossed across the room. One of the men hit Jean-Pierre so hard that blood spurted out of his mouth; another kicked him.

"Get up, you fucking queer. You're going to get just what you deserve."

Before Phillipe could move, Jean-Pierre was dragged out the door and into one of the cars. Phillipe could hear only his mother's weeping and Anne's screaming from her crib.

"I tried to warn him. I tried to get him to America."

"Where are they taking him?" Phillipe asked. He touched the trail of blood in the snow.

"Across an ocean. Deeper and wider than you will ever know."

When dawn broke, Rosie, all in black, came in through our broken front door. She and my mother embraced, their quarrel forgotten.

Jean-Pierre was charged with multiple violations of Paragraph 175 and sentenced to three years in prison. It was never served, he was placed immediately in Natzweiler-Struthof. Have you ever heard of it? It was Maman's *worst fear: one of those camps. Surely, a circle of hell, especially for those like Jean-Pierre who were forced to wear a pink triangle. "A mark of shame," my mother was told, "to show the terrible crime Jean-Pierre committed." They told her they had done her a favor by getting him out of her house.* Maman *and Rosie were forced to give up. But I couldn't.*

***

"On a deep level, I knew Jean-Pierre had been killed. He was much like Rory: short and small-boned, unable to protect himself. And those running the camps, they *were* scum. Anyone wearing a pink triangle was fair game for them.

"I knew Jean-Pierre was dead. But I didn't accept it. I developed a fantasy that I could free him, if only I could find this place. I ran away once, looking for Natzweiler-Struthof. One of our neighbors, one we could trust, brought me home."

"You honestly thought you could get him out?"

"Yes. I would knock on the door—I imagined the place as being a large castle, which it was not—and I would ask for Jean-Pierre. And he would be given back to me. Furthermore, I would demand, and receive, a written explanation and an apology from Herr Hitler."

Phillipe touched the Saint Kristen medal. "Had Jean-Pierre not given it to me, it would have been stolen and melted down at the camp."

"And your mother?"

"Ah, *Maman*. That's what changed her. She and Rosie formed an alliance which lasted till the end of the war. Rosie would watch me and Anne while my mother was doing her Resistance work. You know, *Maman* became much like Madame DuFarge. She'd come home and knit. And then, after a while, we'd hear a distant explosion. Sometimes our windows would rattle. Or there would be an uproar in German. *Maman* always smiled sweetly. 'Take *that* for Jean-Pierre,' she said."

"Is your mother back to Alsace?"

"Yes. We all lived in Washington for a while. Anne and I became naturalized citizens. But *Maman* was homesick. She had to go back to the places she knew, and loved, and sometimes blew up. Rory and I were able to visit her in 1977. One might say *Maman* went nuts over Rory. He needed that."

"From what I have heard about Gertrude McCormick, she must have been nothing like your mother."

"Gertrude led a sheltered life. Which was not to say a totally happy life. She was young and innocent when she married Eddie McCormick."

"What I've heard about him!"

"You've heard the truth. My first time in the McCormick home, I saw how he operated. Gertrude couldn't open her mouth without being called a fool. In subtle ways, of course, but Eddie always made his point. Gertrude loved her son. Totally and overwhelmingly. She turned to Rory for comfort. She was the child and Rory the parent. Very destructive. And, like a child, Gertrude didn't realize that Rory had the physical needs of an adult."

"A gay adult, at that."

"Which made things much worse for Rory. I met him for the first time in early May of 1968. I know you've found this hard to believe, but then I really was a priest. Cardinal Corby had just transferred me from an inner city parish to St. Catherine's."

"With whom you had problems?"

"I was nothing but a pain in Cardinal Corby's...well, his side. He felt that my being exiled to Outer Suburbia would quiet me down."

"That's where you met Rory."

"Rory was the valedictorian of his college class and engaged to the Cardinal's niece. When I spoke with him, away from his family, I learned the truth: that he was depressed, anorexic, and willing to consider suicide as the only way out.

"I had to be there for him and listen to him. No one else in his family did that, not even his twin. And not Rosalie."

"How old was Rory when you met him?"

"The same age as Jean-Pierre when he died. Twenty-one. They even looked alike. Yes, I know what you are thinking. My fantasy. I felt I had to save him. That was the start of my own feeling for him."

I felt I should be writing all of this down. That soon I'd be the only one left. Write it down, with words and music. And sing it myself.

Chapter 4

SISTER AGNES EASED THE CONVENT'S STATION WAGON into the flow of traffic on Wheeler Avenue. *I've done it*, she thought, *and it can't be undone."*

She told Longianna that Pat McCormick was married in 1975 to someone whose name began with a 'J,' Johnson, Jackson, or Jones.

Try finding that, she thought.

None of the Sisters recalled the name, she'd said, or had heard from Pat since the wedding. The only thing they were sure of was that it was not an Irish name.

"Maybe this is all for the best," Longianna told the nun. "I was thinking about this last night just before you called, and I thought that contacting his family might not be wise."

"Why did you think that?"

"They might be interested only in his estate."

Sister Agnes had imagined Rory with few possessions, living in a sleazy walk-up.

"Is there an estate?"

"Oh, yes! I'd feel awful if they came out here after not speaking to him in twenty years."

"How much is involved?"

"His house is worth a million, maybe more."

Sweet Mother of God.

"It's in Westwood. There's a pool and pool house in back. Rory used to do a lot of entertaining before he got sick."

I'll just bet he did.

"With his other assets, and his interest in Mighty Joe Young's Safari Lounge, the whole kit and caboodle will be *well* over a million."

"Oh...my. What is this...this...."

"Mighty Joe Young's? It's a gay bar, Sister. I sing there, sometimes."

Lord, have mercy. "I presume he has someone to take care of his estate."

"Yes, he has a lawyer. The best. His name is Phillipe Leveque."

Sister Agnes bit down on a gasp. Father Leveque from Saint Catherine's. So, they were still together.

True, Phillipe had been Rory's first and greatest love. But according to Longianna, they'd gone separate ways in 1981.

"That's what they regret the most; the fact that they split. Each of them was going through too many changes. They still loved one another but decided that breaking up seemed to be their only choice."

"Changes?" Sister Agnes asked, sitting on the edge of her seat.

"Yes. They'd been living in Washington. Phillipe was Administrative Assistant to Congressman Will Watkins and Rory lived quietly in his shadow.

"Will Watkins was one of the leading liberals on Capitol Hill. I guess you know what happened in 1980. He lost his seat, and Phillipe lost his job. He and Rory sold their house and moved to Los Angeles so Phillipe could finish his law degree out here."

Sister Agnes tried to tell herself, it was none of her business, but she couldn't help asking. "What happened then?"

"A change they were not prepared for. In Washington, there wasn't much Rory could do. He gave music lessons and directed choirs. But in Los Angeles, there was plenty. Rory got a great job at Grimalkyn Records and Tapes. The ironic thing was, this was before Grimalkyn was bought by Snappy Cereal. They were much more open-minded about gay people then."

Oh, dear! And Aloysius Sweeney is on the Board of Directors of the Snappy Corporation. During his assembly speech, Sweeney had used the term "lavender plague" and paused, expecting applause or laughter. The students gave him neither. Sister Agnes had wanted to sink through the floor. *Aloysius Sweeney is our biggest contributor. If he finds out!*

"Phillipe was the starving student, while Rory was the successful one. That didn't sit well, especially since Phillipe was used to being the big shot. He and Rory separated before they drove each other crazy. And after that...."

"Yes?" *Tell me, you must!*"

"Rory made some mistakes, Sister. He admits it. He wasn't very mature and was on his own for the first time since leaving home. Plus, he missed Phillipe. So he became addicted to a mixture of Valium and Old Granddad."

Glory be to Saint Patrick!

"There were lots of other men. Some were mistakes. Some weren't. I know that sounds strange."

I might have known.

"It was the early '80's. The worst possible time. Rory probably was exposed to AIDS again and again."

"Oh, dear," Sister Agnes said. "How *very* unfortunate. And Mr. Leveque?" She'd almost said Father Leveque. If she had, Longianna would *know*.

"Phillipe did a lot of the same things. But he finished his degree and was admitted to the California bar. He set up his practice in San Francisco, mostly working for gay rights causes. Until AIDS came along. Now, most of what he does is *pro bono* legal work, making sure those who can take AZT get it, that sort of thing."

"I've read about AZT. Is Mr. McCormick taking it?"

"He did and had a terrible reaction. We've tried everything, Sister. We even went to Mexico. Not one thing worked."

"Oh, I...I'm so sorry. Let me ask you this one thing, Ms. Raimondi. I'm presuming, if Mr. McCormick's twin was a Sister of Divine Compassion, that he's Catholic. Has he had the last rites yet? Has he made his peace with God?"

"No, Sister. He's made an informed decision not to go back to the Church, and I respect him for it. As for his peace with God, he made that long ago."

"But—"

"Yes, I know it's hard to accept. Phillipe played Devil's Advocate once, giving him all the reasons why he had to go back. But Rory shot down all his arguments. He said, 'The Church refused to accept me the way God made me while I'm alive,' he said. 'So they're not going to get me dead.'"

"He won't change his mind, then?"

"I know he won't."

Rory, you're playing a dangerous game. But you always were like that, off in your own world.
"Ms. Raimondi, I don't want to keep you any longer."
"I've been rattling on, I'm afraid, costing you a fortune."
"That's perfectly all right, my dear. If you don't mind, I'd like to call you from time to time, just to see how you're doing. I know you must be under a tremendous strain."
"That's so kind of you."
You're darn right, Sister Agnes thought as she hung up. *But I have to keep up with this situation. Rory's my twin. Whether I care to admit it to this saloon singer or no. He is family. And I must....*

Sister Agnes stopped for a traffic light at the corner of Fifth and Wheeler—where McCormick Ford used to be.

I must tell Ma Rory has AIDS. But I don't know how to do it.

Instead of going directly down Wheeler to the Peaceful Woodland Nursing Home, Sister Agnes turned left and followed Fifth Street to the Good Shepherd Cemetery. She needed to discuss this with her beloved father.

Seeing the tiny crosses, knowing that one day she would be here, tended to put everything in its proper perspective. She walked on through the older section of more elaborate tombs.

"Rory Michael McCormick, born 1888. Died, 1959. My father's father. And his wife, Agnes, mother of seventeen," she read aloud.

In The Garden of the Last Supper she stood before the familiar double headstone near the willow tree: Beloved Husband and Father. Edward Vincent McCormick, 1918-1981. "To Know Him Was To Love Him." Beloved Wife and Mother. Gertrude Mary McCormick, 1925- . "Obedient To The Will Of God."

"Dad, Rory is dying of AIDS."

A breeze stirred the willow's graceful branches.

"What am I going to do? You always told me. What am I going to say to Ma?"

And she imagined Eddie saying, "For Christ's sake, Pat, don't tell your mother *this*. You know she's not strong like you and I are. She'll never be able to take it."

She bowed her head, closed her eyes, and remembered.

***

Pat McCormick had just finished her day at Divine Compassion

High. She was going to catch the bus home when she saw the Ford Galaxie with dealer's plates waiting at the corner.

"Dad?"

"Hop in, Pat. I had to run a few errands and was in the neighborhood, so I figured I'd save you bus fare."

"Gee, thanks." Instead of going directly to Lemon Tree Lane, Eddie drove to a place Pat had never been before. The sign in front said, "Ash Grove Medical Park."

"Dad?"

Eddie eased the car to the front entrance and let the engine idle. He lit a cigarette. "I'm going to pick up your twin," he said.

So this was where Dr. Engel had his office. Rory had been seeing him since that disaster the previous spring.

Had Rory been making progress? The expression on Eddie's face made her reluctant to ask. After a while, he volunteered the information.

"It takes so long. So long, and it costs so goddam much. And, Jesus! Three times a week. Engel must think my name is Onassis. But it's starting to work. Rory's going to be all right, Pat. He's going to be a normal kid, find himself a nice girl and get married."

Pat nodded but said nothing. Eddie had never come out and said, "Your twin is queer." She had heard her parents arguing often enough. *Rory is inverted. That means he likes boys instead of girls.* Just then Rory came out of the building.

"Get in," Eddie ordered and crushed out his cigarette. Rory got into the back seat, and Eddie spun the car around, eager to leave.

No one spoke until they were halfway home. A small voice from the back seat said, "Dad, I think I'm going to be sick."

Eddie didn't turn his head. "Not all over the upholstery in my new demonstrator!" he warned.

Pat saw Rory's face reflected in the rear-view mirror. He looked ghastly. As soon as they pulled into the driveway, Rory leaped from the car and ran inside the house.

"Oh, Edward," Ma said as they came inside. "What is this Dr. Engel doing to my boy? Why does he have to go through this torture?"

"Dammit, Gertrude, haven't I explained it to you enough?" Eddie asked. "Rory's getting *aversion* therapy. Dr. Engel is forcing him to see how revolting this behavior of his really is."

Eddie lowered his voice, but Pat heard. "He thinks about touching another boy. Then, he has to imagine that boy's body rotting alive...covered with sores and flies and maggots...."

"Edward, for pity's sake!"

"Hell, Gertrude, can't you see? It's working. The fact that he's heaving up his insides in there means that he's *getting well.*"

"I don't like this, Edward."

"You want him to stay the way he was, huh? You know what would happen to him if we let this go on?"

"There was nothing wrong with him in the first place."

Rory staggered out of the bathroom. "My poor Rory," Gertrude said. "Are you all right?"

"Yes, Ma."

"Do you think you'd like some dinner?"

"No, Ma."

"Perhaps if I fixed you a little weak tea and toast...."

"I don't want anything." He started up the stairs. "Leave me alone, Ma. Everything makes me sick."

"Weak tea and toast," Eddie complained. "Keep it up, Gertrude. Just go the way you've been going. All the money I've spent on Engel will go to waste yet."

"I'm tired of this," she said.

"*You're* tired?" Eddie countered. "Rory is going to stick with this until he's cured, and that's all there is to it."

Rory stuck with it for two years before Dr. Engel told Eddie his son was cured.

"Everything's going to be all right, now, Pat Honey," Eddie announced. "He's *normal.*"

Both twins graduated from high school and went on to local colleges: Pat to Our Lady of Grace and Rory to Saint Ignatius. All seemed to be going well except that Rory had almost stopped eating.

The scene began first thing in the morning. "Breakfast is the most important meal of the day, Rory," Ma said. "You're not going to make it through your morning classes on black coffee."

"Sorry, Ma. If I stay, I'll be late for philosophy."

It got worse at dinner. If Eddie were present, he often started with a snide remark aimed as a warning shot over Rory's head.

"Yes, indeed. Rory's going to make some nice girl happy some day. Know why? She won't have to learn how to cook."

"Dad, I'm just not hungry."

"And why not, may I ask? I work hard and pay good money for that food. Your mother slaves over a hot stove to fix it the way you like it. So why aren't you eating it?"

"Because I don't feel like it."

"Who cares if you feel like it or not?"

"Edward, please," said Gertrude. "Rory, if you'd only try."

"I do try, Ma."

"I've had it," Eddie said, throwing down his napkin. "When I was your age, I never got away with behavior like this. We were in the middle of a Depression. If there was enough food on our table to go around, we were damn glad of it. And my Pop never took this lip off any of us, you can bet your life on that. If one of us got one step out of line, POW! None of this having your rights read to you. Just, POW!"

"I'm sorry, Dad."

Eddie shoveled in his mashed potatoes. "All seventeen of us knew how to behave. I'm telling you. We had this big, long table and I always tried to sit way on the other end of it. That way, if I did anything Pop didn't like, I could get a running start. Never got far, though. POW! And with those big muscles of his—"

"Edward," Gertrude said. "I think we've heard enough."

"We have not heard enough till His Royal Highness over there understands how lucky he is. I'm paying through the nose to send him to college. I had to drop out of high school, go to work, to help support the other kids. And here's my son, pretending he's too good to eat what's put in front of him. You eat your dinner, young man, or you sit there till hell freezes over."

"Yes, Dad."

Inevitably, Rory sat at the table, doing his homework, as his dinner congealed into a repulsive lump. "You win this round. I lose," Eddie would say as he scraped the food down the disposal.

"Thank you, Dad, may I be excused?"

"May you be excused! There's no excuse for you. And don't pull this crap again."

Eddie believed that Rory's refusal to eat was a challenge to his authority. "He does this to get my goat, Gertrude. And he does. Every time. I *know* him. He goes to that snack bar at Saint Ignatius and fills up with junk food. Then he comes home with no appetite at all."

"He's so *thin*, Edward. That's what troubles me."

What Ma said was true. He became, literally, skin over bone. His blonde hair turned to the color of straw.

Rory looked like the scarecrow in The Wizard of Oz, Sister Agnes remembered. No one thought it was of any great consequence. After all, he was normal.

She recalled how some people made light of Rory's thinness. The Saint Ignatius yearbook called him Mr. Twiggy. It said he could take a shower without getting wet but was in danger of sliding down the drain.

In those days, no one spoke of *anorexia nervosa*. She'd seen cases of it among the girls at Corby High and wondered if that had been Rory's real problem? Was it the price he was paying for being *normal?*

"There was nothing wrong with Rory," she thought she heard her father say. "He was only being stubborn and pig-headed and ungrateful."

Never mind. There was, at least, some happiness when Rory began going out with girls. And there was one in particular who made Eddie and Gertrude beam with joy.

"I'm taking Rosalie out to see *Dr. Zhivago* tonight," Rory told his parents. "It's a long film, so don't wait up for me."

"Rosalie is a fine girl and a pretty one, too," said Eddie. "Here are the keys to the Falcon. Want to show her a real good time? Here's twenty dollars."

"Thanks, Dad. Good night." He planted a kiss on Gertrude's cheek. "Good night, Ma."

"Good night, Rory," she said, planning to wait up for him anyway.

"I'll say this for our son," said Eddie. "He's finally developed some good taste."

"And Rosalie Corby," said Gertrude. "The Cardinal's niece. Oh, Edward, what a fine wife she'd make for him."

"Don't rush them. They're only kids. Still...."

Late in 1967, Pat snipped an article out of the society page of the local paper. "Mr. and Mrs. John F. Corby are pleased to announce the engagement of their daughter, Rosalie Monica, to Mr. Rory Michael McCormick, son of Mr. and Mrs. Edward V. McCormick. A January, 1969, wedding is planned."

Was it ever!

Cardinal Corby himself would conduct the Nuptial High Mass in Mary Queen of Martyrs Cathedral. A reception for four hundred guests would be held in the Grand Ballroom of the Ritz Hotel. Then the bride and groom were to depart for a honeymoon in Waikiki.

Rosalie. Sister Agnes remembered the young woman who almost became her sister-in-law.

Rosalie Corby was so perfect, so *feminine*, with her bouffant hairdo and her Villager wardrobe. She reminded Pat of Daisy in *The Great Gatsby*. Rosalie Corby's voice really did have money in it.

Eddie adored Rosalie, which made Pat even more uncomfortable. "You know, when her parents kick off, Rosalie's going to come into a few million?" Eddie asked once. "And the girl has something money can't buy: *class*. I tell you, Pat, when Benny Corby says they're man and wife, it'll be the happiest moment of my life."

Oh, Daddy, it went so wrong. So terribly wrong.

That wedding was to have been Eddie McCormick's triumph. After years of denouncing the city's social elite as a pack of snot-nosed snobs, he would be accepted as one of them. "It's high time," he said once, "I have more dough than most of 'em." Beyond that, it would say without words the thing that Eddie most wanted to shout. His son wasn't queer.

The wedding never came about.

Sister Agnes sat on a stone bench near her father's grave and wrung her hands. She let her mind drift back to the fateful Spring of 1968.

Martin Luther King had been killed and there were riots all along Grant Avenue. Her best friend Eileen Daley stayed with them for moral support. From Pat's bedroom window they could see columns of smoke rising over downtown.

Eddie set up a vigilante group to protect what he called 'life and property.' But absolutely nothing happened on Lemon Tree Lane.

Pat and Eileen were reading the first paper delivered to the McCormick household after order was restored. "Listen to this." Eileen said. "`Father Phillipe François Leveque, assistant at Saint Martin's Catholic Church on Grant Avenue, repeatedly risked his life to rescue victims of the spreading fires. On Good Friday, Father Leveque will lead a penitential procession down the Grant Avenue corridor.' And look at this picture."

It was Phillipe, covered with soot and grime, carrying a crying baby to its mother.

"Isn't he something?" Eileen asked. "You know, if he weren't a priest, I might change my mind about being a nun. Oh, well."

"He is cute," Pat agreed. "He looks sort of like Jean-Paul Belmondo."

"Lemme see that," Eddie said. "What next? They're calling this Leveque the white soul brother."

"At least someone is showing a shred of decency in these times," said Gertrude.

"Yeah, but something tells me that this is not going to go over too big with Rory's future uncle, the Cardinal," said Eddie. "Benny Corby doesn't care for this sort of thing. I have a feeling, Gertrude. The white soul brother is going to be put under a firmer hand. And soon."

Shortly thereafter, Father Leveque was taken out of Saint Martin's and made assistant to Monsignor Hayes at Saint Catherine's.

"And just when he was doing so much good for those poor people," Gertrude said.

"Hayes will straighten him out," Eddie predicted. "Leveque might start to remember he's a priest, not a TV star."

"What went wrong?" Pat asked herself. "Rory and Father Leveque, who would have imagined it?" Certainly not herself, she thought. She knew from the start they were good friends, but no more so than she and Eileen.

"I don't want to talk about it, Pat," she imagined her father's voice.

They never did *anything* that led her to believe they were more than friends. She remembered how they used to sit on the glider on the back patio and just talk. Father Leveque seemed like such a nice person. Sometimes, she and Eileen would chat with them. They discussed politics, Viet Nam, the latest *Star Trek*. "Who would believe...."

"Pat, please...." Again, she heard her father's voice.

"Was there something we didn't notice, Daddy? That others did? Once Eileen and I walked to a Sodality meeting at Church. This was right after Phillipe's big blow-up with Cardinal Corby. And everybody was talking, but the instant I walked into the room...dead silence. What did they know that we didn't?"

"Pat, will you stuff a sock in it? I don't want to hear about the man who turned my son back into a queer after I had him cured."

"Oh. I'm sorry, Daddy."

"I know, Honey. I just don't want to hear one word about Leveque. It's all his fault."

Sister Agnes sat quietly on the bench. Somewhere in the cemetery, a military funeral was taking place. "Taps" echoed over the hills.

I'm so sorry.

This time, it was much later in the summer of 1968 and Rory was speaking those words to her. "I know you were looking forward to being one of Rosalie's bridesmaids," he said. "But I can't go through with this wedding, Pat. If I did, it would be immoral."

"But, Rory, this doesn't make any sense. You love her, don't you? And isn't she crazy about you? You have enough to buy a house, start a family. Why on Earth shouldn't you marry Rosalie? You know how much this wedding means to Dad."

Eddie stormed in. "Have you lost your feeble mind?" he shouted. "That was Johnny Corby on the phone. He says Rosalie's locked in her room, crying her eyes out. What is this, that you want to break the engagement? Some kind of sick joke?"

"No joke, Dad. I meant what I said. I just don't think I should marry her."

"What in the hell. A girl like that. And you treat her like a tramp. I ought to knock some sense into you...."

"Edward!" Gertrude leapt to her feet and lunged for his fist. "No!"

Eddie turned a deeper shade of purple. "All right, Gertrude," he said. "Kiss your little baby's ass and let him get away with murder. I won't. I'm going over to the Corbys and apologize for this. That wedding is on."

Pat heard the car screech down Lemon Tree Lane. Gertrude collapsed in tears.

"Ma," Rory said, "maybe it would be better if I went away for awhile. Got my own apartment. Let everybody cool down a few degrees."

"That might be for the best," Pat agreed. Eddie outweighed his son by at least a hundred pounds. Pat remembered what had happened that other time when Eddie really lost his temper.

Dad can put him in the hospital. Or the cemetery. This is killing Ma; she's not strong like me.

Gertrude only wept harder at the thought of Rory's moving out. When she finally spoke, she asked, "Rory, is there someone else?"

"I can't answer that one," he said, and left.

Eddie came home late that night. Pat lay in her bed, hearing her father's words coming up through the heat register.

"What does he want, Gertrude? Didn't I give him everything? A good home, plenty of food, clothing, the best education money can buy. A proper start in life. And, Rosalie. I masterminded the whole strategy for his big romance. Everything I've given him, he doesn't want. He throws back at me. What does he want, Gertrude? What is it he wants, that I can't give him? If he'd just come out and tell me, I'd give it to him."

"No, Daddy, you would not have done that," Sister Agnes said. "Because all he wanted was the one thing you couldn't accept."

She no longer felt Eddie's presence. Perhaps he'd been lulled back into eternal rest by "Taps." "Good-bye, Daddy," she said. "You're right about Ma. She'd fall to pieces if she knew Rory has AIDS. I won't tell her."

Sister Agnes got into her station wagon and headed back to the convent. Evening rush was in full swing. She had too much time to sit in traffic and think.

"I never blamed Phillipe, like Daddy did," she told herself. "He was The Wizard of Oz. He didn't give Rory anything Rory didn't already *have*. I guess if I blamed anyone, I blamed Dr. Engel. He was supposed to have cured Rory. By the time we learned that the cure didn't work, Engel was long gone. It was so hard in those years. So many lives, disrupted. Dad's, Ma's, mine, yes, even Eileen's. And Cardinal Corby's."

She dabbed at her eyes with a tissue. "It was Cardinal Corby himself who charged me never to speak of this. The scandal was too great. All right, Benny. I've managed to keep my big mouth shut so far. It's only that my mind won't stay quiet."

Chapter 5

RORY CAME BACK FROM THE HOSPITAL AFTER A WEEK. During that time, I collected a pile of phone messages. Many were for Phillipe, who was supposed to be on a leave of absence from his law practice. And there was one call especially for me.

"McCormick residence," I said.

"Have you given any thought to the future?" asked the familiar Voice of Doom.

"All right, Donna. Don't tell me. Let me guess. You've become a religious fanatic. Or you're selling insurance. Which one?"

"I am serious, Longianna. I heard that friend of yours picked up another infection."

Who told you? I wondered.

"Have you devoted any thought to what you're going to do when he dies? There's no cure for AIDS."

"Thanks for reminding me. And thanks for calling to see how Rory is. How *sweet* of you to inquire," I said. "He's not dead yet."

Donna sighed. "I'm only trying to keep you from making an even bigger mess of your life. Do you have any plans for what you'll do after he's gone? Are you going back to Luxor? Will you be singing in that dive?"

"Mighty Joe Young's is a respectable dive," I countered.

"It's your life, and your career. Mom and Dad are worried *sick* about you, and so am I. You're throwing yourself away on a person who has *nothing* to offer you in return."

I sputtered. After all Rory had done for me. And he had made a generous provision for me in his will, though I wasn't about to tell Donna that.

"Nothing," Donna pontificated, "except his own disease."

"Do you think he's going to give me AIDS? Wouldn't that require a little effort, on both our parts?"

"He *may* have given it to you already."

"Aw, Donna, how many times do I have to tell you—"

"Suppose you have it already? Who's going to give you a job? Or a place to live? Have you thought about any of these things, Longianna?"

In the background, I heard her baby shriek. "Darling, he's wet," her idiot husband called.

"I'll be right there," she said. "I only ask that you practice a little enlightened self-interest. I wish you'd get out of that house while there's still time."

"Thanks, Donna," I said, "I'm overwhelmed by your concern. Rory will be delighted that you called. You're such a cheerer-upper."

"Longianna—"

"Will you please go dry off your kid's bottom before he gets any louder?"

"Very well. We'll discuss this later."

"I don't doubt it."

There was another call, from Sister Agnes. She wanted to know how I was doing and what I did for Rory. Did it bother her that I was caring for someone whose life style was so blatantly condemned by her Church?

"Actually, not that much," I told her. "When he really fell apart, we got a nurse to do most of Rory's personal care. But I've kept the household running and made it possible for him to stay in his own home. Let's see, what do I do? I clean, I cook, I plead with Rory to eat what I've cooked. I pay bills. I see to the cats and take them to their vet appointments. I shop. I get the Porsche serviced. I guess I shouldn't have been surprised when a delivery man said, 'Sign here, Mrs. McCormick.'"

"Oh, my," said Sister Agnes.

"I keep track of all the visitors. I answer silly questions. And if people I don't trust get too inquisitive, I tell them that Mr. McCormick is very ill with a hangover. When the powers that be at Luxor make noises about his medical expenses, I *remind* them about Rory's Oscar. And sometimes, on a really good day, I can make Rory laugh. Maybe that's the most important thing I do."

"You are, then, rather like a wife to him."

"Not in the most important sense. I don't get to sleep with him. That's Phillipe's prerogative. Actually, I'm sort of a *lar*."

"A what?"

"A *lar*, Sister. In ancient Rome, *lares* were household guardian spirits. They sort of kept everything running. And I guess that's what I do for Rory."

"Oh, dear. I should have known. But Latin was always my worst subject. I preferred science and math."

"Funny," I said. "Those were *my* worst."

Phillipe and I never told Rory that I had tried to find his twin. On the night he came home, we spoke of Sister Agnes as someone who'd shown kindness to me.

"Odd," Rory said. "Pat was the same way. She had such a tough time with Latin, she finally gave up and paid me to do her assignments. I translated Caesar's *Gallic Wars* for ten cents a line, payable in cash, in advance."

"Why, *mon amour*, I had no idea you were so corrupt," Phillipe told him.

"Money talks," he said. "And I was glad to do it. For a while the scheme worked. Sister Francis Regis kept complimenting Pat on her homework but couldn't figure out why she flunked the mid-term."

"You knew, you crook," I chided him.

"I loved Latin," he said. "That was one thing I shared with Jimmy Starke. He was my puppy love. Jimmy and I must have seen *Spartacus* at least fifty times. Why? Just to see the scene in which Tony Curtis dies in Kirk Douglas' arms. That's the way we felt about each other. Unfortunately...." Rory let his voice trail off.

"A terrible thing happened, Gianna. Rory's father came along at the wrong time. Hurt him very badly."

"And the ironic thing is, Dad didn't understand what was going on. I heard him talking on the phone with Dr. Engel, this shrink he sent me to. According to Dad, Jimmy and I were performing an act which is impossible, unless we wanted to dislocate every joint and pull every muscle in both bodies."

"Indeed," said Phillipe. "Eddie McCormick had a vivid imagination. And he would leave nothing to yours."

I said, "I gather that you weren't...."

"No! Neither one of us had any idea *how*. We were virgins, good Catholic boys. We were also both fifteen and at the mercy of raging hormones. But we didn't know enough to question why we felt so strongly about each other and not about girls. In fact, lack of interest in girls was considered a virtue at Saint Ignatius Prep.

"On that night in the car, we were only holding on to each other. That was all. Just trying to figure out why we felt this way. Then, the door was pulled open, and there was Dad. The next thing I knew, I woke up in Ma's flower bed with blood pouring out of my nose."

"Oh, Jesus!"

"And I never saw Jimmy again. Dad forced his parents to leave town. In those days, Gianna, it was worse. There was so much guilt and shame."

"And your father sent you to a shrink? He got away with that?"

"Sure he did. Our pastor helped him."

"Monsignor Hayes," said Phillipe. "My boss for a while. A conservative thinker. You must understand that he was basically a good man but well under the thumb of Cardinal Corby. And totally confused by that which he didn't understand."

Rory got out a cigarette, and Phillipe helped him light it. I had raised a stink about Rory's smoking, until he pointed out the sense of locking the barn after the horses have gotten loose.

Even with the cigarette, Rory looked ethereal. He was wearing the white cotton clothing which Phillipe had ordered for him. A generic size small, it hung loose, covering the sores he thought were so awful-looking.

I remembered the day he told me, "Gianna, I have AIDS." I'd been reluctantly visiting my family, the occasion the baptism of Donna's baby. I felt I was there only as the Raimondi sister who had screwed up.

The minute I walked into Rory's house I sensed something wrong. All of George's possessions and FAA manuals were gone. And the kitchen, which was usually immaculate, was full of...*tangerine rinds*....

"You can't stay here," Rory said. "You're a nice straight girl. Find a nice straight guy and forget about me. Don't lock yourself up with a lump of dying flesh."

"If I leave you alone, I'll never forgive myself."

"Gianna, do you remember the time I fell in the kitchen? During the Dallas game? You wanted to see if my knee swelled up and I wouldn't let you. Here's what I didn't want you to see."

He rolled up the leg of his jeans. "That's not poison oak," he said. "That's cancer. I've known it for some time, and I should have said something. It wasn't fair to you, to George, to anyone. But I'm telling you now."

"Who cares about George?" I asked. "*Screw* George!"

"I did, and I'm sorry."

I heard a persistent horn honking outside. "It's Tony," I said, and ran to the window. "Hey, keep it down and come inside like a civilized person."

Tony greeted me with, "Did you forget we have to be at the beach in an hour?"

"Will you please hold it down? I asked him. "You'll disturb...."

"The lovebirds," he said. "Mustn't bother the lovebirds. How are they, these days?"

"George is no longer here. And Rory isn't feeling well."

"Too bad. Did they have a big spat? And what's Rory got—this gay plague I've heard so much about?"

I said nothing. Tony drew his own conclusion.

"Migawd!" he said, and dashed out the door. Halfway down the walk, he turned and shouted, "I'm going to the doc to get tested right now. And you will, too, if you have half a brain."

"Oh, shit," I said. Tony left two strips of rubber in the middle of the street. I haven't seen or heard from him since.

"You heard?" I asked Rory.

"Yeah. It seems we have a mutual problem."

At that point, we both knew I'd stay.

Now, I'm considering Rory. Even with the sores, he's like an entity not of this world. "Fairy" is supposed to be a derogatory term. Yet I think he ought to have wings. Transparent wings, that reflect every color in the spectrum.

"Gianna," he said, "I've been thinking about this project of yours. And I'm so glad to see you're doing it."

"I haven't written down anything yet. It's still in the thinking stage."

"But how many times have I told you to get back to composing your own material? Ten thousand, at least. You always said, 'Oh, no. All that did was get me mixed up with Renzo. Never again!' I tried to make you see that there was more to it than Renzo. And that you couldn't let him continue to run your life."

"Renzo, that creep."

"Yeah. This shows me you're getting over him. But let me ask you one thing. Why is your song going to be about me? Being sick is so boring. What do I do? I sleep most of the time. I upchuck. I catch ugly bugs. What can you say about that?"

"You are a fascinating person, *mon amour*," Phillipe insisted. "Gianna has chosen her subject well."

"Then where do we begin?" he asked. "Day One? I can't remember back that far."

"Perhaps we ought to go back to the time we met in 1968," Phillipe suggested.

"I understand that was one hell of a year," I said. "I was too young to understand it."

"Yeah," Rory said. "The night we met. You had just been transferred to Saint Catherine's Church, and I was about to graduate from Saint Ignatius College."

"Yes, and Monsignor Hayes took me to dinner at your house. To be truthful, I didn't know what to expect. Monsignor said you'd been a wild kid."

"Did he now?"

"But that your problems were 'solved.'"

"A lot he knew."

"*Mon amour*, I did not know what I would find. A Hell's Angel? A spaced-out disciple of Timothy Leary? Or a bomb-throwing Weatherman?"

I began to scribble my first notes. In my mind, I went back to a pleasant spring evening twenty years ago. Two priests were walking down Lemon Tree Lane.

***

"I'd like to give you some background on the McCormicks before we arrive," Monsignor Hayes said. "But not when our dearly beloved housekeeper is around. I suppose you've noticed Biddy O'Toole's hearing aid. Don't be fooled. Biddy misses nothing, and repeats everything. Be warned."

"Madame O'Toole is that bad?"

"Just be warned. She has a tongue like a meat cleaver. Don't tell anyone I said that. Now, about the McCormicks. The family consists of mother, father, one set of boy-girl twins, twenty-one, about to finish college. The father...I'm sure you've heard of him. He's Eddie McCormick. President of McCormick Ford."

"Ah, yes," Phillipe said. "I've seen his commercials."

"Some of us wish he would tone them down a bit," Hayes admitted. "Especially the one in which he appears as a burlesque comedian. 'This little beauty isn't stripped; she's equipped. So go to McCormick Ford and ask your salesman to...*take it off!*' Oh, well, we can't complain, so long as that one's only run late at night.

"Eddie's a generous man, Phillipe. As big as McCormick Ford is, his heart is bigger. Cardinal Corby thinks the world of him. Eddie's always donating to Church charities and giving cars to raffles. He's earned everything he's got. People like Eddie made our country great."

"What of the mother?"

"Gertrude. A lovely lady. Keeps a spotless house. She's in our Sodality and Rosary Society. She wanted a big family, but, well, it simply was not God's will. At least she has her twins."

Monsignor thought for a while. "Patricia," he said. "She's a splendid, big, healthy girl. Has some ideas about being a Divine Compassion nun. Apparently, her best friend is entering the convent this summer and is very gung-ho on the idea. Eddie's not especially thrilled about Pat's being a nun since she's the only daughter. But he's not ready to reject the notion outright. Anyhow, he's persuaded Pat to wait a year and work at McCormick Ford. See the real world. Understand what she'll be giving up if she takes the veil. Sound thinking."

"And the other twin?"

"Ah, yes. Rory Michael."

Monsignor thought for a longer while, long enough for Phillipe to wonder what was wrong here.

"Rory's a great kid. Good-looking, a little on the skinny side. Brilliant mind. A smidgen of musical talent, but his father made him major in business administration because music is no way to earn a living unless you're the equivalent of a Beatle."

Phillipe considered that. Eddie McCormick, who had put some of the most tasteless commercials ever seen on local TV, thought his son had minimal talent. Interesting point.

"And besides, in that milieu, one often meets people who are less than savory. Eddie doesn't want that for his son. He's very particular about who the boy associates with."

Phillipe asked, "Is there some problem?"

"Problem? Oh, no, Rory is a credit to his family, church, school, society in general. In fact, he's engaged to marry the Cardinal's niece, Rosalie. You never saw two young people so much in love."

"Then I'm very happy for them."

Monsignor thought a little more. "A few years ago, Rory was a bit wild. You know how boys are. They tend to develop more problems than girls do. And sometimes, they get a little mixed up."

"Rory had problems?"

"Yes. A few. He never got in trouble with the law, no drugs, nothing like that. Just a little confusion plus the fact that he fell in with an evil companion. But he's all right now; that's the important thing. Everything else is in the past. That's why you might find Eddie to be a little strict with him. Believe me, it's for the kid's own good. Ah, here we are. Three-six-nine Lemon Tree."

Gertrude greeted them and showed them into the living room. "This is my daughter, Patricia," she said.

"Pleased to meet you, Father Leveque."

"The pleasure is mine, Miss McCormick."

"My husband ought to be down soon," Gertrude said. "Edward, dear?"

From upstairs, Phillipe heard, "Coming! Rory, aren't you ready yet?"

"Dad, can we turn the heat back on? It's freezing in here."

"Seventy degrees out and you're freezing. If you're cold, put on a jacket. What do you think my name is? Onassis? Now come on. You're keeping the good fathers waiting."

Eddie was the first to appear. Phillipe greeted him graciously, recognizing a star of local TV.

"Will you have a drink?" Eddie offered. "Monsignor, your usual?"

"A beer is fine."

"You, Father Leveque?"

"Ginger ale, if you have it."

"We do." Gertrude scurried to get it.

"So, ah, Monsignor tells me you're interested in politics," said Eddie, peeling the top off his own beer.

"Of sorts. I've been working with Will Watkins who's running for Congress as a Democrat."

Eddie grunted and took a sip.

"In Saint Martin's, all of our people are black, and many have come from the Deep South. So I'd ask them, 'Are you registered yet?' 'Oh, no, Father Leveque,' they always said. 'We tried to register in Mississippi but had a very bad experience. So never again.' I tell them, 'That is no longer legal, neither is it right. You come with me, I'll get you registered. And you think about voting for Will.'"

Monsignor, knowing that Eddie frowned on this sort of thing, cut in. "Will is trying to ride Bobby Kennedy's coattails, isn't that right?"

"Indeed. We will have to see how Bobby does in California."

"I dunno," said Eddie. "I think that flower-power McCarthy guy is going to give Bobby a tough time. Well, look who's here. Father Leveque, here he is, live and in person, my son, Rory Michael."

Phillipe took one look at him and thought, *A little on the skinny side? This is absurd. What is going on here?*

"I'm happy to meet you, Father Leveque," Rory said. The hand he offered felt as if it had just come from the freezer.

Phillipe couldn't believe that any person could be so thin and in normal health. Something had to be wrong. As soon as Gertrude announced dinner, Phillipe saw what the problem was.

Rory has no thyroid problem. No unusual metabolism. He doesn't eat. Most young men his age eat enough to fill an elephant, but Rory eats nearly nothing. Why should that be so?

Gertrude asked her son to take more brussels sprouts. "No thank you, Ma," he said. Phillipe could feel a defensive wall going up.

There's a problem here, and no one admits it. They pretend it does not exist.

Eddie dominated the conversation. The few points that Gertrude made were shot down.

Whatever problem Rory had did not go away.

***

I stopped and shook out a cramp in my hand.

"There I was, wishing I could get to know Rory a little better," Phillipe said, "but with Eddie around, no one got in a spare word."

"And that went double if your name was Ger-*trude!*" said Rory.

"You were so quiet and shy," Phillipe reminded him.

"I was in awe of you. Remember, you were the great Father Leveque. You had your name in the paper and your face on the six o'clock news. You stood for social justice and civil rights. Will Watkins and Bobby Kennedy. You were a hero to my generation."

"Was I really that great?"

"You bet. You were one of the few people over thirty we trusted."

"I was not that far over thirty."

"Nevertheless, I was feeling overwhelmed being so close to you. Fascinated, too. That's why I invited you up to my room after dessert."

"You did what?" I asked Rory. "You invited a guy this good-looking to your bedroom, with your father right there?"

"Nothing could have been more innocent. I was 'cured', remember?"

"Besides, Rory knew what I wanted," Phillipe said. "A cigarette. His own pack was hidden between the mattress and box springs."

"Ma didn't know I smoked," Rory admitted.

"You really were a wild kid," Phillipe told him. "I never found out how you knew I was dying for a cigarette."

"Easy. I saw you puffing away on the news. Besides, I wanted to talk to you, to see if you were the same in real life as you were on TV."

"On the pretense of looking at some sheet music, we went up to Rory's room," Phillipe said. "No, I didn't learn the exact nature of the problem till later in the summer. But that evening, Gianna, it was a start."

***

Rory's room was a scholar's den. The thing that surprised Phillipe the most was what he didn't see.

There are no pictures of Rosalie. Monsignor insists he is in love with her. This makes even less sense.

They sat on the bed with the electric fan blowing smoke out the window. "I was sorry when I heard that you had to leave

Saint Martin's," Rory said. "But I'm glad you're here. Maybe you can liven things up a bit."

"I loved Saint Martin's," Phillipe said. "The time I spent there was the happiest of my life. The poor, they have nothing, and yet their faith is so great. However, I'm bound by obedience to Cardinal Corby. So I had no choice but to leave."

"And right when you were doing so much good. It's no secret, is it, that the Cardinal is prejudiced."

"Let's say that he has a little difficulty in dealing with persons of other races."

"I have a secret name for him. You must promise not to tell."

"I swear, *mon ami*, it is safe with me."

"Uncle Ben."

"It's perfect." Phillipe laughed. "Soon, you'll be a nephew of Uncle Ben, *n'est-ce pas?* Tell me of yourself and Rosalie. When will the wedding be?"

"Next January, after Rosalie graduates. She's a bit behind me. Uncle Ben often took her to Rome. During the Second Vatican Council, he did a lot of entertaining and Rosalie's mother was his hostess."

"Ah, yes. His parties were the talk of Rome. But what of you and Rosalie? Do you love her?"

Rory was caught off-guard. "Well, yeah, I guess."

"You guess?"

"I mean, I suppose I do."

Phillipe took a deep drag on his cigarette. "Perhaps that was not a fair question," he said. "Because at Saint Martin's, it was always the last one I asked of the young men intending to get married. One might say I got down to the nitty-gritty. And their answer was always the same: 'You bet I love her, Father Leveque. Wow, do I ever.' Even in the middle of so much poverty our weddings were the most joyful occasions. But you say you guess you love Rosalie?"

Rory crushed out one cigarette and lit another. "She's a nice enough kid."

"And she's rich."

"I'm not after her money. In fact, my life would be a lot easier if she didn't have so darn much of it. But Dad says you have to be practical. It's sort of like that Rolling Stones song."

"You mean, you can't get no satisfaction?"

"Oh, no." Rory's ears turned red. "We don't...not that. I was thinking of another song. *Lady Jane*."

"Ah, yes. The future is secure with her. And that is fine, in and of itself. It doesn't hurt to be practical. But...do you love her?"

"I...oh, God. Excuse me. Things are moving so fast. I can't believe the amount of money that's already been spent on this wedding. Three thousand dollars, just for her gown."

"It makes no difference if you and Rosalie are not happy with each other."

Rory thought for a while. "It seems," he said, "that to have a good marriage, you don't need to be madly passionate all the time...do you?"

"*Mon ami*, you know that I am French. Can you tell me you would marry a woman you do not love? Can you even think of such a thing?"

"Dad says you don't have to be in love. In fact, it's best if you're not. It clouds your thinking. You marry a nice girl, you live with her, you raise kids with her, and love...it grows. Besides, maybe it's *me*. I'm just not very passionate. That stuff's not important to me."

Phillipe saw the pain in Rory's green eyes. He told himself: *We are close to where it hurts. Go with care.*

"Most young men your age have the opposite problem," Phillipe said gently.

"I'm just not. And Rosalie accepts this."

"Rosalie is a virgin, *mon ami*. A Cardinal's niece, raised so carefully. There is much she does not know."

"Well, she doesn't mind. Monsignor Hayes always says we can't be alone in the car together, that it's a near occasion of sin. Everybody does it, anyway. Rosalie and I go to this hill behind Saint Ignatius that the guys call Makeout Mountain. We park. I kiss her a few times. Then, we turn around and go home. That's all."

"That is all?"

"But we only go there because it's expected of us. It doesn't mean anything. And besides, I have to get married."

"You *have* to?"

"That came out wrong, didn't it? It's really for my own sake."

"May I ask, why?"

"Well, Dad says I have to."

"Rory, the Church teaches that you cannot contract a valid

marriage because your father, or *anyone*, says you have to. Only *you* can make the choice. A marriage performed under duress is null and void from the start."

"But Dad is right. I do have this obligation to carry on the family name because I'm an only son. Even though there are so many McCormicks around here—I guess you've noticed. My Grandma McCormick had seventeen children."

"Poor Grandma McCormick. That's one of the Church laws that will change soon. That *must* change, if we are to survive. But do you truly feel obligated as an only son to carry on your father's line?"

"Yes. Yes, I do."

"Very well. That may be a good enough reason. Will you do one thing for me, Rory?"

"Sure."

"Just once, when you're alone, turn your reason off. Don't rationalize. Listen instead to your heart. And if it says, 'marry Rosalie,' then do so. But if it does not...will you come and tell me?"

"Yeah. I mean, if you want—"

"I don't intend you any harm. May I ask you something else? You're free not to answer if you prefer."

"What is it?"

"This may be none of my business. If it isn't, tell me. But downstairs, I couldn't help but notice that you didn't eat much."

"I guess I didn't."

"Your mother's a superb cook. Were you feeling a little off tonight? Too much excitement, perhaps?"

"No, I'm that way all the time. I try, Father Leveque. I really do. Dad yells about how much food costs and that his name isn't Onassis. And Ma worries. What can I tell you? I'm not into food, either. I guess I can't please anybody around here."

"Rosalie? Has she spoken of this problem?"

"No. She doesn't care."

Phillipe thought, *This is incredible. Simply incredible. Rory is grossly underweight, and he's being forced to go through with this wedding as if he were a wind-up doll.*

"Perhaps there's something I can do," Phillipe said. "Are you willing to write down how much you eat? For a few days?"

"If you want."

"Yes. And show it to me."

At that moment, they heard footsteps outside the door. "It's Ma," Rory said, and stuffed the cigarettes back under the mattress. Phillipe turned the fan on full to get rid of the residual smoke.

"Monsignor's wanting to get back before dark," Gertrude said.

"We'll be right out, Ma."

***

"And that was your start," I said. "Rory, did you keep the food diary?"

"I did. And I gave it to Phillipe after Mass the next Sunday."

"I used it to count up the calories this wild kid was taking in," Phillipe said. "I came out with an average of six hundred per day. Can you believe it? In one his age?"

"His mother had spoken to me about his weight. She was terribly worried but had no idea of where to turn. Of course, Eddie had to put in his two cents' worth. 'Rory is being irksome, Gertrude,' he said. 'He eats junk, so he can't eat what's on the table, because he knows it irks hell out of me. Believe me, he'll change when he's married. Don't go troubling Father Leveque about it.'"

"You were willing to be troubled," I said.

"Indeed, because I saw that the way Rory was going, he might not have lived long enough to get married. In those days, few people knew about *anorexia nervosa*. But I knew that there was something wrong. So I took it upon myself to encourage Rory to eat more."

"Which I did," Rory said. "That brought about many changes. I'd like to tell you about them, but I'm so tired now. And I don't want to leave anything out."

"Randi?" I said. "Randi, could you help us, please?"

"Sure, Dearie," he said.

Randi was our nurse. He called everyone Dearie. He weighed two hundred pounds compared to Rory's seventy-seven and had no trouble carrying Rory upstairs to his room.

"Pretzel, will you stay with me tonight?" Rory asked.

"Of course I will."

That was a good sign. Rory didn't want Phillipe to spend the night with him if he was having pain or nightmares. I helped Randi line up the impressive collection of pills Rory had to take before he could get any rest.

"This is awful," Rory said. "This one is big enough to choke a horse."

"Can you get it down, *mon amour?*"

"Yeah. It tastes as bad as it looks."

"You feel hot," Phillipe said. "Randi, what do you get?"

"Ninety-nine point five degrees. Not so bad. Do you feel feverish, Dearie?"

"No. Just sleepy."

"In the name of common sense, I think we can omit the sleeping pill," Randi said.

"Being sick is such a bore," Rory told us. "Good night, Randi. Good night, Gianna."

"Good night, Sweetie," I said, and helped Randi cover them both up.

"Gianna," Phillipe said, "don't stay up too late with your project. Randi, you'll see that she doesn't?"

"You bet, Dearie. Sleep well."

Randi turned the light down. Phillipe drew his *petit amour* next to him so Rory could feel his heart beating and the soft rise and fall of his breathing.

"This pleases you?"

"This pleases me. I love you so much, Pretzel."

"And I, you. Peace, *mon amour.*"

That night, I sat by the drained pool, looked up at the moon and thought, *My God, how can I do justice to this?*

Chapter 6

*I*N THE DREAM DONNA STOOD OUTSIDE THE SLIDING DOOR that led to the patio, nagging me.

"Come in like a civilized person," I said. "We don't *often* get guests in our little pest house, and when we do, we want to make them feel *welcome*. Come in and have a tangerine."

The idea revolted her. "I most certainly won't go in there and then go home to my child," she fumed. "I want to talk to you."

"Then, talk."

"You live like a nun," she said. "That house is your cloister. You even observe the Great Silence at night. The real world is passing you by."

"I don't want to discuss it, Donna," I said. "It's my choice."

"People are worrying about you. They say you've lost your mind."

"Who says that?" I asked. "Who, besides you?"

"You were meant to be out in the world and a part of it, Longianna. You're making a mistake and you'll spend the rest of your life regretting it. If you have much of a life left. I think you know what I mean."

"You're an idiot."

"I'm only trying to help you."

"You're only *trying*."

Randi came down from upstairs. "Gianna? Dearie? We have a problem. I need your help."

"Oh, no," said Donna. "Not another fag. That one looks worse than the dippy flight attendant."

"Donna, if you don't like what goes on here, you're free to go. Keep your commentary to yourself. Nobody asked *you*."

"I want you to come with me."

"Go away. Randi, what's the problem?"

"Well, Dearie, it seems...Rory is dead and rigor mortis has set in. I can't pry him loose from Phillipe."

Donna let out a screech, and took off down the street. I woke up with a louder screech.

"Nothing happened, Dearie," Randi said. "You had a nightmare, that's all."

"It was so real. I was fighting with my sister, and you were in it." I told him what I'd dreamed.

"It can't happen," he told me. "I check on both their vital signs every few hours. And if one of them did die, still, it takes a while before rigor mortis sets in. So don't worry about it."

"Randi, have you seen people die before?"

"Lots of times. AIDS is my specialty, I'm afraid. Look, Gianna, I checked on them not two minutes ago. They're both very much alive."

"Silly of me."

"No," he said, "not at all. They look like a pair of angels in a baroque sculpture. In a sense, Rory is fortunate. I know how strange that sounds, coming from me. I see how sick he is and how much he's been through. Especially last week. But he's so lucky to have someone like his Alsatian Pretzel. Few of us have a relationship that profound."

"I have a bit of news for you," I said. "Few of us straight people do either."

"Rory is such a serene person."

"He wasn't always like that. In fact, after he was diagnosed, he was a holy terror. He'd yell, and I'd yell back. Then we'd both to go to our corners and cool down."

"I find that incredible."

"It's true. And for a long time, he didn't want to tell Phillipe he was sick. I was so glad when he finally admitted it."

"Were Rory and Phillipe always like they are now?"

"No. They started out strong twenty years ago. But Phillipe told me once that they fell in love for all the wrong reasons. Rory needed saving, and Phillipe needed someone to save. It wasn't enough to hold them together."

"But consider them now."

"They've changed so much. Each in his own way. Since this AIDS business began, they fell in love all over again."

"For the right reasons," Randi said.

"It would seem so."

"Speaking of changes, Gianna, I've seen a big one in Rory. I honestly thought last Monday was the end of the line for him. But just tonight...wow. I've not seen him this alert in a long time."

"Yeah, well, he's still full of antibiotics."

"No. More than that. His mind is so clear. And I think you're the reason."

"Me?"

"This project of yours. This song you're writing. I think he wants to know how it turns out."

"And here I was wondering if I could do it or not."

"Did I ever tell you I'm a fan of yours? Well, I am. I used to hang around Mighty Joe Young's before my caseload got so heavy. I saw your act. If you can compose as well as you sing, you'll be terrific."

"Thanks. Did you think I was a boy when you saw me?"

"Well, maybe at first. I'd better not keep you up," he said. "Phillipe won't like it. But think about writing the song, will you?"

"I will," I promised.

There were no more dreams that night.

***

"I feel pretty good," Rory said the next morning. "Not like running around the block, but all things considered, pretty good."

It was Sunday. Rory was back downstairs, dressed in his white garments. He'd eaten two eggs and was surrounded by the *Los Angeles Times*.

"And now, do you know what I'd like to do?" he asked.

"What?" we asked.

"Start up where we left off last night. I want to give Gianna as much information as possible before I get worn out."

"You want to give her your side of the story, no?" Phillipe asked.

"Yeah, Pretzel. I do."

I reached for the pad on which I'd scribbled a few ideas. "Where did we leave off?" I asked.

"With the fact that I was anorexic," Rory said. "It's all coming back to me...the reasons why. They made so much sense at the time."

Rory took a sip of water. "You must realize my father always impressed on me that any sign of affection between two men was 'against nature.' There were only a few exceptions. Let's say you score a touchdown and one of your teammates pats you on the back. That's understandable."

"Provided," Phillipe said, "he doesn't pat you on your rear."

"Well put," said Rory. "I grew up believing him. His own father was his example. Grandpa McCormick begat seventeen children and as far as I know, he never touched any of them except to beat them. Which he did frequently."

Rory thought for a moment. "I can't remember once climbing into Dad's lap without being pushed out. He may have allowed it when I was a baby, but that was it."

"You grew up thinking the whole world was this way?" I asked.

"Not for long. I had a lot of Cuban classmates in high school. To them, it was part of their culture, no big deal. Once I was at José's house, and saw his father kiss him. That blew my mind. It got me thinking that the world is not run according to Eddie McCormick's set of rules."

"There came a time when you didn't live by those rules," Phillipe reminded him.

"Yeah, and Jimmy and I got caught, and I paid the price. And I kept on paying till you came along. All right, so I wasn't eating. Ma cared, but all she did was wring her hands and worry. But you really cared. You wanted something done about it. That got to me: you cared so much. It was for your sake that I started eating more."

"Which had side effects?" Phillipe asked.

"Anorexia *is* a cage, but I felt safe in it," Rory explained.

"How is that?" I asked.

"I'd have to go back to Dr. Engel and his upchuck therapy. The whole purpose of that was—may I speak freely?"

"Don't think I'm going to shriek and faint," I told him. "After all, I've been to Mighty Joe Young's."

"All right. I'll tell you. The aversion therapy was designed so that sexual feelings towards men brought on nausea. Naturally, I had no appetite. But I found that the more weight I lost, the less these feelings bothered me. I got to the point at which I had none at all."

"That must be when the shrink thought he had you cured."

"That was it, Gianna. He didn't make me straight. He only thought so. I was dead from the collarbone down. And if I was underweight, who cared? Just so I wasn't getting interested in other guys. There were disadvantages to living in my cage."

"You were always cold," Phillipe said.

"I wasn't comfortable unless it was at least ninety out. But by the time I met Phillipe, I had forgotten what it was like to have what the nuns called an 'impure thought.'"

"Jeez," I said. "You were a plaster statue of a boy saint in a glass case."

"I was like the Infant of Prague on Ma's bureau. An eternal, asexual child."

"People must have though you were perfect."

"A little too perfect," Phillipe said. "For my sake you tried to eat a little more, no?"

"Yes, the changes started almost immediately. I gained a few pounds. I stopped freezing. That was such a great feeling. Like spring had come after so many years. Other things happened, too. Phillipe, I had that dream about you."

"Do tell," I said. "See if you can make me blush."

"Well, all right," Rory said. "I dreamed we were all in Church. By 'we' I mean my folks, Pat, Rosalie, Phillipe, and Monsignor Hayes.

"We had to undergo a ritual in preparation for the wedding. On the way over Dad had been telling me that 'a married man has obligations.' Monsignor Hayes explained it. In order to fulfill my duties as Rosalie's husband, I had to know what I was doing. I had to be 'initiated.' And that Father Leveque had graciously volunteered to perform the initiation."

I couldn't help but say, "How nice of him."

"Nice is right. I was thinking how glad I was, that Cardinal Corby wasn't going to do this. I didn't want a mouthful of cigar smoke and Polident."

I said, "You're blushing."

"When you told me this dream, I thought the ritual was so

beautiful," Phillipe said.

"I guess it was, though the Church would never allow it. Monsignor Hayes pronounced a benediction on everyone present. Then they all left except Phillipe and me and Rosalie. Rosalie stayed in the front pew, reading *Modern Bride*, while Phillipe made love to me in the sacristy."

"You're turning the colors of a glorious sunset," I told him.

"So are you, Gianna. What shocked me the most is that I woke up with wet pajamas. That hadn't happened in years. I was so embarrassed, I washed them myself so Ma wouldn't know. At the same time, I had no regrets. No sense of wrongdoing. It was my secret. It made me think that the way I had been living was wrong. But this was right."

"That was near the end of May, no?" Phillipe asked.

"Yes. I graduated on the first of June. Then something else happened which I remember well. May I have some more water, please?"

I ran to get it.

"That primary election in California," Rory continued. "I'd stayed up late to see the results. I knew how much having Bobby Kennedy win meant to Phillipe. So there I was, watching, and Bobby said, 'On to Chicago.' I thought about calling you up to congratulate you. And then—"

"I remember, too," said Phillipe. "I felt as if I were the one who had been shot."

"My folks were in bed," Rory said. "Dad got up and demanded to know what in hell was going on. I told him that Bobby had been shot, and I ran out the door. Dad came down, turned the TV all the way up, and yelled that the whole world was nuts. He had the whole block wide awake. But I didn't stop running till I got to Saint Catherine's rectory."

"Biddy O'Toole was leaping about like a freshly decapitated chicken," Phillipe said. "Monsignor Hayes was doing his best to help me. 'I'll say a Mass for Bobby,' he promised. 'To be honest with you, Phillipe, a wound like that, it doesn't look good.'"

"I came in then. Biddy was going 'Saints preserve us.' She was dancing in circles with her face buried in her apron.

"I followed the noise of the TV into the parlor. And I said, 'Phillipe, I'm so sorry. I had to tell you.' You got up off the sofa, came over to me and hugged me. No one had ever done it like that before."

"Having you there at that time brought me great comfort. More than all the words and calls and cards."

"I wanted to hold on to you forever. At the same time, you turned me on. I couldn't admit it, but you did."

"You weren't the only one, as you say, turned on."

"I should have realized at the time what was happening to us," Rory said. "I felt so depressed when you went to New York for Bobby's funeral. You were only gone a short time, but I missed you."

"Unfortunately, there was little we could do with an audience present," Phillipe said. "Monsignor Hayes. And Biddy O'Toole."

"Biddy O'Toole," I said. "The housekeeper, right? I've been having strange vibes ever since I first heard that name."

"Ah, Biddy," Phillipe told me. "I should have listened to Monsignor when he tried to warn me about Biddy. Her mouth ought to have been registered as a deadly weapon."

"I have reason to believe that it was Biddy who almost did us in," Rory said.

"Who else?" Phillipe asked. "I tell you, I got off to the wrong start with Biddy, but she aggravated me so much. I'll tell you my first real encounter with Biddy the morning after I had that dinner at the McCormicks'. Biddy was fixing breakfast and giving me an introduction to Saint Catherine's from her perspective.

"'*Her* brother is a no-good, unemployed, drunken bum. *His* son is a heroin addict. *They* say their daughter is at a German university, when in fact, she's in the Home for Wayward Pregnant Girls.' Finally I said, 'Madame O'Toole, can't you say something positive about any person? Or does no one in Saint Catherine's come up to your standards?' Well, she all but threw a bowl of Snappies at me, and stormed out the door."

"Sounds like she had it in for you," I said.

"Later I learned that while I was at Saint Martin's, she called me a nigger lover."

"Good God."

"That was mild, compared to the other names. In a sense, though, I owe a debt to Biddy. She's the one who forced me to confront my feelings about Rory. And now look what we've done."

Rory had curled up in a corner of the sofa, apparently asleep. "Did I miss anything?" he asked.

"Not much. Only Biddy. We've worn you out. Do you wish to

go back upstairs, *mon amour?*"

"No. I want to stay here."

"Very well." Phillipe pulled a blanket over Rory and then resumed his story.

***

Will Watkins was the featured speaker at St. Ignatius College for a seminar on the Viet Nam War. The turnout was huge; Will had just won the Democratic nomination for congressman. Newly registered black voters had put him well over the top.

"Father Leveque," he said, "I never could have done it without you. What can I do for you in return?"

"You can win in November."

"Sheesh, it's going to be a tough fight. That Sullivan, he's so darn slippery. And he fights dirty, too."

"So you had better protect your rear flank."

The incumbent Congressman Sullivan was a crook, getting rich off the war. No one was powerful enough to stop him, not yet.

Such thoughts were far from Phillipe's mind on that day, simply because Rory was with him.

At the end of the day, Phillipe drove back to Lemon Tree Lane in his black Volkswagen. Rory sat in front alongside him. Pat and her friend Eileen were in back.

Eileen was a very religious young lady, certain of her decision to enter the Divine Compassion Order in August. Her view of convent life was highly romantic, something like *The Sound of Music*.

"You may find that your Reverend Mother will give you little time off to sing and dance in the mountains," Phillipe advised her.

She and Pat giggled. The ride home was a chance to dispel some of the legends that had preceded the great Father Leveque.

"You mean, that I fixed a tuna on rye, extra lettuce, hold the mayo, and turned it into five thousand? That isn't true at all," he said. "But, Pat, one of the stories *is* true. I did have a cousin who was in a concentration camp."

The mood in the black bug grew solemn. Both Pat and Eileen said, "Oh, wow."

Eileen spoke first. "Is he...all right?" she asked. "I mean...did he survive?"

"No. Jean-Pierre was murdered by the Nazis."

The two girls regarded each other. Pat spoke. "Is your family Jewish?" she asked.

"No, Pat, we've been Catholic since the dark ages," he said. "Besides, if we were Jewish, the SS would have taken us all, including myself. Jean-Pierre was a political prisoner."

Yeah. Right, Phillipe thought. Even Rory had been told that Jean-Pierre was taken in on political charges. In a sense, he was.

"This is what you must tell people," Phillipe's mother had warned him. She'd explained the charges against Jean-Pierre when Phillipe was old enough to understand them. He knew the meaning of the pink triangle. *"But you must say he was a political prisoner, so that his dear memory won't be held up to ridicule. The world hasn't changed that much."* Then, *"You must be ever so careful, Phillipe."*

"Then he's a martyr," Eileen said. "Perhaps the Church will make him a saint."

"That is unlikely," said Phillipe. "The memories—they are difficult. We know that Jean-Pierre has the highest place in heaven. But none of us wishes to deal with a Devil's Advocate."

"I'm sorry," Pat said.

"I was only a little kid when Jean-Pierre was taken away. He was a guardian angel to me. I still miss him."

Phillipe guided the bug into Eddie's driveway. Rory had been looking at him with concern as he spoke of Jean-Pierre. Perhaps, even then, Rory suspected there was more to the story.

"Good-night, *mon ami*," Phillipe told him. They made plans to meet the following Wednesday for a Watkins rally.

"Rory? Patricia?" they heard Gertrude call.

"Yes, Ma."

"You had better come in and eat your dinner."

"Yes, Ma."

"Good advice," Phillipe told Rory.

He felt a sadness as Rory went into the house. It was getting more and more difficult to be away from him.

What is wrong with me? he wondered. *Lord, give me a sign. Why do I feel this way about Rory Michael McCormick?*

Phillipe turned on the bug's AM radio. To the great distress of Monsignor Hayes, he kept it on the local black music station. It was a bit of Grant Avenue that Cardinal Corby couldn't take away.

There it was. The sign he'd asked God for came right out of the radio. Tina Turner was singing to him, telling him that he was just a fool. He knew he was in love.

Oh, no, he thought. *Not that.*

He drove the short distance to Saint Catherine's, parked in the lot, but left the radio on, listening to Tina Turner's words. Every one described how he felt.

It's true. I was once a child, telling Jean-Pierre, "I want to be just like you." I'm not a child anymore. And I'm like Jean-Pierre. Exactly like Jean-Pierre.

"*You must be so careful, Phillipe*," his mother said. "*The camps are gone. But the world is not going to change that much. Bring no harm to those you love.*"

"You're right, as always, *Maman*," he said. To avoid bringing harm to those he loved, Phillipe Leveque had taken a vow of perpetual chastity. That should have settled the issue.

"But it's not working."

Perhaps it had worked for a while, in a place like Saint Martin's, where Phillipe could bury himself in never-ending tasks. Yet he'd have found someone, he thought, as now he'd found Rory McCormick, who even looked like Jean-Pierre. "Lord, what shall I do now?" Phillipe said aloud.

There was no reply except for the soft hum of crickets and night insects.

"Father Leveque? Is that you?"

"Yes, Monsignor."

"Glad you're back. May I see you for a moment in my study, please?"

"But of course."

Monsignor shut the door. Phillipe knew Biddy wasn't around. He heard her TV droning in the background. Still, it was a wise precaution.

"I have been, ah, shall we say, going over some figures," Monsignor Hayes said. "In the short time you've been here, attendance at Sunday Mass is up twenty per cent and climbing. Mostly among students and young marrieds. But I have also found that older persons, who've been away from the Sacraments for years, even decades, are coming back. Phillipe, you have no idea of how happy this makes me."

"Why, thank you, Monsignor. But my own thinking goes against coming down hard in the confessional. If someone admits he has been away for many years, I say, welcome back. The fact that such a person has come is a symbol of his good will."

"Ah...yes. And the results you're creating are...very good. Very good indeed. Baptisms are up, enrollments in our school for next September are up...."

He was wringing his hands. Phillipe knew that something was wrong.

"However...." Monsignor said.

"Yes? Is there some problem you wish me to solve?"

"Ah...well...I'm afraid...it's difficult, Phillipe. Not easy, what I have to say. But...how shall I begin? I understand that when you were in college, you studied chemistry. Surely, you remember that one of the properties of hot air is that it *rises*."

"Monsignor, what has this got to do with—"

"Let me finish," he said. "I want to get this over with. Hot air. It gets around. And I'm afraid there has been a certain amount of hot air rising in connection with...."

Monsignor looked at the crucifix on the wall for guidance. Then he charged ahead again.

"Consider, if you will, a boy like...like Rory McCormick. I mean, look at Rory. There's nothing wrong with him, you realize, he is small-boned, blonde, rather delicate-looking. A bit— just a bit—on the skinny side. Phillipe, what I'm trying to convey to you is that sometimes—some people—will entertain wrong ideas about a boy like Rory Michael."

"Wrong ideas?" Phillipe felt a chill invade the summer night. "Precisely what are these ideas, if I may know?"

"That...that...he doesn't look very masculine. And is capable of attracting the wrong sort of attention from certain types of men."

"*Mon Dieu*," he said. "Monsignor, are people saying such things about Rory and me?"

Hayes shook his head. He looked as if he wished he were a million miles away.

"Now, you must understand that Rory is nothing like that," he said much too quickly. "He has never been like that. If he were, I don't know what Eddie would do. Eddie's a fine man but he has a terrible temper. Something like this, if he got word of it, I don't know what he'd do. You understand, that's why Eddie's so strict with the boy. And why he's so eager for this wedding. There's...there's more."

Hayes took a deep breath. "You know our Eminent Lord Cardinal Corby," he said. "And that Rory Michael is engaged to His Eminence's niece. Well, let me tell you, Cardinal Corby adores that little girl. Always has. There's nothing he won't do to insure her future happiness. That means her own home. A husband. And babies. Lots of beautiful babies. If anything comes along to endanger that happiness—such as a rumor that there is something *wrong* with her fiancé—need I say more?"

"You need not," Phillipe said. "I understand *perfectly*."

"Now, don't—please, *please*, don't—lose that Gallic temper of yours. While you were out today I have, I trust, put a *stop* to this idle talk. What I'm asking you to do is, as the kids say, 'cool it.'"

"I can't even be seen in public with Rory, is that it?"

"Mercy, no. You're his friend, you will go on being his friend. His mother says you're such a good influence on him. But it might be a good idea if you didn't spend so much time together. When you're together, I don't believe you ought to be touching him."

"*Incroyable!* Shall I stay five feet away from Rory at all times?"

"No, no, no. It's just that that sort of thing can easily be misunderstood. All right, I'll give you a specific example of what to avoid. You picked up Rory and his sister and her friend after Mass this morning, am I right?"

"Rory, Pat and Eileen waited for me in the vestibule. What's so scandalous about that?"

"On the way out to your car, you said something to Rory that made him laugh. And then you patted his fanny."

"What? I may have patted his back, but certainly never did I make contact with his fanny."

"All right, I take your word for it. But sometimes we must consider how things look to others. It seems—at least, I was told—that this gesture of yours made our parking lot look like—" Monsignor appeared agonized, but went on, "Fire Island."

Phillipe remembered who had been in the vestibule, watching them. *Biddy. Miss Bridget Bedelia O'Toole.*

"I only say this as a guide, Phillipe, so you'll know which specific gestures to avoid," Hayes said. "Now, I know there's not a word of truth to this rumor. And that neither you nor the

McCormick boy is anything like *that*. Besides, Rory's very much in love with Rosalie."

A lot you know, Phillipe thought. *That's not what he's telling me.*

"As far as I'm concerned, the whole thing's finished and done. The only reason I'm telling you this is so that it doesn't crop up again. I'm saying nothing to Rory. You're almost nine years older than he is. You've seen more of the world than he ever will. So you set the example. Be aware of how your actions look. And...please...cool it."

"Thank you, Monsignor," Phillipe said. "I shall cool it. I understand how difficult this was for you. May I go, now?"

"Ah...yes. You may."

***

"And then what did you do?" I asked. "Take a fire axe to Biddy?"

"I should have, Gianna. I was livid. Biddy was still watching her TV, soaking her hideous feet in epsom salts, as was her custom. I wanted to turn her upside down and drown her in the basin."

"You didn't!"

"No, I couldn't give her the satisfaction of knowing how mad she'd made me. I considered saying to her, 'Why, Madame O'Toole. I had no idea that you had ever been to Fire Island. Or that you know so well what goes on there.'

"Instead, I went to my own room. I had to think. What made me so furious was that Biddy'd been right. Not that I patted Rory's fanny, which I hadn't. But that I cared deeply for him, even though I wasn't yet able to admit that I loved him. To myself, to Tina Turner, to God. And if this hot air didn't stop—if it rose to Eddie or the Cardinal, great harm would come to Rory. That, I couldn't permit. You see how it was in those days. Always, the secrecy, the guilt."

Rory stirred. "The matter resolved itself, didn't it?"

"I thought you were asleep," Phillipe said.

"You thought. No, I wasn't sleeping. I didn't want to miss this. Besides, I'll have to tell Gianna what I did next."

"Ah, yes, it was quite spectacular."

"But, Pretzel, if I had known what Biddy did to you on that day, I'd have chopped her up myself."

Chapter 7

We weren't able to continue for a while. Rory really was worn out by the effort of speaking. He refused to go upstairs, saying he wanted to hear me work out my ideas for my song on his synthesizer.

I was in awe of that synthesizer. Here's where Rory composed the score of the film LYNX. The Oscar he won for it stood on the mantle, watching me.

I thought of how the LYNX theme conveyed the vastness of interstellar space. I wondered if his family heard it. Of course they had. Did it occur to them that Rory had written it? Had they seen LYNX, or noticed R.M. McCormick in the closing credits?

I wondered about Pat, if she was still married to the same man, if she had any children. Did they know they had an uncle?

And what about his mother? Was Gertrude still living? Phillipe had spoken of a role reversal in which Rory was the parent and Gertrude the child. Certainly, not healthy for either one.

Rory had said of his family, "They're better off without me." Eddie's obituary didn't even speak of a son. He'd carried his anger into his grave.

I began to develop a theme of pain and alienation. Rory had been cut off from his roots, thrown out of his home and Church. I thought of Dante as I worked, exiled from Florence.

Phillipe thought the music didn't sound right.

"And why not, may I ask?"

"Because, Gianna, as bad as the McCormicks might sound, you must understand them in context. Perhaps I'm at fault here. I have been telling you terrible things about Eddie. It's true that for years I hated him. But I came to understand him through knowing Rory so well. Rory would tell me things—between the sheets—which is where you really get to know another person.

"Eddie McCormick never outgrew being an abused child. To the end of his life, he carried a little boy inside him. A hurt little boy, crying, 'Please don't hit me any more, Daddy.' I can understand because there's a little boy inside me asking where Jean-Pierre went, when he'll come back.

"Eddie could never acknowledge the child inside him. He had to be tough. To be a real man."

"Real men don't cry."

"So Eddie preached. But the anger inside wasn't directed so much at his son as at his father. He had a compulsion to best his father at his own game. Why do you think Eddie wanted eighteen children?"

"Eighteen?"

"Yes. He'd have one more than his own father had. He'd have finally 'beaten' Grandpa McCormick, proven himself more of a man.

"But Gertrude had only two babies. Twins. She wasn't able to have any more. And Eddie never forgave her. He couldn't divorce her. They'd been married in church. But he could make her life miserable."

"I gather Gertrude was passive enough to accept this."

"I don't think it ever occurred to her to ask Eddie for a divorce no matter how bad he got. She had no means of supporting herself and her children.

"She feared that real poverty wasn't *nice*. She was a nice person, Gertrude was. Always, close the wound, cover the scar. Tell the world that all is well at 369 Lemon Tree Lane. The day after Eddie beat up Rory, she wanted Rory to go to school as usual and tell his teacher he'd fallen down the back stairs."

"What a terrible thing it must have been," I said. "I suppose he beat her, too."

"Rory told me that to the best of his knowledge, his father never struck his mother. He had other ways of causing her pain. Rory found her once in tears over the dirty laundry. Eddie had dropped one of his shirts into the hamper. It was smeared with lipstick. A bright red that Gertrude thought no decent woman would ever wear."

"Right where she'd find it. What a rotten thing to do."

"She could have used it as proof of adultery. Instead, she put it into the machine with detergent and bleach. She offered up her pain to God, as her Church told her to. She never knew he was trying to strike back at his own father."

"So, it's nobody's fault," I said.

"Only ironic that Eddie and Gertrude produced a child as beautiful and loving as Rory. And a great tragedy, that they couldn't accept him as he was. They're the ones who were hurt the most, Gianna. They didn't hurt Rory as much as they hurt themselves. If your song must speak of them at all," he said, "say *that*."

***

Sister Agnes called, wanting to know how I was holding up and how Mr. McCormick was.

I told her about my project and that Rory seemed interested. But I had to tell her that he was greatly weakened by the latest infection. Sister Agnes promised she'd pray for him. She also had a request. "I was wondering what you look like," she said.

"Me?" I asked.

"Yes. Sometimes it helps me to concentrate my prayers if I know what the person I'm praying for looks like."

"I can send you pictures if you'd like."

I gathered some 8 X 10 glossies used in ads for Mighty Joe Young's, making sure they didn't look too risqué. I added a picture of Rory and me that George had taken the previous summer, out beside the pool. Rory wore Levis 501s to cover that rash he didn't want anyone to see.

"They say the camera never lies," I told myself as I stuffed them into a manila envelope. Rory looked too old and tired in that picture. I should have realized something was wrong the first time I saw it.

Still, I thought, if Sister Agnes has this hang-up about praying for people she's seen, this ought to help her.

The following morning, Rory announced that he was ready to begin again.

✳✳✳

"What was I to do?" Phillipe said. "Cool it?"

"What could you do, with Biddy watching you?" I asked.

"Darn little," Rory said. He was back in his place on the sofa. Randi had just washed his hair and was drying it with a towel. "It's so beautiful," Randi kept saying. "Real gold."

"I'm so glad I didn't confront Biddy," Phillipe continued. "That would only have made things worse. At the same time, I couldn't take Monsignor's advice to cool it. What was I to say? 'Rory, we must see less of each other because Biddy says we're a couple of queers, and Biddy's is the only opinion that counts around here?'"

"Oh, please," Rory said.

"If I did cool it, that would have been devastating to Rory. He was learning to trust me. If I pushed him away, what would have happened? He'd have stopped eating again and withdrawn into his cage. So I made a moral decision. Instead of avoiding Rory, I'd avoid Biddy."

"Swell idea," I said.

"But didn't Biddy have her ways of avenging herself on you?" Rory asked. "What did she do to your socks?"

"My socks? *Mon amour*, you remember that?"

"Of course, I do."

"Every time Biddy washed my socks, she delivered them back to my room with each pair tied in a tight knot. Little things like that. Still, I was determined that she wasn't going to get the best of me. I wouldn't go down to her level."

Rory said in a solemn tone, "You hid her epsom salts."

"I admit it," Phillipe said.

"This sounds like open warfare." I said.

"He'd hid them under my bed," Rory said. "And when Biddy trashed her room, looking for them, you blamed the Viet Cong."

I almost fell off the sofa. "I don't believe this," I said. "Didn't she know there wasn't a chance against the two of you?"

"Gianna, you must understand that in those days, we had a terrible problem with Viet Cong on Lemon Tree Lane," Phillipe explained. "Not only did they steal Biddy's epsom salts, and hide them under Rory's bed, they replaced the salts with a substance a good deal more effervescent."

"Nothing harmful," Rory said. "Just enough to get her dancing out of that basin going woo-woo. Consider what she'd done: challenged the son of Sophie Leveque. She's lucky her epsom salts didn't go ka-BOOM!"

"You got revenge," I said.

"Biddy was like a rattlesnake," said Rory. "We could handle her, provided we stayed away from her mouth. Because—seriously, now—I never needed Phillipe as much as I did when I came out. And shortly after that, I did come out. It all started with yet another blow-up between Dad and me. But this one was bigger than any of the others. This time, I fought back."

***

"Patricia," said Eddie, "will you say Grace?"

Pat dashed through the blessing and made the Sign of the Cross. Gertrude began passing around the spaghetti and meatballs. Eddie glared at Rory. He was starting to eat now, but there was something new about him that troubled Eddie. Something that made Eddie nervous.

Things should have been going well. Rory had his degree and a job at an accounting firm. To Gertrude's great relief, his draft status was 4F. The wedding plans were proceeding smoothly.

So what was wrong? Why was Eddie uneasy? It was the way he'd felt when Rory was running around with that Starke boy.

Rory's hair. That was it. He was letting it grow.

"So," he said to his son, "I understand you're spending the weekend at the lake with Rosalie and her parents."

"No, Dad," said Rory.

"No? What do you mean, no?"

"I had to turn down the invitation. I had a prior commitment."

"Prior commitment to what, may I ask?"

"I have to be at the Watkins headquarters to stuff envelopes. I promised Father Leveque."

"For Christ's sake, Rory Michael, you have a chance to spend time with the woman you love, and you turn it down for that politician!"

"Now, Edward," Gertrude ventured. "Rory will have plenty of time to see Rosalie after the wedding, won't you, dear?"

"Yes, Ma."

"And this is such a splendid opportunity for Rory to learn how the two-party system works."

"Jesus Christ!" said Eddie. "He'll learn a lot, Gertrude. Yes, he'll learn plenty, working for that ding-a-ling Watkins. Because Watkins is going to get creamed in November, do you hear me, young man? Sullivan is going to emasculate—"

Gertrude's fork dropped to her plate with a delicate tinkle. "Edward," she said, "will you refrain from using language like that at the table?"

Eddie spun spaghetti around his fork. "I was merely trying to point out to your son certain realities of which he is not aware." He gulped a mouthful. "And another thing. You have spent a lot of your time hanging around with Father Leveque. Far be it from me to speak a word against an ordained priest. But I don't think you're aware of how much trouble he's trying to start. Those few words he said during Mass last Sunday. Wait till the Cardinal hears that Leveque's been telling all the girls it's all right to take the Pill."

Pat spoke up. "It probably is all right, Daddy. The Pope's got that Commission, and everybody's sure he's going to listen to them and drop the ban on birth control. Father Leveque's only being practical."

"Practical? If he were practical, he'd keep his mouth shut and let the Pope do the talking. Who put Leveque in charge, I'd like to know? If Leveque were Pope, he'd turn Pat and Eileen into Cardinals. Until the ban is officially lifted, these girls will have to go on using rhythm."

"Father Leveque has a sister in Washington who uses rhythm," Rory said.

"See, what did I tell you," said Eddie.

"Anne's been married eight years and has had seven kids. She knows about real poverty."

"Then she's not doing it right," Eddie insisted.

"I hardly think that birth control is a suitable topic for discussion," Gertrude said.

"All right," said Eddie. "All right. We'll drop it. Christ, why is it that every time I say something, Mr. College Graduate over there has a snappy answer."

"I'm sorry, Dad," said Rory. "I only said...."

"What is your problem? When I was going out with your mother, I'd have jumped at the chance to spend some time with her. Yes, even with her own mother along. And you know how the old bat felt about me. Hell, Rory Michael, don't you know how that *looks?*"

"Dad, I'd rather not—"

"Who cares what you'd rather? And that hair of yours. When are you going to get it cut?"

"Ma," said Rory, "I think I'd better leave."

"No, Rory."

"Do you know how that looks?" Eddie demanded.

Rory turned pale.

"Dammit, Rory, if it gets any longer, do you know who you're going to look like? Zsa Zsa Gabor. So get it cut, Miss Zsa Zsa, and when you're finished eating, you get on the phone and tell Rosalie you're spending the weekend with her. Otherwise people are going to start talking about you. *And I think you know what they're going to say."*

Gertrude gasped. Pat winced. Tears of outrage sprang to Rory's eyes.

The feelings he'd lost for so long, which were only now coming back, had been held up to contempt and ridicule in front of his mother and sister. Eddie had called him a queer. If Eddie had kicked him below the belt, it couldn't have hurt more.

"Rory," whispered Gertrude. "He didn't mean it. Now settle down and finish your dinner."

"Yes...Ma."

Suddenly, an explosion of spaghetti, meatballs and tomato sauce landed on Eddie McCormick's head.

"Stick it up your asshole," Rory shouted. He turned, and walked out of the house.

An alien sound emerged from Eddie's throat. "If I ever did this to my old man," he whispered in awe, "he'd murder me."

"Oh, dear," Gertrude peeped.

"And I'm going to kill that kid! Right now."

Eddie got up from the table. Strands of spaghetti fell out of his sparse hair as he stormed after his son. His voice rose from a whisper to a roar.

"Edward, no! Don't! The neighbors!" Gertrude couldn't hold him back.

"Come back here, you little queer!" Eddie thundered from the sidewalk. "Come back and get what you deserve. I'm going to tear you limb from limb."

"No, Edward, stop!" Gertrude begged. The Reilly children, who'd been playing on the sidewalk, fled screaming about a spaghetti monster. They'd tell their parents, who would tell the whole neighborhood. All of Saint Catherine's would know. Eddie continued his verbal mortar and rocket attack till Pat distracted him.

"Daddy, please, they can hear you in Siberia."

"What am I going to do?" Eddie dissolved into a high-pitched whine. "I gave that boy everything. And look at what I get in return."

"Come inside, Daddy," Pat urged him.

"What have I done to deserve this?"

Rory rang the bell of Saint Catherine's rectory. "Good evening, Miss O'Toole," he said. "Is Father Leveque in?"

"That he is, Rory, but he's on the phone. Got a call from Washington, he did," Biddy said. "No doubt someone of importance. I'll see."

"I can wait," said Rory. Even Biddy sensed something wrong.

She opened the door and looked into the study. There was no hiding her disapproval of the Father Leveque uniform: blue jeans, and a work shirt instead of a Roman collar. Phillipe had just hung up.

"Rory?" he said. *"Mon ami*, there is something wrong?"

"Dad and I just had a big blow-up."

Monsignor Hayes came in. "Have we a visitor?" he asked. "Rory Michael?"

"I had a fight with my father."

"Oh, no, don't tell me. The famous Eddie temper?"

"Yeah."

"Holy mother, help me." Monsignor Hayes opened the door and heard a blast of profane language in the distance.

"Phillipe, come here a minute," he said, leaving Rory alone with Biddy, who strained to hear through the study door.

"I want you to take that kid in that bug of yours," Monsignor said. "And I want you to *get him out of here*. Right now. Before Eddie does something he'll always regret. *Never mind* what I told you before, just do it."

Phillipe hurried toward the door. "Come on, *mon ami*, we're going for a ride. *Vite!*"

Monsignor whispered a brief prayer and took off down the sidewalk.

"I know a safe place," Phillipe said, as they pulled away from the curb. "Where Madame O'Toole can't hear. Always, she must know. Who was that at the door? Who was on the phone? I get a long-distance call and she thinks it's Lady Bird Johnson. It was Anne. You might think I could rap with my own sister in peace. Rory, I hate myself to say this about any woman. But Biddy, she is a bitch. She assumes the worst and spreads it all around. Now tell me—"

"Phillipe, I don't feel too well."

Phillipe regarded Rory when he stopped for a red light. His friend was a sickly white and shaking.

"What is this?" Phillipe asked. He reached into the back seat, pulled out a blanket, and put it around Rory.

"Thank you, but...."

The light changed and the driver behind the bug honked. "Very well," Phillipe said, and took off again. "I gather that this was more than an exchange of words between yourself and your father."

"I threw my dinner at him. He said that—"

"Rory, I've felt since we first met that there's a hurt buried inside you. I'd like you to tell me what it is."

"Suppose I *can't?*"

"Nothing is that terrible."

"Suppose it is?"

"I'll still be your friend."

"If you can't."

"No, I will still be your friend. Hold on. We're almost there."

Another red light was at Fifth and Wheeler. A huge sign greeted them:

SALES - FORD - SERVICE
EDDIE MCCORMICK

"My name is Eddie McCormick, king of kings; Look on my works, ye Mighty, and despair," said Phillipe.

"Ozymandias," Rory remembered. "Shelley."

"Just hold on."

They turned into a neighborhood that was as alien to Lemon Tree Lane as the surface of the moon. Most buildings were boarded up and covered with graffiti. Debris littered the sidewalk. Acrid smoke still hung in the air.

The VISTA volunteers' house was right across Grant Avenue from Saint Martin's. Another VW pulled out from in front of it, yielding Phillipe the only place to park.

"You see? When you must do something, you're given the means to do it," he said, backing his bug into the space. "Come along. Rory, you're safe with me. I'm your friend, no matter what."

"You might not be for long."

"Come with me. No harm will be done to you."

A black woman wearing a dashiki came out of the house. Phillipe got out to greet her. "Kitty," he said.

"Hey, Father Leveque! What a surprise."

"Kitty, my friend and I, we're in an awful bind. May we use your conference room?"

"You can use the whole house. I'm the last one out and I have to run to a home visit. But here's the extra key, so lock up when you're done, all right? Help yourself to anything you need. The refrigerator's full. After all you have done for me. Hope your friend feels better."

"If I had a million dollars, I'd give it all to you."

Phillipe helped Rory out of the car and into the house. "Is it that obvious?" he asked.

"That you hurt inside? Yes." Phillipe turned on the lights in Kitty's office. "Sit down. Would you like a drink of water?"

Rory shook his head.

"Listen to me," Phillipe said. "nothing is that bad. Just relax. Try to breathe deeply."

"I can't." He was shaking so hard Phillipe was afraid his bones would break.

"Do you wish me to hold you?"

"No, don't touch me! If you do, you'll never forgive yourself. People like me are dirty. I'm a fake. Dad's right about me. Phillipe, you asked, so I'll tell you. You'll regret the fact that you ever came near me. I'm nothing but a fucking queer."

"Sweet Jesus," said Phillipe. The same words came back to his memory, this time in German.

"It's true, and I can't deny it any longer." Rory's confession was like an abscess bursting. He spoke of Jimmy, and how Eddie had driven Jimmy away.

"That night, I sat on the edge of the tub with Dad's razor. I thought I should sink the blade into my wrist. I don't know why in hell I didn't. Then Dad said I had to see a shrink. I wanted to! I thought Dr. Engel was going to help me. He didn't do me any damn good at all. He just made me into this disgusting fake. I don't want to live any more. I never had a right to live at all. I should have died when I had polio—stayed a kid—never grown up into one of God's mistakes."

"Rory, no!"

"Don't touch me."

"Hear me: God does not make mistakes. Neither did He make anyone dirty. You're not sick. You're not crazy. You're not evil. You're like Jean-Pierre. He was perfect just the way he was, and so are you."

"Jean-Pierre was...?"

"Yes. I loved him very much, and I always will."

"You mean you don't hate me?"

"Never. Come closer. Don't be afraid, I won't hurt you."

Rory was to remember that the longest journey he ever took was from one end of that sofa to the other. Phillipe gathered him up and held him close. Still the knife twisted inside him. Eddie had said, *"If he turns queer, he's no son of mine."* Gertrude simply denied it. And there was every kid in the schoolyard who'd made fun of him, called him the class queer. Every priest and nun who said that feelings like his were mortally sinful.

"It hurts," Rory said. He didn't want to cry but couldn't help himself.

"You let it out," Phillipe said. "You're safe with me, my precious one." The front of Phillipe's shirt was soaking wet. Still, he held onto Rory and loved him.

"Little one, I know how much it hurts. You must never harm yourself. Never, my precious."

Gradually, the tears stopped. Phillipe could tell by Rory's breathing that he was sleeping. Only then could he say it: *"Je t'aime."*

Darkness fell. The harsh mercury vapor streetlights came on. Keeping one arm wrapped around Rory, Phillipe reached for Kitty's phone and dialed.

"Saint Catherine's Rectory," said Biddy.

Ah, Biddy, he thought. *Biddy, if only you could see this.*

"This is Father Leveque," he said. "May I speak with Monsignor, please?"

"Where did you go?" Biddy asked. "Mrs. McCormick is worrying out of her mind."

"Tell her not to. May I please speak with Monsignor Hayes?"

Monsignor Hayes came on the line.

"Is the coast clear?" Phillipe asked.

"The storm has passed," Hayes said. "Eddie has finally calmed down. And, you? Just where did you take the kid, anyway? Timbuktu? Are you aware of what time it is?"

"Very much, I'm aware. Give us a bit longer. We'll be back. Tell Madame McCormick there's no reason for concern."

"All right," said Hayes, "but try not to be too much longer. I don't want to risk another Eddie tantrum."

Phillipe hung up, then woke Rory. Rory stirred and sighed. *He's so beautiful*, Phillipe thought. *So much I want to make love to him. But not here, not now.*

"Would you like something to eat?" Phillipe asked.

Rory rubbed the sleep from his eyes. "What have we got?" he asked.

"I'll see what Kitty left."

***

"You mean, after that, the two of you got up off the sofa, ate dinner, and *went home?*" I asked. "Back to Eddie?"

"That's just what we did, Gianna. Really, we had no choice. What was I to say? 'Hey, Biddy, I'm going to spend all night loving the McCormick kid. You can like it or lump it.'"

"Hey, Gertrude," Rory added, "we're in the middle of the riot zone. Is that funny?"

"So, you...went home."

"After we cleaned up Kitty's kitchen, yes. I think we both knew what was inevitable."

"Sure we did," said Rory.

"But I knew if we did make love then, it would have to be done quickly. That's not what we wanted."

"And I was strictly a virgin," Rory said.

"I would not have his first time hurried."

"On the way home," Rory said, "Phillipe had me make two promises. One, that I wouldn't come out to anyone else for a while, and second, that I wouldn't go to Whitney Boulevard."

"Whitney Boulevard was the only meeting place for gay men back then," Phillipe said. "Very dangerous."

"When we got home, Monsignor said Dad had quieted down.

So Phillipe and I went inside. Dad was sitting in his recliner. I said, 'Dad, I'm sorry I threw my dinner at you. And I want to apologize to Ma and Pat for using such awful language.'"

"Your father?" I pictured Eddie, seated like a king on his throne.

"He tried to lay a guilt trip on me. He told me that Ma had been down on her knees, picking bits of meatballs out of the carpet. He said that he'd accept my apology but that he hoped I was satisfied."

"I left then," said Phillipe. "Not once did Eddie apologize to Rory for calling him Zsa Zsa. Besides, there was no reason why he couldn't have cleaned the carpet himself. I recall thinking, *Eddie, your son is homosexual. He is also twice the man that you are.*

"Monsignor Hayes met me back at the rectory. 'Rory is the most frustrated kid I have ever seen,' he said. 'He blows up because he can't wait to get at Rosalie. And I can't wait till January, when he's safely married.'"

"He knew the truth, all along," I said.

"Yes, and he was trying along with all the others to keep it buried."

"I knew what I had to do the next day," Rory said. "I was going to call Rosalie and make a date. I'd take her out to a place where we could be alone, like Makeout Mountain. And I'd tell her, 'Rosalie, I want out.' Not, 'I'm having second thoughts' or 'I want the wedding postponed.' Simply, that I wanted out, that the marriage would never work. Of course I couldn't tell her why. That would have been too much of a shock for a girl like Rosalie."

"Did you?" I asked.

"Well...not for a while. Something else came up."

"Something in the form of a hundred-megaton bomb, launched from the Vatican, and on course for Lemon Tree Lane," Phillipe said.

"What on Earth?" I asked.

"This has to do with Ma's least favorite topic for discussion," Rory said. "Birth control."

"On the next day, *Humane Vitae* was released," said Phillipe. "That affirmed the Church's ban on birth control. To put it as delicately as I can, Gianna, on that day, the excrement hit the fan."

Chapter 8

"You must think I'm the most boring person you've ever met," Rory said.

"What?" I said. "Having heard all this, how can I imagine that for a minute?"

"You think all I ever do is sleep. I don't." His eyes grew heavy. Randi made him comfortable on the couch. "I go for walks along the beach. And I can hear you. It's like you're in another room. Please go on."

Walks along what beach? I wondered. Wherever it was, Rory was already there. In his hand, he held Phillipe's Saint Kristen medal. Randi did a quick check of his vital signs.

"He's all right, just pooped."

"Where were we?" I asked. "Birth control."

"Yes," said Phillipe. "In those days, it was the hottest issue in the Church. So many, including myself, took it for granted that the Pope would lift the ban. I felt strongly about it myself, mainly because of my sister Anne."

"She had seven? In eight years?"

"That wasn't at all unusual. Consider the way Anne was forced to live. Her husband was stuck in a boring, dead-end civil service job. He had to work evenings and weekends, stuffing bags in a supermarket. Anne couldn't work, of course. Who would watch those kids? Still, they couldn't make ends meet.

"Anne and Jerry rented a little box of a house in an unstylish suburb of Washington. It had three bedrooms and only one bath. Only one. And no air conditioning. You wished to know what hell is like? You visited Anne in the summer.

"I hate to call the kids disorderly. But they were. No one ever had enough time and energy for all of them. The house was always noisy. You couldn't finish a sentence, or a single thought, in there. Anne looked thirty years older than she was.

"Finally, I had enough. I tore an article out of *Newsweek* and showed it to her. 'This is as easy as taking vitamins,' I said. 'Why don't you ask your doctor about the Pill?' 'Oh, no,' Anne said. 'The Church doesn't allow, the Pope forbids.' How could I, a priest, even think of such a thing?"

"That's pathetic," I said. "How could you not?"

"Precisely. And I saw the misery Anne went through as only a tiny part of the suffering caused by this doctrine. I asked myself, 'This is the purpose of marriage? More children than you can care for or afford? This is God's will?' Sorry, I didn't buy it. Still, those higher up insisted that rhythm worked. Anne was a perfect example of how well it worked."

"What amazes me is that Pope Paul didn't listen to that commission."

"He didn't need a commission. He only needed to spend one hour watching Anne's kids. But he was safe in his own little world and couldn't reach out to the real one."

"I gather you opposed *Humanae Vitae* when it came out."

"Not only did I oppose it, I was the spokesman for the opposition. Cardinal Corby always considered me the ringleader."

"What a great guy he must have been," I said.

"Uncle Ben was a terrific human being. Forgive the sarcasm."

I thought of the irony. Sister Agnes had asked me to send the pictures of me to her at Cardinal Corby High School. A school for teenage girls.

"Did Rory know how strongly you felt?"

"Indeed. I recall once, the radio was on, and we were listening to a Beatles song. 'Lady Madonna.' That was a perfect description of Anne's life. I told him how I felt, that the Pope *had* to approve the use of the Pill. If he failed to do so, I'd consider requesting a release from my vows."

"That's pretty serious."

"Rory was worried. He'd read horror stories of priests who left and weren't able to find jobs or support themselves. But, Gianna,

I was so sure of myself. I honestly thought I was on safe ground. I was such an idiot in those days."

Rory stirred and said, "No, you weren't."

"Oh, yes, I was. I criticized Pope Paul for not being able to make up his mind. Do you remember when I called him a donkey?"

"Yeah. Pat and Eileen heard that, and Eileen said you were going to get your hide nailed to the wall."

"As I did, thanks to Uncle Ben."

"Wait a minute," I said. "Why a donkey?"

"Place two bales of hay at equal distances from a donkey. He'll starve before he makes up his mind which one to eat first. I compared the Pope to a donkey, little realizing what a donkey I was myself."

"When were you ever a donkey?" Rory asked.

"Over you. The night you came out, I was finally able to admit to myself that I was in love with you. But I had a choice to make. I'd known many priests who weren't keeping their vows of chastity. Some had kids. And some were, like me, in love with other men. It seemed no way to live; to keep the one you love in a shadow. To make sure Uncle Ben never found out. I loved you too much for that.

"And yet, here was my big mistake. I thought that by remaining a priest, I was doing the most good for humanity. I say, for humanity. For every worthy cause. What I failed to see was that I was taking care of everyone except myself. I loved Rory McCormick. But the next morning, when news of *Humanae Vitae* hit the wires, I was torn in half. I decided I had to stay and fight. What a spectacle I made of myself."

"Phillipe, you didn't," Rory said. "But you sure scared me. I heard the news on the car radio on the way to work. I honestly thought it was a joke at first. Then I knew: this was real. I kept trying to call you without going through Biddy. So when you called my office, you couldn't get through. But I got your message. All it said was, 'Channel two at six.'"

I said, "More open warfare."

"It was like my playing David to Rome's Goliath," Phillipe told me. "But without the same result. This time *they* won."

"No, they didn't," I said. "They lost you."

"I couldn't go on as I was. Thank God I lost that war. It gave me a second chance to choose what I really wanted. Because, without Rory to love, I could never have gone on."

"I'll tell you want happened, Gianna," Rory said. "After work, I drove straight to Saint Catherine's."

***

Biddy opened the door. Before Rory could speak, Monsignor Hayes ran into the parlor. "Father Leveque?" he asked.

"No, Monsignor, it's me, Rory. Have you seen Father Leveque?"

"I was about to ask you the same thing. Dear Lord, what has Phillipe gone and done now?"

"He left this message at my office." Rory showed him the note on the "While You Were Out" sheet.

"He's gone on TV," Monsignor Hayes said.

"Saints preserve us!" Biddy chimed in.

"It's just after six. Biddy, quick. Channel two. Oh, mercy on us."

"...for worldwide reaction to Pope Paul's ban of all forms of artificial birth control," the anchorman said. "Channel Two's Kathleen O'Hara was at the residence of Benedict Cardinal Corby today for this statement."

"The teaching of *Humanae Vitae* is clear," Corby said. "Every marriage act *must* be open to the transmission of life. There's no room for further debate of this matter. As we say, Rome has spoken, and the cause is finished."

"Oh, no," said Hayes. "He's hardlining. Benny, couldn't you soften up, just a wee bit? Give us a smile?"

"Kathleen, is it true that not all area priests are conforming to the Pope's pronouncement?" the anchorman asked.

"That's right, Bob," she said. "We met with a group of dissident priests from all over the area. Their spokesman is Father Phillipe François Leveque, of Saint Catherine's on Lemon Tree Lane."

"Lord, help me," said Hayes.

"Glory be to Saint Patrick, it's Father Leveque himself!" Biddy screeched.

"Biddy, *hush!*"

Phillipe looked into the camera. "This encyclical is telling us that the purpose of human sexuality is that of reproduction only," he said. "We must respectfully request to differ. We hold that human sexuality is a gift from God, created to bring comfort and spiritual union even at times when it isn't practical to bring a child into the world."

"So your group feels that means of preventing births, such as the Pill, are morally permissible."

"That is correct."

"Thank you, Father Leveque. Back to you, Bob."

"Why, oh why, couldn't he have lost his temper?" Monsignor Hayes demanded. "Why couldn't he have lapsed into that mixture of French and German? No one would have understood him. This would have blown over. As it is—"

The telephone sprang to life. "I'll get it, Biddy," Monsignor said. "Hello? Ah...yes, Your Eminence. Yes, in fact, we do have Channel Two on right now. No, I'm afraid he's not come home yet. Oh, I will, Your Eminence. You may be assured of that. Yes, I'll tell him, the very instant he gets back. Thank you, Your Eminence. Goodbye."

He hung up. "What did they say in the Western movies? 'Big Chief Red Bird on warpath. Him heap mad.' If only Phillipe had consulted with me before he stormed out this morning. I'd have told him to...to cool it. I've never heard Benny so furious. He makes Eddie McCormick sound like the soul of patience."

"I think I'd better go home now," Rory said. "You know how my Ma gets if I'm late for dinner."

"Yes. Yes," said the weary pastor. "Rory, if you should happen to see Father Leveque first, tell him to call the Cardinal's residence immediately. You might also add that he's in a peck of trouble."

"Yes. I will."

"Thank you. You're a great kid."

***

Rory paused for a drink of water.

"You went home again?" I asked.

"Right. I can just imagine Hayes saying, 'Father Leveque isn't back yet, Your Eminence. Would you like to speak with his soon-to-be lover?' And I'd say, 'Hi, Uncle Ben, how's your converted rice?' No, that's not how we did things. I went home, ate my din-din without throwing any of it, and worried. After dinner I was out on the front porch, reading the paper when I heard Phillipe's car coming around the corner."

"You could hear it?" Phillipe asked.

"You didn't drive the quietest car in the world, you know. So I ran down the sidewalk and you pulled over."

***

"I saw you on Channel Two. God, you were great. But I saw it at the rectory. Uncle Ben called. You're supposed to call him the second you get in. He's out to get you, Phillipe. He's hopping mad."

"Oh, he is, is he? Let him hop a while. Get in, Kid."

"But Cardinal Corby—"

"Screw Cardinal Corby."

Rory got into the bug. "We're not going far," Phillipe said. "Just up to Padgett's Park for a minute. There's something I want to explain to you. Away, of course, from Biddy."

Padgett's Park was an open field and playground at the end of Lemon Tree Lane. Rory and Phillipe sat down at one of the picnic benches.

"I said it once and I'll say it again," Phillipe said. "Screw Uncle Ben. And let him wait. Rory, this has been the worst day of my life. No, the second worst. I was so damn mad today. It was all I could do to keep from blowing up on camera."

"You were terrific. You make a fantastic spokesman."

"No doubt, a splendid performance," he said. "When I first heard the news this morning, I thought this was someone's idea of funny."

"So did I."

"Then I knew it was real. I called Anne to see how she was taking it. 'It's the rule,' she said. 'It won't be easy, but Jerry and I have to obey.' Very nice, no? Anne will soon be pregnant again, if she isn't already."

Phillipe got out his cigarettes and offered one to Rory. They lit them off the same match.

"But it's more than Anne," Phillipe said. "Last night, I spoke to you of Jean-Pierre."

"Yeah," Rory said. "You said he was...like me."

"Rory," Phillipe said slowly, "when you studied the history of the Third Reich, did any of your professors speak to you about pink triangles?"

"Pink triangles?" Rory asked. "*Pink* ones? No, I'm sure they never did. I'd remember that. All of that stuff was on the final exam."

"Ah. As I thought. It's still one of our civilization's best-kept, dirty little secrets."

"What did the pink triangles mean?"

"Do you know why the concentration camps were built?"

"To kill off all the Jewish people," Rory said. "And others the Nazis didn't like. Gypsies. Political prisoners. Those who didn't fit into their stupid Master Race."

"That's all true. But there's more that your teachers didn't tell you. Another purpose of the camps was to kill off men like Jean-Pierre. Men who loved other men."

Rory choked on a mouthful of smoke. "You mean...that was why...?"

"That was the charge against him, yes. All these years, I've been forced to say he was a political prisoner. Even today, if people knew the truth, they'd laugh. Or say he got what he deserved. No one deserves that, Rory. And I regret that he wasn't a political prisoner. They got off easy in the camps, compared to what the Jewish prisoners got. And the men forced to wear pink triangles, as Jean-Pierre was."

"But why doesn't anyone say anything about this?"

"For the simple reason that few of these men survived. Those in the SS had a sick notion of how to amuse themselves. And of those who did make it through, many ended up insane. Or died shortly after the war of abuse suffered in the camps. Or are unable to speak out, for fear of being ridiculed."

"Oh, Jesus."

"My mother kept telling me that the camps are gone but the world hasn't changed that much. That's why I told you last night not to speak to anyone else of the way God made you."

"I won't. I don't trust anyone besides you."

"Very good, *mon ami*. Now, you may wonder why I've told you this about my dear cousin. I say this in order that you may understand the kind of atmosphere there was in Europe in those days, that justified the outright murder of homosexual men.

"I regret to say that those in the Third Reich had a strong belief concerning the meaning of human sexuality. They, too, thought it only for reproductive purposes. Anyone who wasn't increasing one of their 'approved' races was guilty of a crime.

And two men, they may love each other, but the expression of their love isn't going to make a baby, no?"

"No," said Rory.

"So, since those like Jean-Pierre didn't qualify as 'real men' willing to breed everyone else off the face of the Earth, they deserved to die."

"I had no idea," Rory admitted.

"That's why I had to do what I did this morning. This limited notion, that we're permitted to make love only to make babies, whether it's practical or not...it's wrong. I heard this, I heard an echo of the charges against Jean-Pierre. That's an extreme example. But it was close enough to frighten me. I honestly thought the Church would see this. In fact, I still have faith. The world is in an uproar over *Humanae Vitae*, Rory. I believe it will be rescinded within a few days."

"Phillipe, suppose it's not? I've never heard of an encyclical being rescinded."

"If it isn't, I'll still stay and fight. I see by your expression, you're probably wondering why I became a priest in the first place."

"Well...yeah. Especially since this birth control business has always been the official Church teaching."

"You're not the only one who wonders. My mother, she was very much opposed to it, and let me know. She's not at all religious. The evidence of history is on her side. The Church did precious little to save the Jews, and absolutely nothing to save the men like Jean-Pierre. How, then, did such a mother produce two children like Anne and myself? That's one of life's mysteries.

"But I'd say to her, '*Maman*, it doesn't have to be so. I can make a difference. From inside, I can make the Church more gentle, more loving.'"

"More of Pope John XXIII. Less of Cardinal Corby," Rory suggested.

"Precisely. That's why I had to do what I did today. And why I'll stay on the front line, till *Humanae Vitae* is rescinded."

"Phillipe, I'm scared for you. I don't want Uncle Ben to do anything really rotten to you. Because at this point, you really are the only friend I have."

"And I'll continue to be your friend, Rory. Forever."

Only a faint rose glow remained in the night sky. Rory noticed the medal that Phillipe was wearing. "You had that on TV today," he said.

"It's Saint Kristen of the Order of Divine Compassion," said Phillipe. "This belonged to Jean-Pierre. I put it on and said a prayer: "Please don't let me look like a blathering idiot on the six o'clock news.""

"It worked," Rory said.

"Naturally it did. Jean-Pierre, he still watches over me. We'd better go, now. Your mother."

"All she ever does is worry. She gets on my nerves, sometimes. I can walk back home."

"That's best. Rory, I must tell you, it wouldn't do for us to be seen returning to the rectory together. I shall spell out the reason. B-I-D-D-Y."

"What has that old harridan been up to?"

"Any time she sees me in the company of another person, she has to cross examine that one. I don't want her bothering you. Besides, she may take up spying for Uncle Ben."

"Phillipe, I couldn't stand for you to get hurt."

Phillipe embraced Rory in the darkened parking lot beside the VW. "Don't fear for me, Little One," he said. "Jean-Pierre really is in the highest place in heaven. He takes good care of me."

***

"What a donkey I was." Phillipe said. "I couldn't even admit to you, the real reason why I was trying to protect you from Biddy. And I wanted to kiss you so badly."

"If you'd started something, I never would have been able to stop it," Rory said. "Gianna, I'd better explain how unsafe that was. Padgett's Park looked like such a tranquil place. But during that summer, a lot of the kids went there at night to smoke pot. So, naturally, the police patrolled it after dark. Suppose we'd been caught? We would have both been arrested, for sure. That would have made our day complete."

"Uncle Ben's, too," Phillipe remarked.

"I was so worried," Rory said. "I remember watching your bug sputter off. And I thought, *there goes the Titanic at full throttle towards the iceberg*. In fact, I was so caught up in your problem, I had forgotten my own."

"Rosalie," I said. "You forgot to get rid of her."

"I got halfway home and it hit me. 'My gosh, I haven't even spoken to Rosalie yet.' And I was so eager to break the engagement quickly, before any more money went down the drain. I arranged to see her the next day. It was something I had to do by myself." Rory puffed on another cigarette, "I rushed into it. I felt like I'd performed a sloppy execution. And when my folks found out...."

His eyes grew heavy again. He dropped the cigarette, I grabbed it and put it out.

"Another one of hell's circles was raised," said Phillipe.

"Pretzel, we weren't doing anything right back then, were we? All we did was mess up."

"No, *mon amour*, not till we were able to admit our true feelings towards each other. Then, and only then, did our new life begin."

"I want to tell Gianna the last part, but I just can't stay awake much longer."

"It's all right. I have some ideas I can try with what's here."

"Then I'll tell you tomorrow. I *know* I'll tell you tomorrow. And it's the best part of all."

Chapter 9

$\mathcal{L}$ATELY, SISTER AGNES FOUND IT DIFFICULT TO SLEEP. At times, drifting between sleep and wakefulness, she heard her father tap on the door of her cell. "Patricia," he said. "Seven-thirty. Up and at 'em. Rory Michael, aren't you ready yet?"

"Please, Dad," she said. "I'm not in high school any more." She worried that he would disturb the other nuns. Eddie was never a quiet man. Then she would wake up at three and be unable to get back to sleep.

Insomnia, she knew, was bad for her blood pressure.

Tonight was different. Instead of tapping on her door, Eddie walked right in. "Pat?" he asked. "I have to talk to you."

"Sure, Dad. Come on in. Quick, before the other Sisters see you."

"Yeah, I'm not used to being in a convent. Awful quiet around here at night."

"We call it the Great Silence."

"Yeah," said Eddie.

He was dressed as he'd been in one of his most outlandish McCormick Ford commercials, as a burlesque comedian. He wore a green and orange plaid suit, a hula girl tie down to his knees, and he held a crushed hat. "Mind if I sit down?"

"Please do."

Eddie sat in Sister Agnes' desk chair. "Do they let you smoke in here?" he asked.

"No. I'm sorry. I wish they did."

"Aw, never mind. It can wait. Listen, Pat, I want to ask you if you've been to the nursing home *yet* to see your mother."

"I'm really sorry, but I haven't. Not since before I found out Rory has AIDS. You know me. I put things off. It's my worst fault. In fact, that desk is full of things I've been meaning to do."

"I think you'd better go see her," Eddie said. "And soon. You know how she is. You don't show up, she starts getting suspicious. Imagines all sorts of things."

"Dad," Pat began, and paused to think of what to say. "I know you remember her as being the one who took care of you when you were so sick. But, since her last stroke, she's changed. Her mind comes and goes. I swear, she spends most of her time serving tea and crumpets to people long dead."

"Nevertheless," Eddie said, "she probably understands more than she's letting on. I want you to go see her, Pat. Even if she acts like she's not all there, I want you to talk to her. Distract her. Tell her everything's great. Because if she figures out that Rory's sick, you know how she'll get. 'Oh, my poor little baby.' She'll want to go to California. There'll be no shutting her up."

"All right, Dad," Sister Agnes promised. "Let's see. I know I can't make it tomorrow; I have to meet with some of the parents. Then, we have SATs coming up. Sunday is the only chance I can get out there. Sunday afternoon, I'll go."

"Good girl, Pat. I knew I could depend on you. Remember, cheer her up."

"Dad?"

"Yes, Honey?"

"What's it like where you are now?"

"Aw, it's getting awful. The place is full of queers and they get the best tangerines."

"Tangerines?" she asked. "Why tangerines?" Eddie faded into a mist. Sister Agnes woke in her darkened cell, the clock in the parlor ringing three.

Again, it was Wake Up and Worry Time.

She rolled over and tried to get back to sleep. It was no use. The events of the previous day ran through her mind. Things had been so chaotic lately, with representatives of colleges coming by, parents calling. The phone never stopped ringing.

"My twin is dying and I can't tell anyone."

Sister Agnes had gone to the Golden Galaxy Mall to pick up some Dr. Scholl's insoles. Aloysius Sweeney was there with his breath that would stop a speeding train. She tried to avoid him but it was too late.

He'd purchased a copy of the tabloid paper, *Nightfall*. Sister Agnes saw the headline. "TWO-HEADED BABY FATHERED BY SPACE ALIEN."

"My group and I are collecting signatures," he said. "We wanted to set up a booth in this Mall but the management wouldn't allow it. Most regrettable. It's quite clear to me that they don't understand the importance of our work. They will, some day, mark my words. Here's my petition. We want mandatory AIDS testing for everyone over the age of five, and quarantine of those testing positive. Sister Agnes, I know it sounds extreme, but believe me it's the only way to put a stop to this lavender plague before it spreads into the general population. May I ask you to sign it?"

She thought of ramming it down his throat.

"There's an interesting article on the subject in this very paper," Sweeney said. "Now, some of this, like the two-headed baby, you have to take with a grain of salt. But this. Some prominent scientists agree that this plague must be halted before it's *too late*. Before respectable people—"

"Why...I don't seem to have my pen with me...." Sister Agnes had at least five pens with her at all times.

"Perhaps I have one." Sweeney blundered through his pockets. "I know that you, working as you do with innocent young girls, must surely be concerned with—"

"Excuse me, Mr. Sweeney, Sister Irene is calling me."

"Ah...yes. Remind me to bring you one of these petitions. You'll want to make some copies and hand them out to your staff."

Aloysius, I'll do no such thing, she thought, and tried to lose herself in the crowd of shoppers. Sister Agnes knew the importance of being polite to Sweeney. He paid for most of the construction on the school building. Most people regarded him as harmless, but she didn't know. He had some strange ideas and a house full of firearms. And there were some who said he had a problem with the drink. He scared her sometimes. "Lord," she mumbled, "what if he finds out about Rory?"

Suddenly, she felt dizzy and sat on one of the benches. Everything seemed too loud: the shoppers' chatter, the water in the fountains, and the organ music blasting out of Schwartz's Fine Pianos. A teenager sat beside her and took a bite of an aromatic pizza. Her stomach lurched. For an instant she was afraid of either passing out or throwing up.

A clerk from B. Dalton's stopped. "Are you all right, Sister?" she asked.

"Yes. Yes, I'm fine."

Sister Agnes sat for a while, then carefully got up. The insoles would have to wait for another day. She had to get out of this place. It was full of people who didn't know or care that her twin had AIDS.

Once in the parking lot, she felt a little better. Then it dawned on her. She didn't know where she'd parked the convent's station wagon.

Sister Agnes spent the better part of the afternoon looking for it. She didn't dare ask the Mall security for help. People would think she'd lost her mind. After all, she was the principal of Corby High.

Once back at the convent, she gathered the mail and dropped it on her desk.

***

Sister Agnes rolled again and the springs squeaked. It was useless. No more sleep for her tonight. Perhaps she ought to see a doctor, get some prescription sleeping pills. Of course, she could never tell the doctor the real reason.

She sighed, got up, and turned on the light. She'd go through the mail, she thought.

She came across an appeal from the Traditionalist League that started out, "Dear Friend." The letter said the same things Sweeney had told her in the Mall, but this time, he wanted a minimum of twenty-five dollars.

"Into the trash with *you*," she muttered, tossing it into the waste basket.

Then she saw a manila envelope with a picture of a grinning gorilla holding a martini with an olive in it. "Mighty Joe Young's Safari Lounge, Los Angeles, California," she read.

Sister Agnes tore it open and glanced at the photos. At first glance, Ms. Raimondi appeared to have nothing on. Closer inspection revealed she wore quite a lot, mostly feathers and sequins. There were three pictures of her singing and dancing. She was small, dark and intense. Sister Agnes couldn't help but notice, Longianna Raimondi had a marvelous pair of legs. Then, she found the other picture, a shock after not seeing her brother's image for twenty years.

Turning quickly from it, she picked up the accompanying note. "Dear Sister Agnes," she read. "I hope these don't cause too much of a scandal, but they'll give you an idea of what I look like. I appreciate your prayers for me, but I'm enclosing this one of me and Rory so you can pray for him, too. It was taken by the pool last September before he was diagnosed. I was an idiot for not knowing something was wrong by looking at this. I'm sorry to say that he doesn't look much like this anymore.

"Please pray for Rory, Sister. He doesn't complain but I see what he goes through. He needs your prayers a lot more than I do."

Sister Agnes studied the image of her twin in the dim light. In Africa, she knew, they called AIDS the slim disease. She could easily see why. "Yet Rory really doesn't look so different from the way he did twenty years ago," she told herself. "Of course, if he really was anorexic then...."

He was.

"At least Dad would be happy that he got his hair cut."

She stuffed the pictures back into the envelope and hid it in her bureau drawer. Rory had been looking right into the camera. Directly at her. There had been a plea in his eyes, which were also Ma's eyes: *Something is wrong. Help me.*

Sister Agnes decided she'd have to phone Longianna and thank her. Yet....

There was reason for concern. Sister Agnes had been calling Longianna from the phone at her desk in school. She alone approved payment of that bill. But suppose someone else were to see it, and question a large volume of Los Angeles calls?

"Another thing to worry about, at this unholy hour."

Besides, as she'd said in the dream, her time was limited. College entrance exams were coming up. Certainly, she didn't wish to be interrupted or overheard while speaking with Longianna. Some of their conversations bordered on the incredible.

"Doesn't it bother you?" Sister Agnes had asked during their last chat. "I mean, isn't it a rather intense physical relationship?"

"Intense?" Longianna had asked. "Rory and Phillipe are lucky if they can hold hands."

"At one time...."

"Yes. At one time, it was highly intense. They both remember. It means so much to both of them, to stay quietly together and share those memories."

"I see," said Sister Agnes. "And this doesn't bother you?"

"Should it?" Longianna asked. "They're two people who love each other."

They're both men, Sister Agnes had wanted to say. She bit her lip.

"Of course," Longianna added, "theirs isn't an everyday attorney/client association."

"Gracious, no," Sister Agnes agreed.

Longianna said something about a song she was writing for Rory. "Why that sounds...most interesting," Sister Agnes had said. "I should like to hear it."

"I still have a way to go on it," Longianna admitted.

Sister Agnes turned out the light and went back to bed. *If I could sleep*, she thought. *If only I could sleep.*

"I'll call Longianna," she decided. "I promised I'd go see Ma on Sunday. No, Dad, I won't forget. Sunday, that's right. After I get back, I'll call Longianna and thank her. Long-distance rates will be down. It was kind of her. So very kind. And I'll tell her so. On Sunday. All I have to do is hold out till Sunday. And all will be well. Forever and ever, world without end, amen."

Chapter 10

THAT NIGHT I DREAMED THAT RORY AND I WERE IN A CAVE in Sicily. He looked like he did last winter, very ill but able to walk. Still, I had to support him over sharp rocks.

"We ought to turn back," I suggested. "It's awfully cold and dark down here."

"No, Gianna. We must go on."

"If you say so. Why?"

"Because we have to see Ma."

I had a Coleman lantern which I held up. The terrain ahead looked forbidding even for a person in perfect health. "I'm beginning to doubt that this was a good idea," I admitted. "Why did I let you talk me into this?"

"Believe me, Gianna, it's the only way."

"Rory, who is that?"

Ahead of us was a woman. It was clear that she wasn't Gertrude McCormick. I had a quick impression that she was incredibly old. Her skin was unwrinkled and her hair had stayed a shiny deep brown.

"Who is she?" I asked.

"My mother," he replied.

She called to him in a deep, operatic voice, "Rory Michael."

"No. Don't go," I said. "I don't like the look of this. Let's go back."

"Gianna, this is something I have to do."

"But not yet."

"Look at me," he said, and took off the suede coat he bought and never had a chance to wear. "How can I go on like this?"

I held up the lantern and saw him as he was, thin and covered with open sores.

"Then, go to her," I said. "If this is the only way."

"It is," he said. I held his coat and let him go.

The woman handed him something that at first seemed like a large tangerine. Curious, I held the lantern up and saw that it was instead a pomegranate.

The moment he ate it, he changed. He gained at least fifty pounds. The sores grew smaller and vanished. His hair turned back to shiny gold.

"Now my dear son will live forever," the woman told me. I called her by name. "Persephone." She smiled and nodded.

I woke up, made a leap for my pad and pen, and began to scribble.

***

"Where were we?" Phillipe asked. "Still in 1968, with both of us making an incredible mess of our lives."

Rory was upstairs, going through the elaborate ritual that got him ready to face the day. "Randi, do I have to take that pill?" he asked.

"You should. In case there's any pain."

"It makes me feel a little spacey. No, we're going to do the important part today. I'd rather have my mind clear."

"Very well, Dearie," Randi said. "But if you start feeling uncomfortable, you tell me right away."

"Don't worry. You'll know."

"Ah, Rory is ready to come down now." Phillipe said.

"I didn't miss anything, did I?" Rory asked as Randi carefully placed him on the sofa.

"Not yet. As I was saying, things were worse for both of us. When I got back to Saint Catherine's that night, I managed to squeeze a call to the Cardinal's residence into my oh-so-busy schedule."

"Was he mad?" I asked.

"All I got was this frozen, controlled wrath," Phillipe said. "His Eminence informed me that I had twenty-four hours to get back in line. Not only to get back in line, but to go on TV with my gang, as he called the other priests, and issue a public recantation. Twenty-four hours, he said, or else. Naturally, I had to find out what 'or else' was."

"Wow, did you find out," said Rory.

"All of us were relieved of our duties," said Phillipe. "Myself, Father Jackson from Saint Martin's and four others. We had to leave our rectories immediately. That was because the Cardinal feared a public demonstration of sympathy towards the six of us would take place the following Sunday."

"It did," said Rory.

"A pity we weren't around to enjoy it. As it was, we six moved into a house on Tenth Avenue. We made it our commune. We settled in for a good long siege."

I said, "No more Biddy."

"What a relief, to see the end of her," Phillipe said. "Yet I was amazed. The Church, which took five hundred years to make Kristen a saint, moved so fast when it had to."

"The might and splendor and glory of Imperial Rome," said Rory. "It never died."

"Yet in my last twenty-four hours at Saint Catherine's, *mon amour*, you were getting into your own problem," Phillipe reminded Rory.

"Oh, yes," he said. "Rosalie."

I served Rory a glass of ice water with a lemon slice and he began.

"Again, I wasn't thinking," he said. "Phillipe told me once that the French invented the most merciful form of execution: the guillotine. So I thought that was how I'd end things with Rosalie. One swift blow. I made a date with her for the following day. Gianna, I thought if we could discuss this alone, without her parents, or mine, or, God forbid, her Uncle Ben, we could end our engagement like two civilized adults. That's not how it worked out. I guess I overestimated her."

"She cried?" I asked.

"Did she cry!" said Rory. "My problem was, I had to tell her I didn't want to marry anyone, without letting her onto the real reason. I couldn't trust her with that. Fine potential we had for a happy marriage, right? The whole thing brought out a side of her personality I just couldn't deal with." Rory took a sip of water. "Was she spoiled? That's putting it mildly. Never before had anyone said, 'Rosalie, dear, you can't have that.' Anything she wanted, she could manipulate her parents to get. Or her loving uncle. The best clothes, a stable full of horses, summers in Europe.... Rosalie wants? Rosalie gets."

"She wanted the wedding of the century. You said she couldn't have it."

"God, it was a mess. Rosalie started yakking about *Humanae Vitae*. It wasn't going to be a problem for us, she said, because she could afford nannies for all our children. Can you believe that? It made me realize that not only didn't I love her, I couldn't stand her. I told her once. She asked if we could name our first son Benedict. I told her again. It sank in. She said, 'Waaaah!'"

"So you were stuck with her, with the water running."

"Rosalie reminded me of the guest list. We were going to invite the mayor, the governor, even that crook Congressman Sullivan. What was I trying to do? Embarrass her? Humiliate her in front of the whole world? I told her what Phillipe said, about marriage being a sacrament, not an extravaganza. I tried to say that a divorce or annulment would be much worse. She wasn't listening. At that point she just plain hated me. 'Take me home, you creep.' she said. Which I did. All the way home, 'Waah. Waah.' She told her folks, who told Eddie before I even had the chance. Things got so bad, Gianna, I had to move away from home. I knew of a walk-up apartment with a monthly lease that just happened to be on Tenth Avenue near the commune. So, I took it."

"Meanwhile, our Eminent Lord Cardinal saw himself in a state of trench warfare with me and my 'gang.'" Phillipe said. "We were known as the Tenth Avenue Six. He was too crafty and too Roman to take on all of us at once. So he made up his mind, it would be one at a time. Each of us would go to a monastery outside the city for a weekend. He said it would be to pray, do penance, and consider our respective futures. And that I, being the ringleader, would go first."

"Whatever did he have in mind?" I asked. "Whips and chains?"

"No doubt the thought occurred to him," said Phillipe. "However, I wasn't able to avail myself of that opportunity. Rory had visited our commune briefly. Recall, we were being so careful. He did tell me that he'd broken up with Rosalie and was forced to move out, without giving any details."

"Yes. You told me about the fun weekend the Cardinal had planned. So I invited you to stop off for dinner and see my new place Friday evening on your way over. To the monastery. Of course. Only later—much later—did it occur to me that I'd propositioned you."

"And I said, *mon ami*, nothing would please me more."

I gave them both a knowing look. It didn't take much of an IQ to figure out what happened next.

"It seemed like such a dark time for both of us," said Phillipe. "I'd worked so hard for Will Watkins. For a while, he was catching up to Sullivan. But there were rumors, that if Humphrey got the nomination, there would be hell to pay at the Democratic Convention. That could hurt Will. And on top of everything else, on that Friday, my car dropped dead on me."

***

Rory decided that although he'd never done any real cooking before, this meal wasn't going to be bad at all. He'd selected the steaks and salad ingredients with care. At half past six, there was a knock at the door.

"Phillipe!"

"*Mon ami*, here I am. I believe you've met Father Jackson?"

"Sure. Great to see you."

"And here are a few goodies I've brought you. Some wine, some eclairs."

"Wow," said Rory. "Looks like you bought out Suzette's Bakery."

"Enough calories here to fatten up the French Foreign Legion," said Father Jackson.

"Rory, there's one more favor I must ask of you," Phillipe said. "You know where this monastery is? On Route 198? Might you take me there after dinner?"

"I'd love to."

As if either one of us had the intention of actually going there.

"Father Jackson was kind enough to bring me over. It seems my little bug, she died."

"Yeah," said Father Jackson. "Right out in the middle of the street."

"I pushed her to the curb," said Phillipe. "I called a crane to take her to *Der Beetle Haus*. They charge an arm and a leg. I have Heinz examine her. Heinz tells me, 'Father Leveque, you've thrown a rod. The patient is in critical condition.' I say to him, 'Very well, Heinz. Fix her on Monday. Don't worry about it, I will not need her this weekend.' Of course, that will cost my other arm and leg. One grows philosophical about these things."

"Right. All six of us are turning into philosophers," said Father Jackson. "I've got to be getting back. Enjoy your dinner."

"Hey, thanks for bringing Phillipe over," Rory said.

"It was most gracious of you," Phillipe told him.

The minute Father Jackson was gone, Phillipe gathered Rory into a strong embrace. "God, Kid. I've missed you. And I've been so damn worried. What did happen?"

"I broke up with Rosalie. My dad found out. He said he was going to knock some sense into my head."

"No, never. I feel responsible. I was off trying to save the world, being Fighting Father Leveque. And I left you to face Eddie alone. If he'd hurt you, I'd never stop blaming myself."

"But Ma and Pat were right there. Ma wouldn't let him do anything. Then he went over to the Corbys, and told them the wedding was still on. Phillipe—"

At that instant, the phone rang.

"I'll watch the steaks," Phillipe said. The phone was beside Rory's bed, which was a mattress on the floor covered with a tie-dye spread.

"Hello?" he said. Then, "Yes, Ma. Yes, Ma. Yes, Ma." And, "No, Ma, everything's fine. In fact, I have company right now. One of the guys. Just one of the guys from the office. We were talking about that. We think we'll be leaving later on, heading up to the lake. Yes, the lake. That's just it, Ma, there's no phone there. No, nothing's going to happen. Ma, I'll call you on Monday, all right? Monday. I know. Goodbye."

"These steaks look just about ready now," Phillipe said. "I'll take them out, and...."

"Phillipe, she's driving me insane. Ever since I moved out, she's been worse than she was before. She's always coming over here with no warning. That's why I handed her that crap about going to the lake, so we could have some peace and quiet. She started right in. Those woods are full of bugs and snakes and poison ivy. And the lake is full of *water*. I tell you, I can't take much more of this Irish Madonna act."

"My poor little one," Phillipe said. He went over to Rory, sat beside him, and took his hand. "Your mother loves you very much. You know that."

"Too much, I think. You know what she did Sunday? I heard all this noise in the stairwell. There she was, struggling up, with her huge vacuum cleaner. Her Hoover with a headlight. I said, 'Ma, it must be one hundred degrees outside. What do you mean, dragging that up four flights?' 'I was only trying to help,' she says. I wanted to scream. It's like, if she can't attain martyrdom in her own home, she'll attain it in mine."

"Married to your father, attaining martyrdom ought not to be too difficult," Phillipe said. "As the saints bore their crosses, your mother bears her Hoover. Gertrude silently suffers."

"Oh, Jesus," Rory said, and began to giggle. "But the way she still acts like I'm a little boy. It gets on my nerves."

"I look at you and know you're not," said Phillipe. "Rory, perhaps I should not say this, because your mother's love for you is real. However, she may be trying to make you feel guilty about leaving her."

"I think Ma is manipulating me," Rory said. "I can't move back to that house. Dad is furious with me over Rosalie. Plus, he says I'm crazy to pay rent on a dump like this when I should be saving up for a home. A dump, he calls it. I don't think it's so bad. Well, I guess it's a dump, compared to Lemon Tree Lane. But I'm so much happier here, being away from the constant bickering. I can sleep all night without hearing one 'goddamit, Gertrude' or 'oh, Edward.' Besides, Pat's so mad, she won't even speak to me. She says if Dad has a coronary, it's all my fault."

"Your father is many years away from his first coronary."

"It's true about Ma. She wants me back so badly, I think she's obsessed with it. But on her terms. Everything has to be as it was. I'll be her good boy and go through with the wedding. As if nothing ever happened that night on Grant Avenue. Phillipe, I absolutely can't do that. And I can't tell them why. What am I going to do?"

Phillipe put his arm around Rory. "In the first place, you're not going to be skipping any more meals. I can feel that you've lost a bit of weight you had gained, no?"

"Well...I guess so."

"Sit down and I'll fix the rest of our dinner."

"But—"

"But nothing. I've been doing most of the cooking for the Tenth Avenue Six, you know. And I'm not so bad. None of us has gotten food poisoning yet."

Rory sat at the table and listened. "When Anne and I were young, we were banned from *Maman's* kitchen. And rightly so. *Maman* had too many ingredients that weren't just inedible, they were highly volatile. Your typical French cuisine, no? During the war, it was. We kids had to stay out. Somehow, later in my life, I learned how to cook. A good thing, too. Last winter, I was visiting Anne. All of her kids had the flu. Anne was up and waiting on them. She felt ten times worse than the whole pack of them combined. So I said, 'Enough, young lady. Get into that bed. I'll fix dinner, wash the sheets, and read the little monsters a story. But you're going to take care of yourself.' Dinner is served."

"Phillipe, this is great."

"For pity's sake, dig in. I worry about you, you know. I will not have you losing any more weight."

"I've been worried about you, too. The way you stood up to Uncle Ben. And what about Will? How's the campaign going?"

"It goes along. This weekend, Will is out of town. He's making a speech to the Enlightened Order of Caribou."

"Sounds like he's in Sullivan's territory."

"He is. It won't be easy."

The TV news was on with the volume low. Rory switched it off after Chet and Dave wished each other good night.

"I'm worried about Ma," he said. "I know she's lonesome right now. This is Eileen's last weekend before she goes in the convent, so Pat's giving her a big party. And Dad's in Detroit."

"Rory, I know this is very difficult. But your mother must learn two lessons. First, that you're no longer a child. Your life is yours, not hers. And second, that she's married to Eddie, not to you."

"That," Rory said, "is going to be the toughest thing of all. I don't know what you did to the steaks, they're terrific."

"A few little seasonings you had in your cabinet. Would you like some eclairs now or later?"

"Can we have them later? I mean...you don't have to leave right away, do you?"

"Not at all. They said to be there at eight. But I don't think the abbot will care much if I'm there by nine."

"We have a little time, then."

"Would you like some wine? A bit won't go to your head."

"That'd be nice."

They sat on together on the sofa. The lights were low and twilight was falling. Rory lit some incense.

"Seriously," he said, "I don't know what to do with myself. With the rest of my life. You're the only person I ever—well, told the truth about myself. And it meant so much to be able to admit it to myself as well as to you. But I don't think I'll ever—I mean, ever...do anything about it. Phillipe, do you think I should enter a monastery?"

"You mean, resolve the issue by taking a vow of chastity? I'll be honest with you, Rory. I do not."

"I didn't mean become a priest like you are. I've known too many guys who dropped out of the seminary. They all said it nearly drove them insane. But to be a monk...you don't think it would work?"

"Rory, would you like me to tell you a true story about that?"

"I'd love it."

"Then, come closer. You're comfortable now?"

"Very."

"When I lived in Washington, long ago, there was a boy of seventeen. Much like you. He was a French boy. He'd been in this country for some time but in many respects, he was just off the boat. Very idealistic and incredibly naive.

"This boy worked during the summer as a translator for a distinguished businessman three times his age. One night, they worked late and were alone in the office. The man said to the boy, 'I love you. I'll love you forever.' The boy, being only a kid, believed him. I think he needed a father figure. His own father had died when he was quite young. Perhaps the older man did love him, but only for a while. I should like to think so. Then it was...over. And great pain was caused. The man's wife found out—not about this boy but about several others—and divorced him. The boy was confused and hurt. He became quite promiscuous for a while."

"What happened to the boy?" Rory asked.

"You may assume that his mother learned what was going on."

"His mother? She must have had a fit."

"No. His mother, she was most understanding. It's said that

this runs in families, and it had happened in her family before. She said to her son, 'I wish you'd told me that you were having these problems. You're the way God made you. Nothing will change that. But please, stop and think of what you're doing. Bring no more harm to those you love.'

"The boy gave her his promise. But he saw no way to avoid doing harm. There seemed to be no place in the world for one such as he. So he went to another area, kept his past a secret, entered a seminary, and was later ordained."

"He took a vow of chastity."

"With the best intentions. He learned they're not enough. I can't be less than honest with you, Rory. What you're thinking is true. I'm the boy in that story."

"I never thought that...."

"That I could be one of *them?* Rory, I've never felt attracted to women."

"I thought I was the only one. Outside of Oscar Wilde, and a few guys in ancient Greece and on Whitney Boulevard."

"Far from it. You weren't even the only one on Lemon Tree Lane."

"Dad says that everybody who's queer—that's what he says— runs wild, can't control himself, hurts little kids."

"That's simply not true."

"You said you would never cause harm."

"Never, to one I loved. I made that vow long before I vowed poverty, chastity and obedience. It means the most to me."

"Then you really are like Jean-Pierre."

"I'd prefer to think so. Actually, I'm a donkey. I go chasing after every worthy cause, in search of what I'm looking for. Always, I have been looking in the wrong places."

"Phillipe, you don't...have to leave just yet...do you?"

"Cardinal Corby wants me to go to this monastery to make up my mind about my future. I don't believe that will be necessary. My mind is already made up. My future, it doesn't lie within the Church. The Church doesn't have the answers I'm seeking. *I don't have to go at all.*"

"You could...stay?"

"If you so wish."

"I want so badly for you to stay."

"Rory, I've cared for you since I first saw you. You, above all, I will not harm."

"Suppose...something happens with the two of us here alone? I mean...you might end up hating me. My friends say they don't understand me. My whole family is mad at me. I can't risk losing you."

"Very well. Let us say for the sake of argument that something did happen. And I loved you more than ever because of it."

"But I've never done anything like that. What if I can't do it right? What if I can't stay still?"

"Who said you had to stay still?"

"Wouldn't I have to?"

It occurred to Phillipe that Rory's mind was an index of misinformation. Who was going to tell him how to love another man? Eddie?

"I'll tell you another secret. Nowhere is it written that you must stay still. In fact, the less still you are, the better it is."

"Really?"

"That's an absolute."

"Does it hurt?"

"*C'est impossible!*" Phillipe felt his command of the English language slipping. "I will not do anything that doesn't delight you, my precious."

"But I could never do it. Not with someone I...loved."

"Little One, may I at least hold you?"

"I want you to hold me so much. I want you to wrap yourself around me like a pretzel."

"Then I'll be your pretzel. If that's what you wish."

Rory snuggled up as he had that night on Grant Avenue. It took a while for the tension to leave his body. *Patience*, Phillipe told himself. *He's worth waiting for. He's a virgin, and what virgin isn't apprehensive? Perfect love casts out fear.*

After a time, Phillipe unbuttoned his Nehru shirt and felt Rory's warm breath on his bare skin. When Rory kissed him, over his heart, he knew how Saint Teresa felt impaled on the angel's fiery sword.

"*Mon amour*," he called Rory for the first time. "My beloved." In the dim light he saw that Rory looked more angelic than human.

Rory stirred and gave him a light kiss on his mouth. Phillipe responded with a kiss that was deep and lingering. "Pretzel," Rory sighed.

"*Je t'aime, je t'adore.*"

Phillipe loosened Rory's clothing, placed him on the bed and kissed him again. Rory was beyond awareness of anything besides his lover's body. With their third deep kiss, so was Phillipe.

Chapter 11

"There were," Rory admitted, "a few intervals of reason over that weekend. Can you think of anything else we did?"

"Wild kid," said Phillipe. "We used up all the hot water, several times. We fed each other the goodies from Suzette's. And we talked. We had to make plans."

"Gianna, you're so young," Rory said. "You can't remember what it was like to be gay, back then. But we knew we couldn't let anyone else know about us. In those days, it would have been suicidal. Phillipe had to find the rules his mother made for Jean-Pierre and we lived by them."

"Eddie," I offered.

"God, yes," Rory said. "If my father had known we had made love, he'd have shot us both. No question. I could have been fired from my job. And Phillipe was in the process of becoming a former priest, which was bad enough. His whole life could have been destroyed."

"When Monday finally did come around, Rory went back to his office, pretending that nothing of importance had occurred. I, however, had to face Cardinal Corby. I must tell you this, Gianna. I went to his residence wearing a Roman collar which I felt I no longer had a right to wear. But it was the only thing that would cover the pash mark Rory had put on my neck. Wait," he told me. "It gets better."

✱✱✱

Cardinal Corby liked to play games with the telephone. One of his favorites was to take calls during appointments with people he was out to make miserable. The sooner he took a call, the lower your status was. Rumor had it that if he were really out to get you, he spoke with his bookie.

"Show Father Leveque in," he ordered his secretary. He was already on the phone.

Phillipe could hear what the person on the other end of the line said. "Waaaah!"

At least this wasn't the bookie.

He reminded himself that hell hath no fury like a Corby woman scorned.

"Now, Princess, don't cry," the Cardinal said. "Yes, I know, you're quite right. You won't give him up without a fight. You'll be coming over later tonight. You, your parents, Mr. and Mrs. McCormick and Pat. We'll get to the bottom of this, don't you worry. Yes, and if there's someone else, we'll get rid of her. Princess, I've lived a lot longer than you have, and I know this to be true from experience. *Everybody has a price.*"

Phillipe looked around the Cardinal's study. He thought of the Biblical verse, that if one offered wealth for love, he would be mocked.

There were pictures everywhere. Here was Cardinal Corby with the Pope and President Johnson. Here he was, blessing the show room of McCormick Ford. And there was Rosalie riding her horse.

"See you tonight, Princess. And wipe those tears away." Corby finally hung up. He nibbled on the butt of his Cuban cigar. He was never without one, and God only knew how he came by them.

"Father Leveque," he finally said, "I understand that you never showed up at the monastery."

"That's correct, Your Eminence."

"I don't seem to be able to get any information out of that gang of yours. Would you mind telling me why you never showed up?"

Phillipe looked as solemn as he could, and intoned, "I threw a rod, Your Eminence."

***

Twenty years later, Rory said, "Now look at what you went and did to Longianna."

"Apparently she finds this amusing. A pity the Cardinal wasn't amused at all."

"She's turning purple. Gianna? Are you all right?"

"I'm fine. Please continue."

***

"You threw a rod," the Cardinal said.

"Yes, Your Eminence."

"Well," he said, "since you never did go to the monastery, may I be so bold as to inquire where you did go?"

"It's a long story. Like Dante, in the middle of my life's path, I got lost. Unlike Dante, however, I didn't go to hell."

A vein was standing out in Corby's neck. This was a well-known danger signal; it always meant he was ready to blow. He rose to his feet, which showed Phillipe how short he really was.

"Just who do you think you are?" he asked. "Ever since Day One, you've done precisely as you please. You and your gang think obedience is a joke."

"Your Eminence, I beg to differ. I take the notion of obedience as seriously as anyone else. Therefore, since I can no longer in good conscience obey you, I'm requesting a release from my vows."

Corby was taken aback; he'd not been expecting this. The vein became more prominent.

"You think I'm going to permit this?" he shouted. "You think that I'm going to let you turn around and walk away, after the damage you've done? You got all the Negroes in Saint Martin's stirred up. That riot was your fault. Then, in Saint Catherine's, you gave the women these insane ideas. Telling them there's more to their lives than self-sacrifice. Why, they'll be coming to me, demanding to be ordained, because of you."

Corby's voice grew louder. It was totally out of proportion to the rest of him. He screeched, roared, and denounced. The verbal abuse continued till his upper plate slid loose. It bounced twice on his desk, landed on a bare spot on the floor, and shattered.

What do I do now? Phillipe wondered.

Corby tried to speak but inarticulate sounds came out. He sputtered in rage, picked up his cigar butt and left.

His secretary came in. Phillipe gestured at the hideous thing lying dead on the floor. The poor man was trying with all his strength not to crack up. He failed.

"Permit me to show you to the door, Father Leveque," he offered.

"Thank you," Phillipe said. "I'll contact His Eminence in writing."

***

"Which is precisely what I did, Gianna. As soon as I got back to the commune, I wrote Cardinal Corby a letter. I respectfully requested release from my vows but made it quite clear that I wasn't going to sit around and stagnate while waiting for an answer from Rome. And that was the last I ever saw of Cardinal Corby."

"Of course, that meant you had no job, no income, no nothing," Rory reminded him.

"I had you."

"You needed more. You told me you asked for another sign. And you got it."

"Father Jackson met me when I returned from the mailbox. He asked me if I'd heard the news. Congressman Sullivan had just been indicted on six counts of bribery and four of perjury. I remember he said that Sullivan had been caught with his hand in the cookie jar all the way up to his armpit. And that it looked like my man Will was in like Flynn."

"You were the first person Will Watkins called. You got together with him and told him that you'd just left the priesthood."

"Which put us both in a tough situation. He kept asking me, 'Phillipe, are you sure you want to do this?' I told him there was more to this than the fact I couldn't get along with the Cardinal. I had been thinking of this step for some time and I had no choice but to take it now. Will wasn't Catholic but he understood just how serious this was."

"And then," Rory said, "he made you that offer."

"He said, 'Phillipe, it appears that unless I screw up spectacularly between now and November, I have a seat in Congress. I'll need a staff I can trust. I was reluctant to ask you as long as you were in the Church. But you say you're out now. Are your free to think about coming with me to Washington?'"

"You mean, he didn't know?" I asked.

"Absolutely not. I had to tell him. Politics being what it was, many people would be more offended by Will's having a gay staff member than they were by Sullivan's corruption. I said, 'I must tell you this. I'm in love.' And he said, 'But, that's great.' So I admitted it. 'Will, I'm in love with another man.' Then, 'Will, it's a good thing your teeth are your own.'"

"I met Will and Cynthia Watkins when they visited Rory last May," I said. "They both seemed so decent."

"They both always were. As Rory showed me love, they showed me friendship. They accepted me totally. The thing that surprised them so much was that they had no idea I was gay. That's how careful I was.

"At first I refused Will's offer. I was so afraid that he would, indeed, screw up before November, and that I'd be the reason why. He told me, 'No one has to know. I'd tell you to be careful, but you are. I can assure you, you won't be the only one on Capitol Hill. What does the public know about you, Phillipe? That you're a former priest? That may cost me a few votes, but what of it? Corby was never going to vote for me anyway.'

"I asked him if he would mind if my special friend came with me. He said that if this person was as discreet as I was, it was fine. I didn't tell him who my special friend was."

"That night, Phillipe told me about Will's offer," Rory said. "All I could say was, 'yes, yes, yes. Call Will back and tell him. Yes, I'll go. I'll find a new job there.' It meant a whole new life for us, in a new place, where we could live together in peace."

"Away from Eddie and Gertrude," I thought out loud.

"Yes," said Rory, "and the Corbys. Phillipe told me about that little conversation he'd overheard. I was worried that the Corbys might hire a private investigator to find out if I'd dumped Rosalie for another girl. A good private eye—and they could afford a good one would find out about me and Phillipe no matter how careful we tried to be. Sooner or later, we'd slip up. Can you imagine what would have happened? Jesus, if that had gotten into the papers...."

"I told Will that my answer was yes," Phillipe said. "Rory was quite right. We couldn't stay in that city, feeling as strongly as we did about each other, with so many people taking an interest in us. In the time between then and the time we left, you never saw two more careful people."

"You both must have been going insane."

"Gianna, if you've ever read *Dark Night* by Saint John of the Cross, you know precisely what we were going through," Phillipe explained. "We met only at night, for a few hours of frantic lovemaking. It was never enough."

"It was a trying time," Rory said. "At least I was still able to think. At work, I told my boss I was going to have to resign. 'Rosalie is the reason,' I said. 'I consider our engagement over but she doesn't. Mr. Becker, I don't love her, and I can't marry her. I think my moving away is the only thing I can do to cool things down.'

"He said, 'Rory, I wish I had your brains when I was your age. Believe me, a divorce is one thing you don't want to go through. Especially if there are kids involved. We sure will miss you around here. If I can give you a reference, or do anything else for you, just let me know.'"

"As it was, the reference from Becker and Becker got Rory the job he needed in Washington. He was the first to leave; we felt it wise that we not leave together. Rory got us an apartment on Capitol Hill, a short distance from the House Office Building. That was our first real home. So when Will won, as he did, everything fell into place for us."

"Not that we were living happily ever after, you understand. My father was furious when he found out I was leaving the area. I couldn't even give out my address, that's how bad he was. I had to get my mail at the Post Office."

"At least, he never found out," I said.

"That's the problem. He did."

"He did? How on earth...?"

"He added things up, though it took him a long time to do it. At least, by the time he figured it out, Phillipe and I were out of his reach. One day, many years later, I got a letter from him. He called me and Phillipe the most vile names you can imagine. Including 'catamite.' I had to look that one up."

"He said that Cardinal Corby agreed with him, that Rory and I were a pair of...well, Gianna, I will not say such words to you."

"One thing he did say was that this scandal was so shocking that the Cardinal wouldn't let anyone speak of it, but from now on, I was dead as far as he was concerned. Sincerely, Edward V. McCormick."

"Migawd," I said. "The Cardinal got in on this."

"Yes," Rory said. "That wasn't till the mid-'70's, when being gay was coming to be more accepted. Well, not to Cardinal Corby, it wasn't. Thank God the Cardinal decided to keep quiet about this so-called scandal.

"You may ask, how did Eddie and the Cardinal find out? We don't know."

"Might it be possible that Biddy O'Toole was involved?" I asked.

"Quite possible," Phillipe said. "As you know, she could be inquisitive. But Biddy wasn't nearly as important as she thought she was. The important thing was...no regrets."

"Absolutely none," Rory agreed. "Well...one."

"One, *mon amour?*"

"I wish we'd had sense enough to stay together, yes, even after Will lost the election and we had to move out here. Because, Pretzel, you know the ironic thing? I was listening to this jerk-off artist on TV a while ago. Aloysius Sweeney was his name. Yes, I know, Gianna doesn't want me to listen to that fool, but I did anyway. He said the usual, that AIDS is divine retribution for what we were doing. Now, here's the strange part. It dawned on me, that if we had managed to remain together, this wouldn't have happened to either one of us. And that's all I regret."

"My precious," Phillipe said, and held him carefully. Then he said, "We can't undo the past, no? We can only make the best with what we have."

"Pretzel, you never told me. Do you regret anything?"

"Only the part about your family. How badly I wanted to tell them: Eddie, Gertrude, I love your son. Rory Michael is the most important person in the world to me."

"You could never do that. Not with Dad so angry, and Ma so passive."

"I still wish. Consider my own family. My mother says you're the best thing that ever happened to me. And Anne. Do you remember when we came out to Anne?"

"How can I forget? She came over to see us in our apartment with all of her kids. And one of them had to shriek that we must be poor, because we had only one bed."

"Do you remember what followed? Absolute silence."

"Did Anne accept this?" I asked. "You said she was very religious."

"Gianna, Anne was so nervous, because she came over to tell Phillipe she'd gone on the Pill. Here she was, not knowing how he would take that, after he told her so many times to do it."

"Yes, she did accept us," Phillipe said, "because she remembered Jean-Pierre as I remembered Papa. And she knew that we were doing no wrong."

"Excuse me," Randi said softly, "Phillipe? Your AZT. It's past time, but I didn't wish to cut in."

"It's all right, Randi."

***

"Gianna," Rory said, "I worry about him. Look at Phillipe, he seems so healthy, compared to me. But he's had this for so much longer. How long is the AZT going to work? And what's he going to do after I'm gone?"

"I could keep an eye on him, if you'd like."

"I'd like that. But, Gianna, I worry about you, too. Look at you. You never get out any more. That's no life for a person like you. You're beautiful, you're talented, and you're wasting away."

"Rory, after all you did for me. You got me out of that dump and off Valium. Isn't this the least I can do for you?

"That night you got so sick and Phillipe and I took you to the hospital, he asked me why I was staying with you. I told him I didn't know. I still don't. I wish I did. I wish there was some name I could put on it."

"Some day," he said, "some day, you'll know. When you do, you'll say the name out loud."

"You're sure of that."

"You bet I am."

Rory traced a pattern in the quilt. "I was thinking about my family," he said. "My father died a while ago. And I always kind of envied Phillipe for being so close to Anne. I don't think Pat is very fond of my guts, to put it mildly. But I wondered about Ma, and if...then I said, no. I don't know what would happen to her if she walked through that door and saw me like this. Phillipe was right, though. Ma did love me. In her way. And even though I was so happy with Phillipe, I missed Ma terribly. There are still so many things I want to tell her. Now, I never will."

"Dammit, Rory Michael," I said, holding him.

He's only a few more days left. Then he's going to Persephone, like he did in my dream.

I began singing to him, little bits of the song that were drifting around in my mind. Like different colors and shapes, they came together and formed a pattern, the pattern of all the love and happiness Rory had experienced, all the pain he'd overcome, the beauty he'd created and shared. That was going to last forever.

Forever.

"I think he's sleeping now," I said to Randi. "Or he's gone to that beach."

"Let's leave him," Randi said. "I'll take him up later. And I'd like you to sing that song for me and Phillipe after I do."

"Sure," I said. "Did you like it?"

"Dearie, it was terrific."

"I hope Rory liked it. It's his."

Rory stayed still for a while, then suddenly woke up with a sharp cry.

"Randi," I said.

"It hurts," was all Rory told us. "It hurts."

Chapter 12

ON SEVERAL OCCASIONS, SISTER AGNES TOOK OUT THE pictures of Longianna and studied them.

Sometimes she became indignant. "So, this is a Divine Compassion girl," she told herself. "Longianna didn't learn to dress like this *there*. And singing in a gay bar. Lord, have mercy on us all."

Gradually, her indignation dissolved. *She really is beautiful*, Sister Agnes thought. *I wonder if those men appreciate it in that...place.*

At least there were no more Eddie dreams. And then, it was Sunday.

"I didn't forget, Dad," she said as she backed the station wagon out onto Wheeler Avenue. "Yes, I know. I promised I'd go see Ma today. But really, you don't know how bad she's gotten. She lives in the past. I get so fed up with hearing the same stories, over and over again."

She let her mind go back to the last time she'd seen Rory. The words between them, she remembered, were harsh. He was living in that apartment on Tenth Street, and she'd been sent there on a specific mission.

"I probably blew it, Dad. I'm terrible at gathering information."

She stopped for a red light. She and her parents had been invited to Cardinal Corby's residence to discuss the Rory crisis.

Then the cardinal's secretary called and put off the appointment. There had been, he explained, a "dental emergency."

When the meeting did come about, Corby wasn't in the best of moods. His new upper plate didn't fit.

"I'm telling you, Eddie," he said, "whatever you do, keep your teeth. Don't let anybody talk you out of them, no matter how bad they get."

Rosalie was there. The light turned green. *Rosalie wore no makeup, and her eyes were puffy and red.*

Snob, she remembered thinking. This whole affair made her glad in a sense that the wedding was supposed to be canceled. It showed her just how childish Rosalie could be. Besides, Rosalie had chosen powder blue dresses for the bridesmaids, the worst possible color for Pat. And the style added twenty pounds to her middle.

But I mustn't think such uncharitable thoughts, she'd reminded herself. *This wedding must go ahead no matter how awful I look in the pictures. For Dad's sake, it must.*

"Princess, I don't want you to change any of your plans," Cardinal Corby said. "You go right ahead and have that fitting for your gown. I can promise you that wedding is going on as scheduled."

Rosalie nodded, and sniffled.

"Eddie," Corby asked, "what do you think your son's problem is?"

"Could be a case of pre-wedding jitters," Eddie said. "I remember, I was so scared, the good Father had to prompt me word-for-word. 'I, Edward, take you, Gertrude.' I'd rather have faced the whole Japanese navy. But, hey, it didn't stop me."

Johnny Corby spoke up. "My daughter is under the impression that there may be another girl after Rory."

"Did any of you notice other girls around? Or any strange letters or phone calls to your home?"

"No," said Eddie. "Gertrude?"

She shook her head. It was amazing, how Ma got through that entire meeting, without uttering a word.

"Pat?" asked Eddie. "Did Rory show interest in, say, any of your friends?"

"No, Dad, except that he used to walk Eileen home after dark."

"Yes, and Eileen just entered the convent," said Eddie. "We

can count her out."

Pat bit her lip. Eileen had departed for the Divine Compassion Motherhouse the previous week. Pat missed her terribly. She couldn't write or call Eileen. That was against the rules.

The course of action was decided. Pat would go to Rory's apartment and speak with him. Further action would be taken based on what information she got.

"You can find out what's going on, Pat," Eddie said as they drove home. It was raining and she remembered the *thump, thump* of the windshield wipers. "He'll talk to you. God knows he won't talk to me."

Eddie paused and aimed his next words at Gertrude. "Except to call me an asshole. His own father, an asshole, can you believe that? Lovely vocabulary your son has."

"Oh, Edward." It was the first thing she'd said all evening.

Feeling tired, Pat went straight up to bed. She couldn't sleep; she felt the tension in the Cardinal's residence clinging to all of them, and heard her parents' words as they prepared for bed.

"I don't know, Gertrude," Eddie said. The bed springs squeaked beneath his weight. "Pre-wedding jitters? Another girl? There are times when I wonder if it might not be—oh, Christ. I don't even want to say it."

"What were you thinking?"

"I keep telling myself, no. But I still wonder: another man."

There it was. He'd spoken the words he didn't dare say in the Cardinal's presence. All of that was supposed to be in the past. Suppose it wasn't? *Suppose Engel was a fraud, and his cure hadn't worked?* For the first time, Ma blew up.

"Now see here, Edward Vincent McCormick. Say what you will, but I know my son. My son isn't queer, and never was. Don't you dare speak that way of him again."

"Goddamit, Gertrude, I only—"

"I will not hear such talk." And Ma stormed off to sleep alone in Rory's abandoned bedroom.

Suppose it's true? Pat thought. *Who might the man be?*

"Christ, there's been no talking to Gertrude since Rory moved out," Eddie muttered.

After work the next day Pat went to Rory's apartment. She was tired, and in no mood for nonsense. Eddie had been having his end-of-model-year clearance and McCormick Ford had been a madhouse all day long.

She rang the bell. There was no answer. She waited ten minutes, rang again and gave up. Then she saw an incredibly good-looking young man coming up from the basement laundry room with a basket of clean clothes. He was Rory. How different he looked since he started gaining weight.

This is the way God intended Rory should look.

"Pat," he said.

"Rory, I need to talk to you."

"Sure," he said. "Only, it might help if certain people called before they came over. So they don't get stuck out in the hall. Come on in. Can I offer you anything?"

"No, thank you."

His apartment was surprisingly neat. Her eyes darted around, trying to get evidence of another feminine presence. *What was I looking for?* she asked herself. *A frilly nightie? A whiff of perfume?*

She saw a paper with a picture of Will Watkins kissing babies. A carton of cigarettes was out in the open; Pat knew about Rory's smoking. Comic books about Mr. Natural were strewn over the bed.

A half-empty bottle of a light German wine stood on the kitchen counter; propped up by the cabinet, a loaf of French bread.

"That loaf looked like a Saturn 5 pointed at the moon," Sister Agnes remembered. "Even then, Rory's apartment was a sanctuary of *plaisir d'amour*. Was I really so ignorant that I couldn't guess who had been there?"

Rory got out an ironing board and proceeded to press his shirts.

"Why do you do that?" she asked.

"So I won't go to work looking like a slob," Rory explained.

"What would Dad say if he saw? You know Ma always did the ironing. And you'll have Rosalie's maid to do that for you once you're married."

"I don't want Ma to press my shirts. And I especially don't want Rosalie's maid to go anywhere near my shirts."

"Rory, are you serious about breaking this engagement?"

"Yes, I am. I don't love Rosalie. She's spoiled rotten, self-centered, and she bores me out of my mind. I don't love Rosalie's money. I've no intention of spending the rest of my life with her. I said I wanted out and I meant it. All right?"

"I wish I knew what's gotten into you."

Rory set down the steam iron. He started to reply and thought better of it.

"Don't you know what this wedding means to Dad? It's as if his whole life depends on it. Married to Rosalie, you can afford to give him lots of grandchildren. *McCormick* grandchildren. Doesn't that mean anything to you?"

"Aren't there too many children in the world already? For that matter, aren't enough of them named McCormick? How many grandchildren does Grandpa McCormick have? Wasn't it around seventy-five, at the last count? Isn't that plenty?"

"It's not the same. You're his only son; he's depending on you. Can't you at least do this much for him?"

"Pat, listen to yourself. You're asking me to spend the rest of my life stuck with a woman I don't love. Making babies whose parents can't stand each other. Yes, it's too much to ask. It's my life and I'm not going to play these Eddie and Gertrude mind games any more."

"Let me ask you something, if it's not too personal. Did you go to Mass last Sunday?"

"No, Pat, I didn't. I had other things to do."

"What about next Sunday?"

"I've no intention of going."

"Oh, this is great! What would Dad say? And you know Ma would be heartbroken. Now you've gone and lost your faith."

"I said I wasn't going to Mass. I didn't say that I've lost my faith."

"I think you ought to go to Confession."

"Pat, for pity's sake—"

"I think you ought to go as soon as possible. Tell God you're sorry for all the misery you've created. And stop all this idiocy."

"It isn't idiocy."

"You're doing a lot of damage."

"I'm fed up with being held responsible for everything that goes wrong. You and Dad are going to have to learn that, Pat, *and so must Ma*."

"All right, Rory Michael," she said with a sigh. "I've tried to get you to listen to reason. I'd better go."

"I'll see you to the door."

"I can find my own way out, thank you very much."

She'd paused at the door, wondering if she ought to tell Rory what Dad had suspected. *Another man.* Then she decided against it, walked downstairs and to her car.

And I never saw him again, Sister Agnes told herself.

Shortly thereafter, Rory left town. The only address he gave was a post office box in Washington. Biddy O'Toole made it a point to tell Ma that if she thought Grant Avenue was bad, she ought to see the riot zone in Washington. "And that's not all. They have these long-haired kids going there, setting off bombs," said Biddy. "There's not a safe place in the whole city." Sick with worry, Ma took to her bed.

Dad raged. He began drinking heavily and spent election night in a drunken stupor.

As the years went on, her parents' marriage continued like a machine that had slipped a gear but went right on functioning anyway, serving no useful purpose.

Ma cooked, shopped, cleaned, attended Mass, and made excuses for Eddie. Eddie drank. They rarely spoke.

McCormick Ford fell apart. Eddie's best salesmen quit. The service was awful. His lawyer advised him to sell the business and retire. Eddie got a good price for it and devoted his attention to his drinking.

As a professed Sister of Divine Compassion, Sister Agnes was free to visit her parents. Gertrude was always the same, still putting on an act that everything was fine. Eddie rarely went outside.

Sometimes he sat up at night, shouting "Fire One! Fire Two!" over Lemon Tree Lane. He wrote long, rambling letters to Anita Bryant that never got mailed. He would denounce Gertrude, claiming that she deliberately turned his only son into a queer in order to make his life miserable. Therefore, he had to drink. It wasn't his fault. Nothing was his fault.

Gertrude offered no argument. She believed that his abuse would turn into jewels in the martyr's crown that awaited her in Heaven.

"My wife is one hell of a woman," he would tell an unseen guest. "My daughter's a nun, you know that? And my only son is the sugarplum fairy."

"Dad, please," Sister Agnes would say. "Studies show...."

Eddie didn't want to hear about any studies that said it wasn't Gertrude's fault, not Father Leveque's, not even Rory's. For the truth, indeed, had come out much later. Biddy O'Toole, in her zeal for cleanliness, had found a referral to Dr. Engel for Rory. The diagnosis was "sexual inversion." Biddy had no idea what "inversion" meant, but she knew "sexual" meant something dirty. Therefore, this really ought to be called to the Cardinal's attention.

"Jesus, Mary and Joseph," the Cardinal said when he read it. That confirmed Biddy's opinion: here was a matter of grave importance. "Eddie should have told me this," Corby said at first. Then he concluded: "Something like this in his family? I can hardly blame him for wanting to keep it quiet. At least my little Princess never married that...that...."

It tied in with the research Cardinal Corby had been doing on the former Father Leveque. There had been some irregularities in his family background. Corby had traced one particular rumor to a place called Natzweiler-Struthof, only to learn that the record he needed had been burned just as Allied forces were moving in. Nevertheless, he assumed enough to draw a conclusion.

"Leveque and Rory both went to Washington," he told Eddie, who had sobered up for the occasion. "My understanding is that Leveque is working for our pea-brained congressman. We know that Rory is close by; therefore, we must assume that they're living in sin together."

"Oh, Jesus," Eddie said. "Rory wasn't cured at all. If I could find Engel, I'd sue him for every dime he's worth."

"This is indeed a heavy cross to bear."

"We'll call the papers," said Eddie. "We'll destroy that Watkins once and for all...have him impeached."

"Can we do that, Eddie?" Corby asked. "How can we destroy the reputation of a man who is promoting civil rights for a bunch of queers? We can't have my name, and yours, in the papers over this. The scandal is too great. It may be the hardest thing we will ever do. But we must keep silence."

Cardinal Corby had called Phillipe and Rory catamites. Before getting drunk again, Eddie looked up 'catamite' in the dictionary. He wrote a nasty letter to Rory and included that word in it.

Monsignor Hayes fired Biddy O'Toole, then retired himself. He could no longer stand to see the good work Father Leveque had done falling apart. He died soon thereafter. Biddy was placed in a nursing home at Cardinal Corby's expense.

Gertrude didn't change her mind. She continued to recite her private litany: "Holy Trinity, my son is not queer. Mother of God, my son is not queer. All the angels and archangels, all the saints and martyrs, my son is not queer."

Eddie grew sick; Gertrude waited on him. He was hospitalized briefly in December of 1981, when it seemed he was near death from alcoholic cirrhosis. He improved and was ready to go back home.

Eddie seemed so well that Gertrude didn't hesitate to leave him alone to attend Christmas morning Mass. When she returned, a Tarzan yell was ringing out over Lemon Tree Lane. Eddie had died in his recliner in front of the television. He still held the remote control, with the volume all the way up.

Gertrude was alone. For a while, she seemed to adjust well. She took the trip to Ireland that Eddie had promised and never delivered, then seemed guilty about having such a good time. Shortly thereafter, she fell in the vestibule of Saint Catherine's and broke her hip. A series of debilitating strokes followed.

Sister Agnes recalled all too well the final stroke that had put Ma in the Peaceful Woodland Home. She'd found Ma on the floor holding a news magazine. The word "AIDS" was on the cover with a picture of Rock Hudson.

"Ma," she said. "Were you reading this?" Gertrude was unable to speak.

Sister Agnes called the fire department ambulance and discreetly stuffed the magazine in the back of the rack.

And so it went. They had a first-rate therapist at Peaceful Woodland, and Ma got most of her speech back. Still, she couldn't walk, and her mind was never the same.

She never spoke of Rory, which wasn't to say, Sister Agnes thought, that she didn't think of Rory.

She parked in the Peaceful Woodland lot, signed in and took the elevator to the third floor. Ma wasn't in her room. Her Infant of Prague was on her bureau, as was a picture of Pat and Rory on their First Communion day.

Another fashion disaster, Pat thought. Her dress had a sash around the middle that emphasized the baby fat. But Rory looked like something from a Christmas tree.

When staff members asked, "Who is that adorable little boy?" they were told that Rory had died long ago. He was killed in Viet Nam. Or in an accident. The important thing was, he was no longer living, and that poor Mrs. McCormick was heartbroken.

Ma was in the day room, chatting with some of the nurses. *Thank God they didn't have a party going on.* Sister Agnes found the parties here to be incredibly depressing. Saint Patrick's Day was the worst. They had all these senile beldams wearing funny hats, singing "When Irish Eyes Are Smiling."

"Ma," she said. "I've come to see you. I'm sorry I couldn't stop by sooner, but at this time of year, you know how it is."

"Why, Pat, what a nice surprise," Gertrude replied. "I believe you all know my daughter? The principal of Cardinal Corby High School?"

"Oh, yes, glad to see you, Sister."

"Mrs. Rizzo's daughter just got married, and she was showing me the wedding album."

"Is that so?" Sister Agnes joined the others in admiring the beautiful bride. It got Ma into a loquacious mood.

"I remember my wedding day," she said.

Aw, Ma. Don't get started again. It was too late. Mrs. Rizzo and the other nurses insisted on hearing all about it.

"It was in September of 1945. Eddie had just gotten out of the Navy. And I was so much in love."

"Isn't it great to be young and in love?" Mrs. Rizzo asked.

"But not with Eddie," Ma said.

"Why, Ma," Sister Agnes said. She'd never said this before.

"No, I was in love with Frank Sinatra," Gertrude admitted. "I never told you that, did I? Well, I was. My friends and I went to New York as often as we could in those days to catch Frankie's act at the Paramount. Each time he came on stage, I pretended he was singing to me, personally. I used to scream my fool head off."

A smile came to Gertrude's face, showing a trace of her former beauty. "But you married Mr. McCormick," said Mrs. Rizzo.

"Yes. That's the way it was. I knew I couldn't be a bobby soxer forever. And in those days, the war had just ended, the fellows were coming home. Everyone was getting married. We girls didn't think about having careers. There was nothing worse than being an old maid.

"I'd known Eddie for quite some time. He joined the Navy the day after Pearl Harbor. He asked me to write to him, which I did, all during the war. I'd be writing to Eddie, and Frankie would be on the radio or the victrola. Perhaps I told Eddie more than I intended to say. And as for what he told me...."

Ma stopped to think for a minute. "Don't tire yourself out, Ma," Sister Agnes warned. She tried to quell a panic inside. *What is Ma doing? I knew she liked Frank Sinatra—at least up till the time he left his wife and married Ava Gardner—and then she said she couldn't stand him. But she's never spoken this way before. What does she mean, she never loved Dad?*

"I'm not tired, Patricia," Ma said. "Let me see...how shall I explain? What Eddie told me...."

Ma seemed to focus her gaze on a distant object. "In those days there was so much we didn't know about. And one of those things was the Manhattan Project."

"The first atomic bomb," said Mrs. Rizzo.

"Yes," said Ma, "none of us had any notion that such a thing could exist in real life. We believed, instead, that the only way to end the war would be to invade Japan. That would have meant a heavy loss of American lives. Eddie was sure he would be one of those who wouldn't make it. So he wrote me a letter that summer. He wanted to know that if by any chance he did survive, would I marry him. I wrote back and said yes."

"Oh, my goodness, isn't that fascinating," said Mrs. Rizzo. Sister Agnes fidgeted.

"Of course," Ma said, "I'd no idea that the war was going to end so quickly. Or that Eddie really was going to come back in one piece, but he did. So I married him. But there were problems."

Oh, please, Ma, don't go on....

"My father had no real objection. He knew the McCormicks from church. Seventeen of them, there were. In our parish, they were our adopted 'poor family.' Every Christmas, when we took up a clothing drive for the poor, we knew our castoffs would go to the McCormicks. My father didn't let that bother him. He saw Eddie as a person with lots of ambition and potential and business sense. 'The content of a man's character is what counts.' That's what he said. My mother, however...."

"That was a different story," Mrs. Rizzo volunteered.

"My mother despised Eddie. She did everything she could to prevent the marriage from taking place. Naturally, that brought out the worst in me. I refused to listen to her. But she said many times that Eddie wasn't good enough for me. She used to say that he was...common."

Ma paused, as if she could still hear her mother's nagging in the background.

"Perhaps Eddie didn't always dress well. Or speak with correct grammar. But my mother knew of the McCormicks, too. She used to pass their house on her way home from the butcher shop. So she told me, one night during one of our quarrels, that she often heard screaming from that house and knew that Mr. McCormick was beating the children. She said she'd seen proof of this. During the summer, she saw welts on their arms and legs. 'I see these things with a mother's eyes, Gertrude,' she said. 'I pity those children. My heart goes out to them. I wish there were something that could be done. But I'll not have my own baby girl marrying one of *them*.' All I did was dig in my heels. It got to the point where my mother had to give up."

"So, you married Eddie," said Mrs. Rizzo.

"That I did," said Gertrude. "I shut my ears to Mother's wailing during the ceremony. And when the priest asked, 'Do you, Gertrude, take Edward?' I said, 'I will.' Then we went to Atlantic City for our honeymoon."

Gertrude again looked as if she were gazing at a distant past. "I guess Atlantic City was different then," another nurse said.

"Different?" Gertrude asked. "I suppose it was. We got to our hotel room. Edward, he...."

Ma! Gertrude had never spoken of this before. She'd always made it clear. Nice people don't speak of such things. We're nice people.

"I tried to tell him, Edward, don't do this. He said he *had* to. That I was his wife, and there was some law about it. It hurt. It hurt terribly. At least it was over quickly. And Edward rolled over and snored."

Sister Agnes then had to speak up. "I don't think my mother is feeling quite like herself," she said. "Ma, do you want to go back to your room?" Even the nurses seemed troubled. They had never heard this from the prim Mrs. McCormick before.

"No, hear me out. I must say this. I have to say it before it's too late.

"I got up. I was bleeding so I put on a pad. I straightened out my clothing so no one would know what Edward had done. And I went out. Out of the room. Out of the hotel. Across the boardwalk to the beach. I remember thinking, *No, no, there must be more to it than that.* I walked down to the ocean, to the waves."

Ma, if you say you went right on walking, I'm going to go smack out of my mind

"The sea. It was so clean, so pure, compared to what Edward had done. I took off my shoes and waded in. The tide was coming in all around me.

"I wasn't ignorant. I knew what Edward had done makes babies. And I knew, *I knew*, at that moment that I was going to have one. No, not one. Because I felt that there would be another baby. One that came to me, not from Edward, but from the sea, a marvelous, enchanted little creature, with a great gift...."

"Ma, I really think...."

"I had my babies. You, Patricia, you were Edward. Put a cigarette in your tiny hand, and you would *be* Edward. I had a terrible time having my babies. I nearly died, so they said. But when I was able, they brought my babies to me. Patricia was first. When I saw the second one, that's when I knew. Here was my enchanted sea-creature, my special one, my very own little darling...."

Ma's voice cracked.

"Mrs. McCormick? Would you like to go back now?" Mrs. Rizzo asked.

"Go back?" Ma asked. "Go back where?" Then, "Yes, yes, I'd love to go back." One of the assistants rolled her wheelchair back to her room. "My poor little darling," Ma said. "They sent you away. If only I'd stood up to Eddie and the Cardinal. If only I could see you once more."

"I'm so sorry, Sister," Mrs. Rizzo apologized. "I'll ask the doctor to check on your mother when he visits tomorrow. She's seemed a bit depressed lately but looked like she was snapping out of it. Still...you're right. She wasn't quite herself. And there was nothing we could pin it on. I gather this second baby she spoke of was your twin brother."

"Yes," said Sister Agnes.

"Tell me, did your twin die at about this time of year?"

"Ah...yes."

"That explains it. An anti-depressant might help her through this. I'll phone you in the morning after Dr. Singh has had a look at her."

"Thank you," Sister Agnes said. "That's probably the only thing she needs. As I'm sure you've gathered, she was very close to Rory."

"A little sea-creature," Mrs. Rizzo said. "The poor dear."

Well, I blew that, too. Sister Agnes berated herself as she parked in the convent's lot. *I was supposed to cheer her up. A lot of good I did. This day has been a total loss.*

She went back to her cell, trying not to take Ma's words too seriously. "Ma's mind is going," she reminded herself. "Still, is any of that true? That she didn't love Dad? That she was more involved in her fantasy romance with Frank Sinatra?"

Just before dinner she went across the street to the school. There was something eerie about Cardinal Corby High on a Sunday with all of the students gone. Perhaps it was the way that portrait of Benny Corby seemed to be waiting for her.

It might be true, what the girls say. He comes to life at night, looking for people to terrorize. She quickened her pace to her office, shut the door, and dialed the number with the 213 area code.

It rang many times. "Perhaps they're not home," she said.

But where would they go?

Just before she gave up, she heard a man's voice say, "Stay where you are, Dearie. I'll take care of the phone. McCormick residence."

"Yes, is Ms. Raimondi there?"

"May I ask who is calling?" he said. "Is this her sister? Is this Donna?"

"Why, no, I...."

"Just a minute," he said. "I'm sorry, what was your name again?"

"If it's not a good time...."

"Ma'am, I'm really sorry. But would you like to leave a message for Longianna? Or call her back later? Mr. McCormick just died and we're expecting a call from the coroner's office."

"Tell her—I'm so sorry." Sister Agnes made it back across Wheeler Avenue, and into the convent parlor. There was a symbol on the wall: an alpha and omega. That's what this day had been. Alpha and omega, beginning and end.

Sister Agnes collapsed across the coffee table.

Chapter 13

Would you like my tangerine?
The question bounced off the curve of the universe.
like my tangerine like my tangerine like my tangerine?
Can you hear me hear me hear me?
Rory Michael, are you there there there?
I come to this beach when I know no one else will be here, because I have to be by myself. I have to shut out the sounds of humanity. Of technology. I need only to hear timeless sounds: waves crashing, sea-birds calling. I need to come to this place and remember.

I remembered Phillipe's beautiful French-German voice at Rory's memorial: "'If I speak with human tongues and angelic as well, but do not have love, I'm a noisy gong, a clanging cymbal.'"

I think of Aloysius Sweeney, whom Rory dismissed as a jerk-off artist.

"'If I have the gift of prophecy and, with full knowledge, comprehend all mysteries, if I have faith great enough to move mountains, but have not love, I am nothing. If I give everything I have to feed the poor and hand over my body to be burned, but have not love, I gain nothing.

"'Love is patient, love is kind....'"

Those last days were hideous. Unlike the minds of many persons with AIDS, Rory's never dissolved into dementia. He knew what was going on.

"This time," he said, "don't save me. Let me go."

He asked to speak with me alone. "Gianna," he said. "Your song. Perfect. I'll take it with me. Remember it." Then he said, "I love you, Longianna."

I turned that moment over in my mind as the waves crash against the rocks.

Would you like my tangerine?

For a while after that, Rory was alone with Phillipe. Then he went in and out of a semi-comatose state. There was still great pain. I thought of being on a world with a giant orange sun that never sets, never stops burning, draws every drop of water out of you, and you still are alive.

Phillipe, Randi and I stayed with him for three days and nights.

No more pain. That was all that mattered.

Randi insisted that I get some rest. Somewhere in the distance, a telephone rang, and Randi answered it. It didn't matter to me. There were no dreams, only a merciful blank.

I didn't feel that Rory was really dead. The next day so many people from the past came to see us. I asked myself what they were doing here. Will and Cynthia Watkins were in the living room, sharing their memories with Phillipe. Anne and I were making coffee in the kitchen.

"I knew my brother was having problems with Cardinal Corby," she said. "Who wouldn't? I wasn't surprised when Phillipe wrote to me and said he was leaving the priesthood. I was worried about him, but when I learned he was coming to Washington to work for Will, I knew things were going to be fine. I should have known a person like Phillipe wouldn't be coming alone."

I asked, "Did you know?"

"You bet," she said. "I was just as opposed as *Maman* to Phillipe's going into the seminary. Because I knew. I'd been told the nature of the charges against Jean-Pierre. My instincts told me that Phillipe was the same and that he was making a mistake in trying to deny it.

"I remember my first visit to their apartment on Capitol Hill. I couldn't get a sitter. Jerry had to work, so I had all the kids with me. Phillipe was trying so much to remain in the closet. Because of his job with Will. He introduced Rory to me as his friend with whom he was sharing expenses. His friend, indeed! Rory was a bit too adorable for a simple friendship."

"One of your kids had to announce that Rory and Phillipe had only one bed."

"Oh, yes. They'd all had Hawaiian Punch before we left home, so they had to go charging for the bathroom the minute we got there. I told them to behave. But they couldn't help but notice: only one bed. Rory handled it well. He said they took turns sleeping on the sofa. But he became the most brilliant shade of red."

"You accepted it, though."

"Oh, yes. I knew that Phillipe had chosen well. And Rory, he was so kind, so understanding. He knew how tough it was, trying to raise seven kids on our income. He used to save the food section of the *Washington Post* for me, so I'd have extra supermarket coupons."

It didn't hit me till after the last guests left! Rory was dead. I thought I'd lose my mind.

"*Ma petite*," Phillipe said, "you must let this out, not hold it in."

A terrible thing it was, to drop on him. *He has suffered enough*, I thought, but he wouldn't leave me to face this alone. I felt the pain would never end.

"Phillipe," I said, "you asked once why I stayed on, even after George left."

"Indeed. It seems so long ago."

"I told you I didn't know. Gratitude? To one who had been a friend when I needed one? Certainly. And pity? At first. But that wasn't enough as Rory got worse. Especially when he got mad at his sickness and took it out on me.

"I loved him, Phillipe. Like I've never loved any man before. I loved Rory Michael McCormick. Completely. *Just the way he was*. I'd not have changed a single thing about him. He was perfect."

"Longianna," Phillipe asked, "how could you help but love him?"

"'Love isn't jealous, it does not put on airs, it isn't snobbish,'" Phillipe had read at the memorial. "'There is no limit to love's forbearance, to its trust, its hope, its power to endure.

"'When the perfect comes, the imperfect will pass away. When I was a child, I used to talk like a child, think like a child, reason like a child. When I became a man I put childish ways aside. There are in the end three things that last: faith, hope and love, and the greatest of these is love.'"

Rory had trusted me with the knowledge of how he'd put away childish things. Of how he'd become a man, without illusions about who and what he was. I'd translated that knowledge into a song. After Phillipe had read Rory's favorite Biblical passage, I stood up and sang that song.

The chapel was full of celebrities. Their presence didn't bother me. Here were executives from Luxor Studios and Grimalkyn Records. The entire cast of LYNX was here.

I had no edge of fatigue in my voice, no problem hitting the high notes. Everything came together, all the love and perfection I'd known in Rory. My lyrics were of a love stronger than sickness and death. The refrain was made of the words of the goddess Persephone in my dream. *He'll live forever now. Forever. Forever.*

Just before Phillipe returned to San Francisco, he gave me a business card.

"I'm getting forgetful," he said. "A gentleman in the chapel gave me his card to give to you. He would like to meet with you when you feel up to it."

"Vice-President, Grimalkyn Records and Tapes," I read. "Vice-President? What do you suppose he wants to talk about?"

I found out. It wasn't long until I was in a recording studio, with my head trapped in earphones, being told to "do it naturally. The way you always do."

I'd come to this beach just after daybreak to be alone. But the day was too perfect, the waves too good for me to have it all to myself. Several carloads of surfers arrived, bringing with them a huge boom box blasting Shadoe Stevens' *American Top Forty*.

"We have a letter from Denise Brown of Topeka, Kansas," Shadoe said. "Denise wants to know if there have been any references to goddesses of classical mythology in top forty hits. Well, Denise, the one most mentioned has been Venus, the goddess of beauty and love. She was featured in "Hey, Venus" by Frankie Avalon in 1959. Again, in "Venus" by Shocking Blue in 1970. That remade song was back on the charts in 1986, by Bananarama.

"This week, a new goddess appears in our countdown. She's Persephone, guardian of the afterlife, who grants immortality to her followers. Persephone is in the new hit, "Forever," by a new artist, Longianna Rae. Here, making her chart debut at Number Twenty-Nine...."

At one time, I'd wanted this. Renzo was going to give it to me. Now, I wasn't even sure.

My manager, Leo Redwyn knows why I wrote "Forever," but he worries whenever AIDS is mentioned.

"Remember that Grimalkyn is owned by Snappy Cereals. Need I say more?"

"Grimalkyn is a business, run by pinstriped people with their eyes on the bottom line. Besides, it's well known that Elizabeth Taylor used to visit Rock Hudson."

"Elizabeth Taylor is an established star. She was big when you were still in diapers. You're just starting out. It's fine if you donate a percentage of your income to the AIDS foundation, but as for what you say, *be careful*. There's a lot of paranoia out there."

"Very well," I said. "I'll be careful. But I won't cater to paranoids and Sweeneyites."

But I'd also be truthful, I thought. *After all, I wasn't going to be quasi-famous forever.*

I got into the Porsche Rory had left me and went home to the house where he used to live. I co-owned it with Phillipe. We decided not to sell it because it's where I want to be. Donna, of course, still won't visit.

Carla MacIvey, my secretary, was there. She'd been referred to me by Michelle Maitland, the star of LYNX. It was strange, at first. to need a secretary, but Carla soon became indispensable.

A pile of messages waited for me. The most important was from Phillipe, the "World's #1 Longianna fan."

"You'll soon be at the top of the chart," it said. "Don't forget who said so. Enjoy."

"I've got to see him!" I told Carla. "Is there any chance I can get to San Francisco later today?"

"Sure, I can get you on a flight. But you have to be in Italy by Wednesday."

The video of "Forever" was ready to be shot in a Sicilian cave. I'd appear as Persephone.

"I have to see Phillipe before I leave. Last time I talked to him he coughed and wheezed a lot. And then he told me nothing was wrong. I have to see for myself. Anything else?"

"Here's a letter from Snappy Cereal," Carla said.

I read through it. "Listen to this," I told Carla. "It says I'm a good example to young people because I don't run around in my underwear."

"Who's it from?" she asked.

"Aloysius Sweeney. Think of it, I have his autograph now."

"No kidding!"

"If he only knew what Rory thought of him," I said. "Or, what I think of him. Perhaps I ought to send him a copy of the lyrics, explaining what every line means. Or a picture of myself stark naked. Too bad there aren't any."

"I saw him on TV," Carla said. "He seems a little strange, especially when he gets on the subject of AIDS."

"He makes me uncomfortable. I guess I'll have to acknowledge this. He's on the Snappy Board of Directors. Let's make our response as 'Dear Occupant' as possible."

"Right," said Carla. "And speaking of being uncomfortable, there's something I've been meaning to bring up. You've been lucky so far, Gianna. Most of your fans are great. But if "Forever" keeps going up the chart, there will be a few who don't know when to back down. After LYNX was released there were so many weird people after Michelle. She had to install an elaborate security system at her house. And I think you should, too."

"That's a good idea." I'd already taken a few precautions, including an unlisted phone number, mainly so Renzo couldn't bother me.

"Look at this, Carla. It's a letter from Sister Agnes."

"Is she the nun you found when you were looking for Rory's twin?"

"Yes," I said. "Let's see. This looks quite long."

"Maybe she's really sorry about Rory."

It was gushy and effusive, as if Sister Agnes had lost someone close to her, not someone she couldn't possibly have known. She promised to remember Rory in her prayers.

Sister Agnes had tried to call me a few times after Rory's number was disconnected, but the operator refused to give her my new number. She seemed somewhat offended by this.

"She makes me feel like she's handing back my homework with a nasty note on it," I said. "Like, 'you could do better if you tried, Longianna.'"

"Nuns can do that," Carla said. "They're supposed to make you feel guilty. I wonder if Sister Agnes knows why you had to have the number changed?"

"I doubt that she listens to the *American Top Forty*," I said. "Or that she *cares* about what's on the pop chart. Oh, well, she was awfully sweet. I'll write to her and explain what happened. But this is kind of odd."

"What is?" Carla asked.

"Here she is, the principal of Cardinal Corby High School, who doesn't move in the same circles as Rory did. Yet, she seems to be taking his death so hard."

Why should she be so concerned? I wondered. I read her letter over. There was an almost childish petulance at the end when she asked for my new phone number. That made me reluctant to comply. It was not only the new number she wanted; it was my attention. *Now!*

Her letter reminded me of the calls I used to get from George when I was still a receptionist at Luxor. *Drop what you're doing. Find Rory, I have to talk to him right this minute.*

I sent her a quick acknowledgement and said that more would follow shortly. I didn't give her the phone number.

"Can you be at the airport in an hour?" Carla called.

"Sure thing."

There was a missing piece here and no time to find it. Sometimes it felt so unfair, getting what I only thought I wanted, at a time when it's so hard to deal with fame. With so many strangers' hands reaching out to me, I didn't need another background voice calling, "Longianna, Longianna."

I cherished every minute I could spend with my own thoughts just to be at the source "Forever" came from. *Because I loved him. I still love him.*

Chapter 14

SISTER AGNES HAD BEEN RELEASED FROM THE SMALL infirmary to the privacy of her own cell. She didn't remember falling. She did remember the squeeze of the doctor's blood pressure cuff.

"Sister Agnes! How on Earth did your pressure get this high?" he asked. "I want you on strict bed rest, do you hear me? No work, no problems, no worries, no *nothing!* If that doesn't get your pressure down, I'm afraid I'm going to have to put you in the hospital for some tests."

No, no, no, she wanted to say. *I'm not sick! You don't know what sick really is!*

It looked as if she'd escaped the trip to Mercy Hospital; her pressure was starting to stabilize. Her cell was filled with get-well wishes from teachers and parents and students.

The other Sisters were taking such good care of her! What would they say if they knew the reason for her attack?

At least, for a little while, Sister Agnes could shut the outside world from her cell where nothing changed. She could try to forget the news she'd heard.

Mr. McCormick just died.

But she couldn't. Sister Irene had visited for a chat, and left a copy of the morning paper. Under "Deaths Elsewhere," Sister Agnes read:

> R. M. MCCORMICK, a composer and arranger, died Sunday at his Westwood home of complications associated with AIDS. He was 42. McCormick won an Academy

Award for the score of Luxor Studio's science fiction film, LYNX.
There are no immediate survivors.

Thank God Ma won't see this, was her first thought. Mrs. Rizzo described Gertrude as more depressed and withdrawn since Sunday. She no longer read any papers or watched TV. Dr. Singh had put her on an anti-depressant but it would take awhile to have an effect.

And just who does that young twerp of an obituary writer think he is? was her second thought. *No survivors?*

She bit down on her ruffled feelings. How would it look to have her name, and Ma's, listed in Rory's obituary after all these years?

So many years. Twenty. She remembered Eddie's obituary. "Mr. McCormick is survived by his widow, Gertrude, of the home address, a daughter, Sister Agnes Mary of the Sisters of Divine Compassion, and twelve brothers and sisters."

At Eddie's request, there was no mention of a son.

There's no way anyone reading this would connect me or Ma with this Hollywood composer. We're safe, for all that's worth. Well, Rory, I guess this is good-bye. I wish it didn't have to be like this. I'll pray for you, of course. I'll ask the students to pray for a special intention.

Her hand gripped the paper. If only it could have been different. If only it could have said, "He's survived by his life's companion, Phillipe Leveque, a devoted friend, Longianna Raimondi, his mother, Gertrude McCormick, and his twin, who feels like a big fat fool."

Easy, now, she reminded herself. *You get upset, your pressure goes up again.* She put down the paper, then went to the bureau and got out the pictures of Longianna.

I wonder what it was like at the end? she asked herself. *If there was much pain. Or was it peaceful?* She didn't know anyone with AIDS or even anyone who knew anyone else with AIDS. She wondered about Longianna, why she wasn't scared, what gave her such strength.

Sister Agnes stared at the glossy photo of Longianna on stage at Mighty Joe Young's. Startled by the sound footsteps in the corridor, she hastily pushed it back into her bureau.

She heard a soft rapping on her door and opened it to see

Sister Edith and the doctor.

"May we come in, Sister Agnes? The doctor wants to see how you are."

"Of course, Sister, come in."

The doctor-checked her pressure and found it still a bit on the high side but much better than it had been.

"Doctor, I'm so tired of being in here," Sister Agnes said. "I'm getting so much rest! It's driving me batty!"

"I think we can turn you loose now, Sister Agnes. As long as you stay on your medication, you ought to do all right. I'm not saying back to work! You stay away from that desk for a few more days. But if you'd like to get out in the sunshine, perhaps do a little shopping, it will do you good."

"Oh, thank you, Doctor!"

Sister Irene drove her to the Golden Galaxy Mall. Once there, Sister Agnes went into the card shop and purchased several tasteful sympathy cards.

So much sickness and suffering. Who knows when I'll need them? she thought.

***

The weeks passed, the days grew short and the nights frosty. On several occasions, Sister Agnes tried to reach Longianna. The familiar number had been disconnected, and she didn't have the unlisted one.

Where was Longianna? Was she still at the same address? Apparently so since it was the return address on the brief note Longianna sent her.

Longianna's note had only a few sentences. Not enough! Still, Sister Agnes kept it in the drawer with her winter underwear as she did the pictures from Mighty Joe Young's.

Sister Agnes fell back into her routine. She did her job well. She dutifully visited Eddie's grave and the nursing home. The antidepressant seemed to work; Gertrude acted more like her normal self.

She never spoke of Rory and had forgotten her outburst.

Mr. McCormick just died.

Each morning at Mass, Sister Agnes said a prayer for Rory. "Eternal rest grant unto him, O Lord, and let perpetual light shine upon him. May his soul and all the souls of the faithful departed rest in peace."

This was November, the month of the dead. Surely, someone up there was listening. She tried, for the rest of the day, to keep Rory out of her thoughts.

Then there came a time when she thought she was losing her mind.

On one occasion, the final bell of the day had rung, and the corridors were full of teenage girls. One sophomore was showing a music magazine to another. For a second, perhaps less than a second, Sister Agnes thought she saw Longianna Raimondi on the cover.

That was impossible! Sister Agnes went back to her office. Surely it was someone who looked like Longianna. The latest teen sensation!

The following Saturday there was a brief warm spell. Sister Agnes was standing on the corner waiting for a green light. A car filled with teenagers stopped in front of her, its radio blasting.

The light changed, and the car took off with a screech. "Wait!" Sister Agnes called, but they didn't hear.

That was Longianna's voice she'd heard on their radio. Or was it?

Am I getting a little loony? she wondered.

She went back to the convent chapel where it was quiet. "If I continue to hear Longianna's voice in here, I know I'm insane."

All she heard was the vigil light sputtering by the altar.

Maybe she hadn't lost her mind. But maybe she should discuss what was happening with a professional. Then she'd have to tell the person about Rory.

There was so much tension in her daily life. Sweeney was trying to get in contact with her, and she was doing her best to avoid him. It could be that a mild tranquillizer was what she needed. Other Sisters had taken them; it was no disgrace. All she had to do was ask the doctor.

But I'm a strong person. Like Dad, she thought. *I can't let this get the better of me.*

The days grew even shorter and sharply colder. Sister Agnes spent more time in her cell, contemplating the pictures of Longianna.

"What became of you?" she whispered. "Where did you go after Rory died? Will I ever see or speak with you again?"

She would look at the photo of Longianna and Rory by the pool.

"Why don't you answer my letter?" she asked. "Don't I deserve more than a form thank-you note? Why won't you give me your new number? Am I nothing to you? Just *who* do you think you are, young lady? Some kind of international star?"

***

On the night of the first major snowfall, Sister Agnes had a dream.

In it she was twenty years younger and being interviewed to see if she should be accepted as a postulant. Saint Kristen herself was questioning her.

"Why do you desire to become a Sister of Divine Compassion, Pat?" the saint asked.

"I have to get away, Reverend Mother," she replied. "They're talking behind my back. I go into a crowded room and suddenly there's silence. I know what they say."

"What do they say that so distresses you?"

"That Father Leveque really left to get married. Then they whisper that Father Leveque married Rory. They laugh. But not around me. They pity me. I see all the pity in their faces. *The poor dear*, they think. *What a terrible thing to have in your family*. I can't stand much more of it. Reverend Mother, you have to help me. Please, accept me, get me away from all that pity."

Sister Agnes woke with a start. She felt a strange relief, as if being able to talk to Saint Kristen took off some of the pressure.

But she also felt restless and knew she wouldn't go back to sleep.

What time was it? One A. M.? The insomnia was getting worse.

There was a thumping sound outside. Sister Agnes went to her window and saw a car with chains on its tires go slowly down Wheeler Avenue. The snow was so deep there was a good chance that the next day's classes would be canceled.

That wasn't good. It would leave her too much time to think.

"Why *did* I become a nun?" she asked herself. "I was interviewed by Reverend Mother Maria Immaculata. I don't remember what she asked, or what I said. Apparently, she was impressed enough to accept me. Having a letter of recommendation from Cardinal Corby didn't hurt. It seemed the practical thing to do. When I was a child...."

Sister Agnes got back into bed. The wind made the windows rattle. Mercy, it was cold.

When she was a child, she had no thoughts of becoming a nun. She wanted to join the Navy. She remembered asking her dad if girls could do that. He said yes. But times changed. There was Viet Nam, which she felt was wrong. And Eileen was a Sister of Divine Compassion. And dear God, she missed Eileen so much.

Pat had visited her the first time it was permitted. She was shocked by what she saw. Eileen had gained at least twenty pounds, her face had broken out, and her fingernails were bitten down. Yet she insisted that she was happy. Pat repressed her thought that perhaps Eileen was just plain miserable.

She spoke to Eddie about her desire to enter the convent after she'd worked for a year at McCormick Ford. At first, he was unhappy about it. "Eileen's father has four other daughters," Eddie had said. "He can spare one. You're the only one I have, Pat!"

Then, all hell broke loose. Rory moved out of the house, then to Washington. So did Father Leveque. It was years before Biddy O'Toole came up with that damning piece of evidence. But there were rumors flying around about those two.

Besides, in 1968, the whole world appeared to be falling apart. Eddie gave in.

"I was hoping you'd change your mind, Pat," he said. "Or, maybe, some decent guy would come along and change it for you. But if you want to try out the convent, go ahead. Maybe it's the only place where you'll be safe. I don't know."

Eddie took another snort of whiskey. "In the convent you'll be all right," he said. "And...it would mean so much to your mother...to walk down the aisle at Saint Catherine's with her head held high."

Pat knew Eddie was also speaking of himself. People talked. From now on they'd say, "That may be true about Rory. But Pat is a Divine Compassion nun."

"Oh, Daddy!" she'd said, and prepared to follow Eileen.

She was accepted the following August, and Eddie and Gertrude took her to the motherhouse. Gertrude wept when she saw Pat dressed in her postulant's habit.

"You look nice, Pat," Eddie said. "You look real nice!" He was too eager to turn his face away.

Her parents left, and it dawned on Pat that Lemon Tree Lane was now a long-distance call away. Calling home except in the worst emergencies was strictly forbidden. Homesickness hit her like a wrecking ball.

Reverend Mother Maria Immaculata was stern and unsmiling. So was her assistant, Sister Margaret Mary, the Mistress of Postulants.

"Make our rules a part of you," Sister Margaret Mary lectured them on the first day. "No talking during the Great Silence. Or at meals, without Reverend Mother's permission. The morning bell rings at five-thirty. You have fifteen minutes to be up, fully dressed in your habits, and in line for Chapel. Don't waste any of them."

"Yes, Sister," they agreed.

"During your time here, you'll learn much," Sister Margaret Mary continued. "You'll learn that, as a Sister of Divine Compassion, you'll love every one of God's children *equally*. Which brings me to an important point, concerning *particular friendships*."

Pat tried to look around. Eileen wasn't here. She had an awful feeling that she would be seeing little of Eileen.

"When I say *particular friendship*, what do I mean? I mean, a pairing off of any two that excludes your other Sisters. Does everyone understand this?"

"Yes, Sister."

"Very good. This sort of thing is always a grave matter, disruptive to the spirit of our community, and it will not be tolerated. Any Sister involved in a particular friendship, who doesn't put a stop to it after being reprimanded, will be asked to leave."

"Yes, Sister."

"It's always sad when someone must leave. But keep in mind, all of you are years away from making your final vows. If anyone is obligated to leave, we announce before the breakfast reading the next day that Sister Mary Whoever is no longer with us. Above and beyond that announcement, *absolutely no discussion whatsoever* is permitted about a Sister who has left. Those who do leave, go out the back door. No good-byes are permitted. Yes, it sounds harsh. But believe me, it's for the best."

Harsh was hardly the word for it. Pat got little sleep on that first night.

The postulants' dormitory consisted of a large room. Each Sister's private area contained a bed and bureau surrounded by sheets. It was strictly forbidden to enter another Sister's area.

Pat could hear the sobs of other homesick girls through the wall of sheets. Several of them went home at the end of the first week.

Pat stuck with it. She tried her best to absorb all the rules. "Keep your eyes down, and your hands modestly folded," Sister Margaret Mary said. "Don't speak unless you're spoken to. If you're corrected by another Sister, you don't offer an alibi! You say, 'Thank you, Sister. I deserve much more.' And remember, except on very special occasions, you're strictly forbidden to touch one another. Do I make myself clear?"

"Yes, Sister."

After a while, the postulants were permitted some brief contact with the novice nuns. It was all Pat could do to keep from hugging Eileen. A voice inside her head warned her, *Don't!*

"So how are things going back on Lemon Tree Lane?" Sister Eileen asked her one day during recreation, as they strolled beside the frozen pond.

"Oh, the same, I guess," Pat admitted.

"You know, it was a funny thing, when I first came here. We're not allowed to watch TV, of course. But one night I was staying with some of the older nuns in the infirmary. They had their TV on. A commercial came on for McCormick Ford. I got so homesick, seeing it! Isn't that odd?"

"Not really," Pat said.

"Pat, what became of Rory? Did he ever marry Rosalie?"

"No. He told me that he meant it when he broke the engagement. So Rosalie went to Europe with her father's American Express card. And Rory moved to Washington."

"That's too bad."

"I think it was for the best. Dad is so mad at him. Rory had his big chance. And he ruined it."

"I can't understand why. I thought he was in love with Rosalie. Pat, there's someone else from Lemon Tree I think about often. Remember Father Leveque?"

"He left. It's said he got married."

"Gee, that's terrible! I'll pray for him. Maybe, some day, he'll come back."

"And we'd better get back before Margaret Mary sends a

search party after us." It occurred to Pat that they were alone together. Sister Margaret Mary had forbidden her postulants to take recreation in groups smaller than three. That looked like a forbidden *particular friendship*.

"Yes. When you write to your folks, give them my regards, will you?"

When Pat heard from her parents, they pretended that all was well, but she could read between the lines. *People are talking. Dad is drinking more than ever. Ma is trying to cover it up, but it's true. It's all Rory Michael's fault!* She prayed for divine assistance but felt a great anger rising within her.

And then one day, she told. She broke the promise made to Cardinal Corby and spoke the words out loud.

Pat had been alone in the Chapel. She'd been severely reprimanded by Sister Margaret Mary for a trivial infraction, shouted at, and made to kiss the floor for humility. Wasn't she humble enough?

"God, what do you expect of me? Is this what Saint Kristen had in mind? Is it really what I want? Margaret Mary hates me. I'm trying my best, but with the trials you've sent, how am I going to make it? How would you feel, with someone like Rory Michael in your family?"

And then, for the first time since coming here, she broke down.

"Pat?" Eileen slid into the pew beside her. "What's wrong?"
"Nothing. Everything!"
"You can tell me."
"No, no, I can't. It's too terrible. You'd never believe it!"
"Pat, if you keep these things inside you, it's not good."
"I can't tell anyone!"
"Here." Eileen offered her a tissue.
"Thanks," she sniffled. "It's...Eileen, it's.... Everything is going wrong! Eileen, I'm afraid that Rory is a homosexual."
"Oh, no!" Eileen said. "That can't be true!"
"It is! *It was*," she said. "He got into trouble over it when he was fifteen. Dad sent him to a psychiatrist."

Eileen's eyes grew wide.

"He was supposed to be cured. I don't think he was. Not really. Eileen, people are saying that so is Father Leveque. That's why he left. And that he married Rory."

Pat was unable to go on. Eileen sat silent for a moment, then said, "Oh, wow!"

"I can't let anyone know! You won't tell?"

"Never, Pat. You can depend on me. Now, come on. Don't cry."

Eileen put her arm around Pat. Pat thought she heard the Chapel door open and shut. She didn't care. Eileen was showing her real kindness, and that was all that mattered. No one else in this place cared if she lived or died.

She didn't see Eileen the following day. Neither was Eileen at breakfast the next morning. Sister Judith got up for the reading.

"The Lord gives and the Lord takes away," she said. "Sister Eileen left us last night. Today's lesson is...."

And I never saw her again.

Even now, after so much time had passed, the wound was still painful. Sister Agnes blamed herself.

Did another Sister see us together in Chapel? she still tormented herself. *Did she think that we were like that? Why did they get rid of Eileen, and not me? Was it because of the Cardinal's interest in me? Eileen, if only you could have called me, or written to me just once! Let me know that you were all right! Or told me that you had left of your own free will, so I could stop blaming myself. Wasn't I your best friend since kindergarten? Didn't you tell me that all you ever wanted was to be a Sister of Divine Compassion?*

Any further contact with Eileen was forbidden. Pat concentrated on becoming the best Divine Compassion nun ever. She learned the rules and lived for and by them. She never let myself get that close to another Sister again. The very word *lesbian* filled her with horror and shame. And yet....

She sat up in bed. It was two-thirty and she was wide awake. Outside, the street lamp cast an eerie glow on growing drifts.

And yet, she was so lonely! A part of her died and she let it. Like Rory died. And she had to stand aside and not do anything. It was for the best! "Wasn't it, Lord?" she asked.

Instead of reaching for her Rosary, Sister Agnes pulled open her bureau drawer and took out the pictures of Longianna.

"You helped Rory," she said. "You stood by him to the end. Please, Longianna, might an old fool have a drop of the kindness you showed him? Won't you help me too?"

Chapter 15

*A*GAIN, I HAVE TO BE ALONE. This time in a church.

Of course, I'm not in an ordinary church. I've come to this place in Sicily. I must be here, I must touch my roots, before I go on with my life and my career.

My one regret is that I couldn't bring Rory with me, as I did in the dream. There are such powerful mystical forces alive in this land. Rory would love it here.

The *Forever* video was finished yesterday and Carla is taking it back to Los Angeles. I'm staying on for a few days to visit the other Longianna, my grandmother. She appeared in the video as the wise crone. I'm afraid she stole the show.

I have to *think*. To go over where I've been in order to see where I'm going, because I'm getting there so fast.

My trip to San Francisco didn't go well. I called Phillipe's home from the airport. His law partner answered and said that since I was in town, I might as well come over. He didn't sound enthused and when I got to the house, I saw why.

"What in the hell...?" I asked.

This person didn't look like Phillipe. He looked like an ascetic one might find living in a cave in India. So thin, from years of fasting. How could anyone lose so much weight so fast?

I knew the only way.

"I'm sorry, Longianna," his partner said. "Phillipe just got out of San Francisco General Hospital. He knew you were going to

Italy, and he wanted you to have a good time. He didn't want to spoil it for you."

"As you see, I no longer have ARC," Phillipe told me. "I now have AIDS."

That did it. I started in again. "I want you to come to L.A. with me. I'll have the gay clinic send Randi back. And I'll take care of you. Like I took care of Rory."

"I can't let you do that," he said. "What about your career?"

"Screw my career!"

"No, Longianna!"

"Phillipe, it's nothing! What have I accomplished? I get written up in these silly teenybopper magazines. And you've heard the Top Forty version of "Forever." Who can understand a single word of it? What good is it doing for anyone?"

"Longianna, they're not listening to it with their ears. Rather, with their hearts. The message is there. The love is there."

"But what about you?"

"Please, don't worry about me! Anne's oldest daughter is coming to stay with me. She's a registered nurse. I'm getting the best care possible. Besides, look at this."

He got out a scrap book. It was all about me.

"You see?" he said. "Here's that picture of you and Rory by the pool. And a note that says I-knew-you-when. Here's some of your publicity from Grimalkyn. And here's that cover story in *American Teen Scene*."

"'Longianna Rae. Can you win her love?'" I read. They even changed my name at Grimalkyn, so it would fit on the record label.

"But this article is bubble gum. Stark, sheer bubble gum."

"Important bubble gum."

"It's a perfect example of what my manager wants."

"Then you must reason with him. I submit to you, now that you're on the Top Forty, you're big enough to do just that."

"You think so?"

"When there's some task you must do, you're always given the means to do it."

"Phillipe," I said, "I don't want to leave you." I was afraid that I'd never see him alive again.

"Longianna, you have to go. You can no longer lock yourself up like a cloistered nun."

He was so much like Rory; skin over bone.

"Please," he said, "don't deprive me of the joy of being a fan!"

I had to tell him goodbye. "If you ever need anything, you let me know," I insisted. "Here's a number. You can reach me anywhere in the world. I'll drop what I'm doing and take care of you."

"Longianna, I only want you to be happy. And to keep on singing. There's so much you must say."

The final image of Phillipe burned into my memory. He'd lost so much weight his Saint Kristen medal looked larger.

On the way home, I had a long conversation with Whoever is supposed to be running the universe. "Here is my body. Here is my blood. Take them and contaminate them with this sickness," I asked. "If you live off human suffering, let me be the human who suffers. Don't do this to the Alsatian Pretzel. I don't care whose set of rules were violated. Phillipe did no wrong."

The conversation was one-sided. I knew the sickness would run its course, Phillipe would die; there was no cure, no hope any longer, no way out except one.

"Who needs You?" I concluded my prayer. "*Per omnia saecula saeculorum*, and that's *Forever*. Amen."

I may have been religious at one time. But I knew that now I was mad at whatever power had loosed this plague.

Yet here I am in a particular Sicilian church. I'm kneeling before a statue of what is supposed to be the Virgin Mary and the Infant Jesus. My grandmother told me about it.

"That statue is much older than anyone knows," she said. "The child is female. Oh, yes, that's true! For they're not Jesus and Mary, they're Demeter and Persephone."

I've come here, to this place, to light a candle for Phillipe Leveque. And to think.

My life has gone from a dead stop to a series of quantum leaps. The first was when "Forever" made it to the Top Forty in the States. The second was when the next barrier was broken. "Forever" is now nearing the American Top Ten and is climbing the European, Australian and Japanese charts.

I had that little chat with my manager. "I want to tell the truth," I insisted. "Can't you see that I'm outgrowing this teenybopper image you're trying to stick on me? I want my fans to know why *"Forever"* was written."

Leo got out his Greek worry beads. "You told me that your friend was gay and that he died of AIDS," he fretted. "Are people going to accept that?"

"I think they are."

We were interrupted by a call about a backlog of orders for *Forever* albums and compact disks.

"You see what is going on, Gianna?" he asked. "The executives at Grimalkyn are ready to sprout wings and fly. This is right on time for the Christmas season. Don't you think that what you have in mind will jeopardize the tremendous profit they stand to make? Think of it in terms of dollars and cents."

"I am, " I said. "I think we'll make a lot more by being honest."

"All right, all right. I'll see what I can do," he promised. "Just remember who owns us! Snappy! With this Sweeney on their Board, it might not go over too well."

"Leo," I said, "I'm not doing it for Aloysius Sweeney."

Good old Leo! He'd called and said that as soon as I got back to L. A., I'd be interviewed for *Circuit* magazine.

"That's terrific," I said.

"I'll need to see you before your interview," he cautioned me. "I'll need to go over what you say. Longianna, *be careful.* You're new at this. *Circuit's* a fine publication, but there are others out there. They won't hesitate to destroy your reputation if that's what it takes to sell their rags. And this AIDS business has to be handled with a lot of care."

"Will you quit worrying!" I told him. "This is just what we need."

The next day, my grandmother and I went to Rome. My three backup singers, Cherie, Roseann and Flo, were there. We appeared in a videotape to be shown on Italian TV, singing "Forever" in English and "Volare" in Italian. After that, it was time to go. There was another good-bye to my fantastic grandmother, another jet heading back to Los Angeles.

I decided to use these long hours to make notes for my *Circuit* interview. Then I heard Roseann say, "Hey, Gianna! Look at this!"

She'd found an American publication in the magazine rack. On the cover was the First Lady. Inside were Christmas treats that any working mother could prepare (if she has a staff of twenty), heartwarming (or gutchurning) fiction, many ads for cleaning products and....

"My Sister Longianna Rae," I read. "By Donna Raimondi." *Dear God*, I thought, *what has that fool gone and done now?*

There were several Ghosts of Christmases past: pictures of

Donna and me in our pajamas ripping into presents beside the decorated tree. There was one of me on my First Communion day. Another showed me with my principal, Sister Jude Thaddeus, when I graduated from Divine Compassion High.

The tone of the article was so sweet I'd caution diabetics against reading it. Of course there was no mention of my wretched marriage and divorce. Certainly not a single, blessed word about Rory. Or of how Donna constantly nagged me to abandon him.

"I don't believe this crap," I said. "Look, it says here that I never express a single thought without clearing it with Donna first. We're soooo devoted to each other. The fact that she wrote this without even telling me shows you how close we are."

"Gianna, what are you going to do?" Roseann asked.

"If there's a phone on this plane, I'm going to tell her off, but good. Is there?"

I got up and looked down the aisle. Then I stopped. I recalled how Phillipe once advised me against dignifying stupidity with a response.

"No," I said. "There are other people on this plane. And if there's one thing they don't need, it's a rock star throwing a tantrum. No, this has to wait."

I folded up the magazine and rammed it into the pouch with the vomit bags.

"When we touch down," I said, "Donna's hide belongs to me. Until then I'll just have to seethe."

"Is it really so bad?" Flo asked. "You looked kind of cute in those Christmas pictures."

"That's the problem I was hoping my being in *Circuit* would solve," I said. "Cute! I'm trying my best to shed this airhead preteen image, and Donna goes and exploits it to get her name in print. What perfect timing. You might think she would have told me."

"Perhaps she wanted to surprise you."

"She did. And there's something else which has been bothering me...something Leo told me."

"What is that?"

I kept hearing my manager's words in the purr of the jet engines.

You're new at this, Longianna. Some of them will print anything to sell their rags. Be careful.

"That's why this *Circuit* interview is so important," I said. "It has to be without illusions."

"Natch," said Flo. "But I don't think Leo was referring to a piece of fluff like this."

"I know," I said. "I've seen some of those papers he was talking about."

It occurred to me that blowing up at thirty thousand feet in front of a captive audience was a good way to get into the supermarket tabloid press. That was another image I had to avoid.

"I'll stay out of *those papers*." Leo's words kept coming back, all the way home.

They'll do anything. Anything. Be careful, Longianna. Be careful.

Chapter 16

"Sister Agnes," the doctor said in a grim tone of medical concern, "is there something you want to talk about? Something that's bothering you?"

"No, Doctor," she said. "It's just that, well, I've been under so much stress lately. My mother. She hasn't been well, you know."

He made an affirmative grunt.

"After that snowstorm, Mr. Bostic slipped on the ice and broke his leg. I had to take his English Literature classes. I simply couldn't find a qualified substitute. I guess it was too much."

After not sleeping for three nights, Sister Agnes had collapsed again, this time in front of an entire class. They had been discussing the wounded fisher king of the *Wasteland* when, suddenly Sister Agnes was no longer with them.

"I can understand that," the doctor said. "Stress will cause these reactions. Would you like to go on a mild tranquillizer? Something to help you sleep at night?"

The doctor had offered it without Sister Agnes' having to ask. Therefore, it was all right to nod a weak *yes*.

"Good. Have you ever taken Valium before?"

"No."

"We'll try it out and see how it works."

Valium, Sister Agnes thought as the doctor scratched out a prescription.

Longianna had told her about Valium. She said that back in the early '80s, when Rory and Phillipe went their separate ways, Rory had become addicted to it.

That was the word she used. *Addicted.* However, Rory had been drinking heavily, and mixing it with God-knew-what.

"Doctor," she asked, "is this dangerous?"

"Not taken in small amounts. All you'll need is one before bedtime and during the day any time you're unduly tense. If you have any problems with it, of course, you'll have to let me know right away."

"Thank you, Doctor. I certainly will."

Sister Edith sent the housekeeper to the drug store at the Golden Galaxy Mall to pick up her prescription. "You'll feel better," she promised.

"I hope so. I could hardly feel worse."

Left alone in the infirmary, Sister Agnes imagined what she might have said.

"Yes, Doctor, there's a problem. My twin died of AIDS. I stood aside and let him. What could I do? And now Longianna—she was with him, to the end, in my place—Longianna is acting as if I don't exist. She won't answer my letters, won't give me her unlisted number. I think about her all the time. I imagine I see her picture on magazine covers. I hear her voice from car radios. Tell me, Doctor, is there a diagnosis for the way I feel? Would you call this a problem? Something I ought to talk about that might require professional help?"

That night she knew she was able to sleep because she dreamed of Eddie.

He was in her cell, still dressed in his comedian's outfit, looking out the window. "Pat," he said, "Rory's here."

"You mean he made it to the other side?"

Eddie nodded. "Got a real nice place, he does, on top of a hill. All the amenities. So they tell me."

"Dad," she asked innocently, "have you been up there to see him yet?"

"No," Eddie said, "I'm not going. If he's going to hang around with that goddam bunch of queers...."

Eddie ran out the door with his face averted. Sister Agnes understood. *Dad's crying. Men cry! That's their secret.*

"Dad, come back. I didn't mean—"

She chased him out through the corridor, down the stairs, and through the door. There was no sign of Eddie and no way to find him in this vast crowd.

A policeman was directing traffic on Wheeler Avenue. Sister Agnes asked him what was going on.

"Big rock concert tonight at Corby High," he said. "All the kids are going."

"I'm the principal. And no one thought to tell me. Who is giving this concert? Some garage band?"

"Longianna," he replied. "This is big-time. Sister, if you want to cross the street, you'd better do it now."

"I most certainly do."

The entire school was lit up. Even the portrait of Benny Corby looked festive. Sister Agnes walked toward the gymnasium. Everyone made way for her, so she could sit right up front.

And then, Longianna came out. The crowd gave her a standing ovation even before she'd sung a single note.

"Thank you! Thank you!" Gradually, the racket died down. "And before we begin tonight, I want to say a special thank you to a special person. The one who did so much for me. Your principal, Sister Agnes."

Again, the applause started. Longianna extended her hand and lifted Sister Agnes onto the stage.

"Oh, my goodness," she said. "I feel so unworthy."

"It's all right," Longianna said.

"You said you were writing a song for Rory Michael. I had no idea...."

"Neither did I." And then, Longianna kissed her. It wasn't a shy peck on the cheek, either. It was smack on the mouth, the way no boy was ever permitted to kiss Pat McCormick.

"Oh, dear," she said as she sat up in bed. "I must not...I must never...."

Sister Margaret Mary had warned her about such thoughts. They must be gotten rid of immediately before they became mortally sinful. Before God notices you're having them.

"But, mercy, that felt so real," she said aloud.

The idea that she'd permitted another woman to kiss her like that, even in a dream, was shocking. Yet her initial reaction was overcome by the fact that *she wanted it.*

It's a well-known fact at Corby High. Agnes Agony of the Jungle has never been kissed. Which is not to say, Agnes Agony of the Jungle should never be kissed. Rory Michael certainly was.

The next day, Sister Edith stopped by for a brief visit. "You look a little better," she said.

"I feel a little better."

"You're getting quite an accumulation of junk mail. However, this came. It looked important. It's from Italy."

"From Italy? Is it from the motherhouse in Rome?"

"Apparently not."

Sister Edith gave her the envelope. It was addressed in Longianna's familiar hand.

"Oh, my. Yes, I know what this is about. Thank you so much for bringing it."

Sister Edith had the good sense to leave. Sister Agnes tore it open.

Longianna first apologized for not writing but explained why. "A recording contract with Grimalkyn," Sister Agnes said. It really was the song Longianna told her about. On the American Top Forty, and with a video. So it was Longianna she heard. She wasn't insane. Longianna was a star, just like in her dream. "Oh, Lord have mercy."

Sister Edith came back to the infirmary. "Sister Agnes, are you feeling well?" she asked, confused.

"Am I well? Certainly not. I'm more than well, Sister, I feel *great.*"

She left her Superior in the infirmary, wondering, *Have I witnessed a miracle?*

***

Even Aloysius Sweeney looked good.

He came, as he always did, to give the Divine Compassion nuns frozen turkeys for Thanksgiving. He regarded this as an act of charity. The Sisters thought of it as charity on their part to accept Sweeney's tough and stringy birds. It was a fair enough exchange.

"Sister Agnes," he said, "I heard you've been ill."

"I'm much better, thank you."

"That's good to hear. Sister, there has been something I've been meaning to call to your attention."

Sister Agnes steeled herself for another idiotic article from *Nightfall*. Instead, Sweeney showed her a letter from Longianna. It was a form letter, she knew, the sort Longianna had to use to acknowledge a deluge of fan mail. Certainly not like the one she got.

"As you know, I'm on the board of the Snappy Corporation, and we own Grimalkyn. Now I've been concerned for some time about the quality of the music coming from Grimalkyn. I know we have to tolerate rock music, but some of the lyrics I found objectionable. I know that many of your students purchase Grimalkyn records. Well, you can imagine how happy I was when I found out that this young lady was under contract. She doesn't run around practically naked, as so many of them do. She doesn't use offensive language. And, Sister, would you believe it? She's a Divine Compassion girl."

"I know, Aloysius," she said, and dropped the bomb. "I know Longianna Rae *personally*."

"You know her?" he gasped.

"Oh, yes."

"Well, now. Isn't that grand."

"How long have you known Ms. Rae?" asked Sister Irene.

"Oh, a little while," Sister Agnes admitted, with a serene smile.

Sweeney left, beaming.

***

The doctor permitted Sister Agnes to go back to her regular schedule after the Thanksgiving break. She found good reasons for going to the Golden Galaxy Mall. There, among the Christmas decorations, was a poster of Longianna in the window of Sweet Daddy's records.

She paused to admire it, then went inside. "Do you have the *Forever* album?" she asked a teenage clerk.

"We have a few left. We're expecting more in the morning."

"Then, I'll take one."

He may have been surprised at a middle-aged nun wanting *Forever*, but he rang it up and gave it to her in a Sweet Daddy's bag. From Sweet Daddy's, Sister Agnes went to check out the magazine rack in the drug store.

"Ah," she said. "My Sister Longianna, by Donna Raimondi." Yes, she did have a sister named Donna, didn't she?

Sister Agnes paid for the magazine, stuffed it into her Sweet Daddy's bag, and went back into the crowded concourse. The noise in the Mall blocked out what was in her mind. The Valium was so helpful.

Mr. McCormick just died.

She smiled at a line of children waiting to talk to Santa. Christmas would be here soon. It would be a good one. Of that, Sister Agnes was quite confident.

***

Indeed, Christmas was marvelous. Even Ma seemed happy and contented.

No wonder, a tiny voice inside of her said. *With the antidepressant, Ma's even more stoned out of her skull than you are. How could she know that her baby's dead?*

Quiet, she warned the voice. *Everything is working out for the best.*

A few days before Christmas, Sister Agnes was watching one of the specials with some of the older nuns. She ordinarily didn't watch these things, but this one was important. Longianna was one of the guests.

Standing in fake snow, before an imitation cathedral, Longianna lead a group of carolers in "Adeste Fideles." In Latin. Ninety-nine year old Sister Dolores enjoyed it thoroughly.

"Sister Agnes, I've not heard that done so well since Bing Crosby was on. Of course, that was so long ago. No doubt, before your time."

"Not really," Sister Agnes said. In her opinion, Longianna was far superior to Bing, but it was best not to tell that to a raving fan like Sister Dolores.

***

Christmas had a distressing tendency: not only to be over, but to dump you at the start of a long, grim winter. This time, the usual letdown didn't trouble Sister Agnes. There was business to transact, mid-term exams coming up, and Las Vegas night to prepare.

Las Vegas night was an annual ritual at Corby High. It was a fund-raiser for the Divine Compassion mission in East Africa and usually held on or about the feast of Saint Kristen at the end of January.

Every year they did the same old thing, Sister Agnes thought as she went through the mail in her basket. A mock casino. Lots of bingo which raised a few hundred dollars and that's it. She wondered if, this year, they couldn't do something a little different.

She thought about that for a while and found an official letter from the Snappy Corporation which demanded her immediate attention.

When Eddie died, he left Gertrude several stocks, Snappy Cereal among them. Sister Agnes had power of attorney for Gertrude since the last stroke. This letter announced that the stockholders' meeting for the Snappy Corporation would take place on January 30th, in the Grand Ballroom of the Ritz Hotel.

"The Ritz," said Sister Agnes. "That was where Rory and Rosalie were going to have their wedding reception."

The Board of Directors was up for re-election. A booklet enclosed a few words about each member. One was "Aloysius Sweeney, president, Traditionalist League." You look better in that picture than you do in real life, Aloysius-Baby," she muttered. "They must have touched it up."

In years past, Sister Agnes simply marked the proxy for re-election of the whole Board. This time, she marked it to re-elect the Board with the exception of one, Aloysius Sweeney.

Wouldn't it be funny if he got thrown off that board? she thought, dropping the proxy into the mailbox. *That would kick the soap box out from underneath him.*

She then paid her mother a brief visit. Gertrude was the same, happy and smiling. She was reading the local Catholic paper which Mrs. Rizzo said was a good sign.

"Your mother is perking up, showing interest in the outside world," Mrs. Rizzo said. "She likes to talk with us about what is here and now, not in the past. I'm very happy with the progress she's made."

Sister Agnes was pleased. But in the background, the only man Gertrude had ever loved was singing that when he was twenty-one, it was a very good year.

Sister Agnes decided to stop off at the Golden Galaxy Mall on her way back. There might be more news about Longianna in the latest crop of magazines.

Already she had quite a volume of Longianna literature cached away in her cell. There were several teen publications. One of the better tabloids had a section called "Fashions on Parade."

"Looking *tres chic* for luncheon at *Ma Maison* are actress Michelle Maitland (*Lynx*) and singer Longianna Rae (*Forever*)."

Why was she going to lunch with Michelle Maitland? That troubled Sister Agnes so much she had to take an extra Valium. A part of her was asking, Why doesn't she go to lunch with *me?* Is it because I'm not a movie star?

Sister Agnes had written several letters congratulating Longianna on her success, assuring her that the Cardinal Corby students were her most loyal fans. Longianna had written back only once to tell her of future projects.

There was something about changing her image. And she might be endorsing products, but she didn't say what they were except that already she was working on her next album. It would include a duet with Tina Turner.

That made Sister Agnes think of the former Father Leveque. Back in the Sixties, he'd been such a Tina Turner fan. Was he, still? Was that why Longianna was doing this song?

The letter also spoke of plans for a North American tour next summer. There was nothing here that one couldn't learn through the fan magazines. Nevertheless, Sister Agnes cherished the one letter.

Longianna had written that she didn't have any details of the tour yet, and Sister Agnes wondered if she'd stop in the area. *If I could get to see her, only once*, she thought.

The idea hit her just as she was pulling into a parking space in the mall.

Who needs this silly Las Vegas night? she thought. What if she could have Longianna give a concert instead? Like in the dream. Was it really such a wild idea? How would she know unless she asked.

Longianna had given her the number of an office somewhere in Hollywood, not her home number. Sister Agnes had called a few times and was only able to leave a message. She wasn't happy that this wasn't *the* number, but it was better than nothing. She'd call as soon as she got back. The feast of Saint Kristen was only a few weeks away, so she had to act fast.

In the drug store she got a refill of her Valium. The pharmacist said something about a limited number of refills left. "Yes, yes, I know," she said. Her attention was on a stock clerk replenishing the magazine rack.

At first she thought she was dreaming again. No, it was real.

The kid put the latest *Circuit* on display.

Longianna was on the cover. Sister Agnes thought she was going to die of happiness.

When she got back to the convent, with more copies of *Circuit* than one person would need in a lifetime, she noticed Sweeney's Cadillac parked in back. He was in the parlor with Sister Edith.

"My plan is to send these petitions to the state legislature," he was saying.

"Yes," said Sister Edith, not really paying attention.

"My group is requesting a mandatory quarantine of all persons testing positive for this plague, and—why, Sister Agnes. How good it's to see you looking so well."

"Look what I found, Aloysius."

"Why, for Pete's sake. Look at this, that lovely young lady is on the cover of the *Circuit*. Sister Agnes, may I take this home with me and read it?"

"Take one. I've got lots of copies. Now, if you'll excuse me, I have an important call to make."

"Sister Agnes," said Sister Edith, "might I speak with you later?"

"Sure thing." She went up the stairs two at a time.

"Of course, if we could, we'd like to build a brick wall around Whitney Boulevard," Sweeney rattled on. "Not that they'd let us, but if they did, I'd pay for it."

***

It paid to be persistent. By refusing to take "no" for an answer, Sister Agnes had worked her way up to someone named Carla, who was supposed to be Longianna's secretary.

Unfortunately, there was little this Carla could do besides take another message. "The fact is, Sister Agnes, that no one knows less about Longianna's schedule than Longianna herself. I don't know if she's free at the end of this month or not. In fact, because of that *Circuit* article, everything is up in the air."

Sister Agnes wondered just what was in that article. If it was anything like the one her sister Donna was nice enough to write, there should be no problem at all.

"The person to talk to is Leo Redwyn. He's her manager. He makes her schedule."

"Is Mr. Redwyn there, please?"

"No, but I can give you the number of his office." Carla gave her another 213 number. Sister Agnes thanked her and hung up. She checked the back cover of her *Forever* album. Sure enough, it said that Longianna Rae was managed by Redwyn Associates, Wilshire Boulevard, Los Angeles, California.

She called Redwyn's office and got his secretary. Instead of getting an automatic turn-down, the party on the other end said, "Wait. You say you're from Divine Compassion High?"

"It used to be Divine Compassion High, it's now Cardinal Corby," she said. "Ms. Raimondi will know what I'm talking about. I happen to be an old friend of hers."

"Sister Agnes, I can't make any promises. All I can say is that I'll bring this up with Mr. Redwyn when he comes back to the office. And I'll get back to you."

Someone in Hollywood was going to *call her back*. On this very phone. Glory be to Saint Patrick!

What would the students say if they knew she'd become a behind-the-scenes big shot? Squirming with delight, she sat down to read the article in the *Circuit*, entitled "Longianna Rae Without Illusions."

There were three black-and-white pictures. One showed Longianna deep in thought, another making a point, and a third of her dissolving into laughter.

How beautiful they are.

Chapter 17

Ms. Rae, why did you write "Forever?"

I wrote "Forever" for a very dear friend of mine who recently died of AIDS. Yes, he was gay. I knew that from the start, and believe me, there were no illusions about it.

I was going through a tough time in my life, a nasty divorce, my ex was a druggie. And I guess it took me too long to wake up and smell the coffee. When I did, I had no choice but to leave him. My immediate family was not being at all supportive. They wanted me to give my ex a second chance. I come from a strict Sicilian Catholic background. There had never been a divorce in our family, up till then.

I was determined to make it on my own. I found a clerical job at a film studio. And that's where I met Michael. No, that's not his real name. I wouldn't be comfortable in giving out his identity. In fact, I don't think it's necessary to do that.

Michael was my friend when I needed one. When he saw the rat trap I was living in, he took me into his home. It was a funny sort of relationship.

During my marriage, I did a lot of songwriting, went to so many auditions. My ex was such a B.S. artist. I was such a dip back then I believed him. After the divorce, I decided I wasn't going to do it any more. All it caused me was trouble. I'd settle down, be a nice little secretary, forget about all this other stuff.

Michael didn't see it that way. He heard me singing while I was running the copier. I showed him some of the songs I'd written. They were really pretty stupid, childish things, which would embarrass the hell out of me if they were ever published. But he said he saw potential.

So he got me a second job, singing in a gay bar. I had some stage fright after so many bad experiences. You know, a drunk in a straight bar threw a bottle at me once? Almost got me before I could duck.

Michael told me that this job was a good way to get over stage fright and practice in front of a live and friendly audience. I came to love that place. There were wonderful friendships with the guys in the chorus. That's why it bothered me so much when so many of them started dying.

Michael told me about AIDS, but not much. I felt as if he were protecting me from it. He would say, "I'm going out," and I knew he was visiting someone who was dying. He never wanted me to come along and see what this sickness does. Always, hide the wounds, cover the scars. He'd tell me, "My mother was like that, and I guess I take after her."

No, he didn't admit it to me, that he had it, not at first. He didn't even want to admit it to himself. Who in his right mind would? It got to the point where there was no denying it. I'd seen signs that perhaps something was wrong. He kept telling me, "It's nothing. I had this rash last year and it went away."

Our funny relationship went on till then. Oh, he used to nag me terribly. "You should at least *try* writing your own material, Gianna," he said. "You can use my synthesizer. Do it." I was scared. Not just of his synthesizer; you ought to see it. Mostly, of trying again, and failing, or getting into another mess.

That was another thing. Michael had a lover. Actually, he had a few, but there was one who was a soul-mate, a former priest. He was French. I won't say his real name either, but I'll call him Jean-Pierre.

Jean-Pierre came to my defense. "Michael, you must understand that perfect love casts out fear," he said. "When Longianna feels no more fear, none at all, she's going to sit down at that synthesizer and astound us all."

I was glad to have someone stick up for me. In another sense, though, this only confirmed what I felt. I'd never compose any original material again. Who ever experiences perfect love? Think about it. With absolutely no illusions, no jealousy, no unrealistic expectations? Very few people. Little did I know that some day, I'd be one of them.

Michael told me that he had AIDS, the tests were back, the doctor was a hundred per cent sure of the diagnosis. The first thing he tried to do was move me out of the house. Besides, he had another lover, not his soul-mate, who had run out on him once the diagnosis was handed down.

I wouldn't go. I couldn't. Michael was terribly depressed. I was scared to leave him alone. I'd ask him, "What do you want for dinner?" and he'd say, "Cyanide."

Then he got mad and took it out on my skin. Plus, he wouldn't tell Jean-Pierre that he had AIDS. "I can't tell him *this*," he'd say. And he'd snap and snarl at me. Everything I did was wrong. Nothing was right. His toast was too damn light or too damn dark. His eggs were too damn hard or too damn gooey. What could he expect of a dumb broad? And one night during this time, I had a mystical experience I'll tell you about.

I had to go up to his room to change his sheets. He was in fine form. He accused me of only doing this because I was after his money. Oh, yes, he was saying these terrible things, that his name wasn't Onassis. So I told him where he could stick his money and walked out.

I got as far as the bottom of the stairs. Everything started swaying and I landed on my fanny. The crockery in the kitchen was rattling. I heard Michael ask what in hell I'd gone and done now. "Earthquake," I told him. All my fault, right? In his mind, there was the Longianna Fault, worse than the San Andreas.

I guess we were lucky in that it was a mild quake. The place I landed was right beside the kitchen. Now, in the kitchen, there was a glass sliding door that led to Michael's patio where he had a pool. At that time it was still full.

There was this eerie light in the sky and the water was sloshing around. And I saw—oh, I must have been out of my tree—I thought I saw an angel above the pool stirring up the water.

I had this...this idea...that this was like the pool in the Bible. The angel would come and trouble the waters. And the first sick person who got into the water would be cured. So I ran upstairs and said, "Come on, quick! I have to throw you in the pool."

We got downstairs. Michael saw what was going on, knew what I was talking about. Then it hit us both. I'd seen an illusion. There was no cure, miraculous or otherwise. No way out. He was trapped and so was I.

We both started crying. He told me, "Gianna, you know, the things I've been saying, I don't mean. You want to stay? Fine. You can stay. If you can stand me."

Yes, I know. That was one powerful experience. It was also a turning point for Michael. He called Jean-Pierre and told him the truth. Jean-Pierre was terrific. He stuck with Michael till the end, and I love him very much.

Just why did you make a choice to stay with Michael?

Why did I stick with him through all the yelling and screaming?

Did you love him?

Yes, absolutely.

Let me clarify that. It didn't start out as love. I was so grateful to Michael for all he'd done for me. When I found out he had AIDS, I felt sorry for him. Pity is never enough. Not enough to deal with a temper like Michael's.

I guess because I lived with him on such an intense level, whatever feelings I had for Michael were transformed into love. It was sort of a metaphysical alchemy: base metal into gold. And by love, I mean a perfect love.

You said Michael was gay. Were you...did you...?

Say no more. I understand. I'll tell you. The answer to your question is no. Never. Obviously, I'm not his type. And by the time I understood that I did love him, Michael was far too sick for that sort of thing. But, well, let me say this about that.

There was a time, after the anger was resolved, when we'd be alone in the house together. Michael went through a stage of having nightmares. He asked me to sleep in his room so he wouldn't be alone, so someone would be there if he woke up. Then, when he did, and it was really bad, I'd stay with him, I'd be there for him till he got back to sleep.

Do you think that turned me on? You're darn right it did. Michael was a very attractive man. Even when he was falling apart, he was a beautiful green-eyed Irish blond. And *I'm* straight. Good-looking guys have that effect on me. I'm only human, right? I'm not a saint made out of plaster. Yet—I understood, this wasn't meant to be.

How's that possible? It's something I can't explain. Sometimes, you can't always have what you want. I know that isn't a popular philosophy these days.

It was disturbing, but there was no sense of being frustrated.

Considering the level of sharing, of intimacy that I had with Michael, there was great satisfaction in our relationship.

What about this lover of his, Jean-Pierre? Did you see yourself in competition with him? Was there jealousy?

No, I wasn't jealous of him. That was never part of it.

In fact, Jean-Pierre stayed with us for the last days. He gave me a lot of help in writing "Forever." You might feel it was ironic. For a few nights, he was able to sleep with Michael, before Michael's pain got too great. I used to help the nurse tuck them into bed at night. Could a jealous person have done that and not gone crazy?

"Love is not jealous." That was part of the Scriptural reading at Michael's memorial. That's true: once you have attained the perfection of love, you're not jealous.

I still ask myself, "why me?" Not, "why did this terrible thing happen to my best friend," but "why, of all people, was I permitted the experience of perfect love for another person? What did I ever do to merit this?" I've no idea. Ask my family about my colorful vocabulary. Ask Sister Jude Thaddeus about some of the practical jokes I used to pull in school. I'm not Mother Teresa and never will be.

Maybe you don't have to do anything to earn it. It just happens.

I had to do something with this experience, and that's what "Forever" came from. The odd thing is, that in so many letters I get, people say it's such a happy, up-beat song. Not a death song.

Would you believe that the first version of "Forever" was pretty awful? It was a protest song: why isn't this plague abolished, why doesn't someone do something, ban the nukes, save the whales! Whiny. Jean-Pierre told me, "No, Longianna, that isn't what you want to say." But I had some of the chords worked out on the synthesizer.

Then, when it finally did happen, it was a spontaneous thing. Michael was talking to me about his family and how much he missed them. He'd had no contact with them in twenty years. He needed some loving. So I sang him the song that became "Forever." He was the first person to hear it.

How did he react?

He upchucked. Then he told me please, please don't accept that as a critical comment. He loved "Forever." It was the one thing he could take with him. That was right before he went into a terminal coma. He was having incredible pain. He said he loved me. And that...*that's* what I'm going to have with me. Always.

Do you still miss Michael?

You're putting it mildly. Things happened so fast with "Forever", it was on the Top Forty before I realized what was going on. Still, I'll go into a mall and see something and think, "Michael will get a kick out of that. I have to get it." Then it hits me, he's dead. I think what bothers me the most is that I'm not able to share my success with him. He was responsible for it. He knew I had it in me, all along, even after I'd said to hell with it.

You said there had been no contact with his family in twenty years?

That's right, nothing since 1968.

In a sense I can understand the way they felt because I come from a such a similar background. As a child, I was told how sinful it is to be homosexual. And if you carry all those arguments out to a conclusion, it becomes morally justified to beat up gay people. Then I thought, "Hey, wait a minute, this isn't right."

I never knew any gays who were out of the closet till after I finished school and got involved in the music business. Some I think the world of, and some I couldn't get along with if they were the last people on Earth. I figured, John is gay, Suzy is a Lesbian, so what? It made no difference.

Michael's family never had the opportunity I had, to break out of a restricted background. I was angry with them for a long time. It was Jean-Pierre who helped me understand what made them the way they were.

And, oh yes, Jean-Pierre. He was a priest back in the Sixties when he and Michael fell in love. Can you imagine how that went over? Plus, Jean-Pierre had to answer to a hard-line conservative Cardinal. No, he wasn't Francis Cardinal Spellman. And, no, I'd better not tell you who he was either.

Did you, personally, make any effort to find Michael's family after he became ill?

I never told Michael this. I didn't want him to be let down. But I tried to find his family before he died. I came incredibly close to finding his sister who is a fraternal twin.

That's one thing I really regret. Michael wanted to make his peace with them before his time ran out. I believe having them with him would have taken the edge off the pain and made his passing easier.

Oh, well, I tried. That's another reason why I'm not going to disclose Michael's real identity. I know his family is out there someplace. And I think that, some day, they might come looking for him, not knowing that he's dead. I tried to put myself in their position. Would I want to learn by accident that my son, or my twin, died of AIDS? And that someone did try to find me in time, but I wasn't available? No way. The guilt would kill me.

***

"No, Longianna, stop this. Stop it, please."

Sister Agnes rumpled up *Circuit* and shoved it under her pillow.

"I must be strong." Her eyes burned. "McCormicks are tough. Dad said so. McCormicks don't cry. I can't cry. If I do, the whole world will know. I'm the one you tried to find, Longianna. I denied Rory, I said, 'I know not the man.' And, now...."

She heard a discreet tap on her door. "Sister Agnes?"

It was Sister Edith. She must not know.

"Sister, I was wondering if we might have that little talk now. Are you all right?"

Sister Agnes dived under the covers and hid her face in the pillow.

"I've been concerned about you, and...."

She came in, presumed Sister Agnes was sleeping, and left. "The poor dear," she said.

At that instant, there was a scream of tires through the alley beside the convent, and a loud crash in back.

"Mercy on us," Sister Edith said. Sister Agnes rolled out of bed and ran into the hallway. Her Superior was peering out the window that overlooked the convent's parking lot.

"Is someone hurt?" Sister Agnes asked. "Shall I call the police?"

"Yes. No, wait. Don't! That car belongs to Mr. Sweeney."

The two nuns charged down the steps, through the kitchen, and out to the parking lot.

Sweeney's Cadillac had collided with a tree in the middle of the lot. The entire front end was shattered. Antifreeze poured out of the bottom and steam rose from the top. Sweeney was in the driver's seat, slumped over, probably unconscious, bleeding, dying in agony.

Sister Agnes did as Eddie taught her. She reached over Sweeney and cut off the engine. Then, Sweeney's breath hit her full.

Of course he wasn't hurt, his body was too relaxed. He was stinking drunk.

"Aloysius, how dare you!" she hissed at him.

"Is he injured?" her Superior asked.

"No, Sister, he's intoxicated."

"Merciful Mother of God. Why?"

Sweeney lurched, then treated the nuns to a rousing chorus of *Sweet Rosie O'Grady*. By then, lights were on all over the convent, and several other nuns were looking out through the kitchen door.

"Back inside, everyone," Sister Edith warned. "The situation is fully under control. No one has been injured. There's no need to call for any assistance." She shepherded her Sisters back inside, leaving Sister Agnes alone with Sweeney.

"Ah, Sister Agnes," Sweeney said, unstrapping his seat belt and staggering out of the car. "You're the one I came to see. The very one." He brandished a copy of *Circuit*. "There's something I wanna show you."

The bitter air had a slightly sobering effect on him, as did the contempt in Sister Agnes' eyes. "There's something I want to show *you*, Aloysius," she said. "Look what you did."

"Hunh? Hey..that's my car! My Caddy. Who in the *fuck*...."

He felt a sharp slap across his face. "Don't you ever use that language in my presence again," she warned him.

"Don't get mad at me. And I'm not drunk, I only had a couple whiskey sours at Danny's. Or three. Or four, maybe. Not enough to get a man drunk. Anyhow, I'm try'na do you a favor. Look at this, Sister Agnes. Just look at this. It says here a girl from Divine Compassion, a so-called decent girl, crawled all over a sick queer. Used to be, I respected her. Hell, she was nothing but a dirty little plague carrier all along. That damn tramp doesn't deserve to live."

This time, Sister Agnes hit him so hard he fell over. He was only briefly stunned. "You don't have to get mad." he protested. "And don't get up on your high horse and blame *me* for having a few drinks after I read this."

Sister Agnes struggled to hold herself back. *If I cut loose now*, she thought, *I'll kill the son of a bitch. If he ever calls Rory a queer, or Longianna a tramp again, I just might. Sweet Jesus, I'm turning into Grandpa McCormick. POW!*

"I only wanted to call this to your attention, Sister Agnes. Some day, you know what? You'll thank me. Yes, you'll say, 'Thank you, Aloysius Sweeney, for protecting me from reading this trash.' The Church should never have got rid of the Index of Forbidden Books. Yes, Sister, sometimes we need someone else to tell us what we have no business knowing about. I'll tell you who understood this. Benedict Cardinal Corby, God rest his noble soul. Now there was a *man.*"

Sister Edith came back. Sweeney pulled himself up. Sister Edith noticed a tiny rivulet of blood coming out of the side of Sweeney's mouth.

"He fell on the ice," Sister Agnes sweetly said. "I tried to break his fall."

Sweeney burped.

"Sister Agnes, we have got to get Mr. Sweeney home. We can't have the police over here. You understand...the *scandal.*"

"Oh, yes," Sister Agnes said to the familiar words. "I was just explaining to Mr. Sweeney the penalties for drunken driving."

"Oh, dear, yes," said Sister Edith. "And for such a prominent member of our community."

Sister Agnes aimed a benevolent smile at Sweeney. "How the court would love making an example of *you.*"

You deserve to hang, she thought. *Only, let me provide the rope.*

"Mr. Sweeney, we're going to have our school janitor drive you home," said Sister Edith. "You understand, we *can't* call a cab."

"What'ja say?"

"You have to go home and sleep it off."

"No, there's work I gotta do. I'm on the Board of Snappy Cereal, did you know that? I own Grimalkyn Records. I'm gonna tell 'em to cancel Longianna's contract. Throw her back in the slum she came from."

Lord, I should have killed him while I had the chance.

"No, Mr. Sweeney. You're going to go home and *sleep it off.*"

"Then I'll do it in the morning. First thing."

"No, you won't," Sister Agnes said, careful to maintain her cheery smile. "First thing in the morning, you're going to have a hangover."

She added, in a whisper, "I hope you enjoy it."

"Oh, dear," said Sister Edith after Sweeney was gone. "I'm so sorry that Mr. Sweeney never married. If he had, there would be a Mrs. Sweeney to drive him home when he gets like this."

"To drag him out of Danny's?" Sister Agnes asked. "I wouldn't wish that fate on anyone."

Back in her cell, Sister Agnes filled a glass with water, and swallowed two Valiums.

"Can he do it?" she fretted. "Does he have the authority to terminate Longianna's contract? How can I stop him?"

Trying to pretend there was nothing wrong, she joined the others for evening recreation. There was a radio on in the corner with a local talk show.

"Welcome to *Talk of the Town*," said the host. "I'm Bill Bradley. We have open topic tonight, so we can discuss anything your heart desires."

Sister Agnes thought, *Let's talk about Aloysius Sweeney.*

"I'd like to talk about an article in the new *Circuit*," said a teenage girl.

"Yes, what's your first name?"

"I'm Robyn. And I go to school at Cardinal Corby."

"Robyn, what's on your mind?"

"Well, I just want to say that Longianna Rae is terrific, to do what she did. I wish I could meet her. And I wish I'd known Michael, too."

"Thank you, Robyn. A most interesting article, bound to produce controversy. Any further opinions?"

"My name is Karl," said a raspy voice. "I have AIDS. I want to say thank you to Longianna. I'll be a fan of hers forever."

"I'm Pauline. I'm a born-again Christian. My son showed me that article. I've never been able to accept homosexuality. But Jesus says in the Bible that 'what you do to my brethren, you do to me.' There are people in my church who won't agree with me, but I say Longianna was right. And I pray that the Lord will bless her."

"Sister Agnes?" said the housekeeper.

"Excuse me, I wasn't paying attention."

"You're wanted on the telephone. Long-distance. He gave his name as Mr. Redwyn. It's still the middle of the afternoon where he is, if it's not convenient, he could call back tomorrow."

"No, I'll take it!"

"Longianna says she remembers you well, Sister Agnes," Leo said. "She wants to repay you, and she'd be delighted to come sing for your students. Only one question. When?"

Chapter 18

*W*HEN? WHEN WOULD IT BE? Why, on the thirty-first of January, of course. The feast of Saint Kristen.

"I suppose it would be a change from our usual Las Vegas night," said Sister Edith. "But, Sister Agnes—a rock star? Won't she try to provoke a riot?"

"Mercy, no, Sister. She was a Divine Compassion girl herself."

"Why, in that case, I don't think anyone will have any objection."

Longianna is coming here. I'll be able to speak with her, to be with her. But, Lord. Suppose Sweeney finds out? Sweeney had been dormant. Perhaps the hangover was bigger than anyone imagined.

The important thing was, Sweeney hadn't been around. Had he made good on his threat to terminate Longianna's contract? Did he dare, with public opinion so much in Longianna's favor?

I'll say this for Aloysius. He's a stupid man.

As the winter days went by, Sister Agnes found herself dipping deeper into her Valium. Who could blame her? She was so excited. The students, when they learned about the concert, had the freedom to shriek, whoop and holler. People expected more of Sister Agnes.

I must remember these three things: calm, cool, and collected.

But it wasn't always easy. "Videos?" one of the students asked her. "You have to be able to get MTV. But sometimes, Channel 30 shows them."

Sister Agnes took to watching Channel 30. Most of its programming consisted of cowboy movies and wrestling. They did have videos. And one day, they showed *Forever*.

Sister Agnes squirmed to the edge of her seat. The video started showing a young man, dressed in brown, going up to the mouth of a cave. An elderly woman was waiting for him, gesturing to him to come closer.

Don't go, Sister Agnes almost said out loud.

He went in, down to the depth of the cave with the crone. Just before the refrain, "My son will live forever," there was an explosion of light. Every possible color flashed on the screen. The crone was transformed into Longianna. She was offering the young man something.

"It looks like a tangerine."

When he took her gift, the hood fell back off his head. *Mercy, it's Rory*, she thought. A closer inspection showed her it wasn't Rory, but someone who looked a lot like him.

It was the strangest thing she'd ever seen.

The video shook her up so much she needed even more Valium. As she lay in her bed that night, she tried to analyze why that was so.

"Perfection of love," she said. "Like a mother for her son. That's what I saw. Was Ma like that? She used to love Rory so much. Sometimes, I wondered if she loved me. Ma always wanted Rory in her lap. Dad used to say, 'Come on, Gertrude.' But Rory was her little darling. Not being able to see him again, that's what destroyed her. But was it really perfect love? Ma wasn't able to let Rory go."

The Valium took over, oozing up to her brain, blotting out any further thoughts of Rory and Ma.

Sister Agnes went on in her pre-concert euphoria. She continued her stops at the mall, looking for more news of Longianna. One day, while walking out of the drug store she saw Longianna's name in print on one of those dreadful tabloids. What could Longianna possibly be doing in a publication like *Nightfall?* Sister Agnes went closer to inspect.

LONGIANNA AIDS SCANDAL was the headline. She felt herself shaking.

There was a picture on the front page. Sister Agnes recognized it as the one Longianna had sent of herself and Rory beside the pool.

"This can't be Rory. Sweet Mother of God."

Someone had gone over Rory's image with an airbrush. The results were grotesque and sickening.

Dizziness swept over her. The sales clerk asked her if she needed help. Quickly, she paid him for *Nightfall*, hating herself for offering money for it, and took it out to a bench in the concourse.

Aloysius Sweeney, if you've done this....

"'Longianna comes off as such a goody two-shoes. Let me tell you, she's nothing like her image at all.'

"George Stephenson, former lover of the late Academy Award winning composer, Rory McCormick, ought to know. In this exclusive interview with *Nightfall* he tells how Longianna Rae, while sharing their house, did nothing but take advantage of McCormick's generosity and try to seduce him on a constant basis.

"'Oh, I mean, it was absolutely revolting, the way they carried on. She used to come to the table stark naked. I begged her to put some clothes on, but it did no good.

"'The fact that Rory had AIDS didn't even slow her down. Obviously, she was after his money. I do believe she's one of these people who goes looking for rich gay men who suddenly start losing weight. Yes, indeed, she knew she was sitting on top of a gold mine.

"'Naturally, I wanted nothing more than to stay with Rory. But I couldn't. Not with Longianna there, and I mean, there was no getting rid of her. So one day I told Rory, either she goes, or I go. He must have had brain damage, to choose her, but he did. Leaving him was the hardest thing I've ever done.'"

Lies!

Sister Agnes tossed *Nightfall* into the nearest trash receptacle. She stormed out of the Golden Galaxy and returned to the convent.

On the way, her eyes overflowed. There was no stopping the tears of rage.

At least it wasn't Sweeney, she thought. But she knew he read this garbage. What kind of monster was this George, she wondered, that he could do such a thing to Rory? How could he desecrate the memory of one he said he loved?

Sister Agnes steered the wagon around the stump where a tree used to be. Sister Edith came out of the kitchen. There was no hiding the tears on Sister Agnes' face.

"Oh, mercy, Sister Agnes," she said. "We didn't know where you were. We tried to get word to you. But I see...you know. Our sympathy is with you, our prayers, always. We'll help you in any way we can. Just ask. You must have come from the nursing home."

"The nursing home...."

"Yes, the Peaceful Woodland, where...."

"Maaaa!"

Sister Agnes dived back into the station wagon and left two strips of rubber in the convent's parking lot. She didn't know how she got to the Peaceful Woodland, but when she got there, Dr. Singh was in the lobby.

"I'm so sorry, Sister Agnes," he said. "I've just pronounced Mrs. McCormick dead. It was another stroke. A massive one. Nothing we could have done. Such a lovely lady, your mother."

"Doctor, may I see her?"

"She hasn't been moved out of her room yet."

"Sister Agnes, I'll take you," Mrs. Rizzo said.

"Please."

"And when she was doing so well." Mrs. Rizzo said. "She was so interested in everything. Whatever she saw, she had to pick up and read and discuss."

Mrs. Rizzo opened up Gertrude's door. Gertrude's body was covered with a white sheet. Carefully, Mrs. Rizzo folded the sheet down so Sister Agnes could see her mother's face. Gertrude looked somewhat stunned.

"Would you like to be alone with her?"

"Yes. Mrs. Rizzo?"

"Sister?"

Her eye had caught what was in Ma's wastebasket. She saw the words LONGIANNA AIDS SCANDAL.

"Was she reading this thing that's in the trash?"

"We found it beside her wheel chair. One of the cleaning people left it in the lounge. Poor Gertrude, she'd read anything, even junk like that."

"I see. Thank you."

Mrs. Rizzo shut the door. Sister Agnes tore the copy of *Nightfall* into tiny shreds.

"Ma," she said. "Ma, please don't do this to me. Not now. Ma, please don't be dead. At least give me a chance to explain."

She thought she heard Ma saying, "Patricia, you knew Rory was sick and you didn't tell me."

"Ma, please, if you die, I'll be an orphan. I'm still too young."

More tears came, tears of grief, of rage and guilt. She grasped her mother's hand. It was still soft and warm. Sister Agnes sobbed like an abandoned child.

"I didn't tell you about Rory. Yes, he did have AIDS, and he died in September. Maybe I should have told you. I don't know. But there was Longianna. That article is a dirty lie. She was good, and kind to him, and, Ma, don't look at me like that."

Sister Agnes cradled Gertrude's lifeless body, as if she were the mother and Gertrude her stillborn baby. She remembered that video, the gentle Persephone giving her son eternal life, perfect love.

Is Rory doing that? Is he offering Ma a tangerine right now?

The door opened. Mrs. Rizzo came in with Dr. Singh. "Easy now, Sister," she said. "We've called your doctor. He's going to give you a shot that will make you feel better and help you through this time."

"I don't want a shot," she said. "I want my Ma. I've killed my Ma."

***

"Begged me to put some clothes on, did he? By the time I'm through with him, he'll have to wear a fig leaf on that cute little crotch of his. If I let him keep it."

I was waving Leo's letter opener around, and I'd turned the air in his office cobalt blue. "Longianna, if you feel you need legal advice...." Leo tried to say.

"You think I need a lawyer? It happens that I know the *best*." And I dialed the San Francisco number of Carstairs and Leveque.

"This is Longianna. Is Phillipe there?" And, "No, I need to consult with him in a professional capacity. I intend to file suit against *Nightfall*, and George Stephenson, as soon as I can. Yes. Yes. Is Phillipe feeling any better? Good. You say he's seen this article? What did he say? This *is* obscene. Will you give him the message, then? He knows how to get me. Thanks. 'Bye."

Leo and the members of the band eyed me nervously. They

knew when Vesuvius had blown. "Phillipe wasn't in," I told them. "He'll get back to me, don't worry."

"Longianna," Leo volunteered. "This sort of thing...it *looks* worse than it *is*. Not that many people buy or read *Nightfall*. It's known to print flat-out lies. And it's only at the check-out counters for a week. Look at the article next to yours—a miraculous image of the Virgin Mary appears on a rutabaga. I mean, come on."

"It's not for my sake," I said. "It's what they did to Rory. See what they did to his picture? That's the worst thing they could have done. He never looked like *that*. Do you know why it was that he got off pills and booze and one-night stands? Because it was messing up his face. That's what he said. And now these jerks have to do a thing like this after he's dead."

Roseann, one of my backup singers, attempted to defend Leo. "Leo's been in this business a while. And like he said, this sort of thing happens to everybody who gets famous."

"Look at this trash," I said. "I *never* went to the table stark naked."

"Nobody said you did," Leo offered.

"George did. All right, maybe...."

Leo looked up. His cigar nearly fell out of his mouth.

"I was anything but naked. I had on my shirt and shorts. The air conditioner broke and George was bitching like you wouldn't believe. It must have been a hundred and ten in that kitchen.

"'I've called the repairman,' Rory said. 'He'll be here as fast as he can. We're *not* the only ones to whom this has happened. So why not enjoy some of this ice cream Gianna bought for us? Or go for a dip in the pool?'

"Then I suggested that George go soak his head. I should have known he was filing that away for future reference. Ooooh, that creep! And this picture of Rory and me—he took it. He had the negative."

"I don't want to second guess that lawyer friend of yours," Leo said. "But I think he's going to advise against filing suit. In this sort of thing, the best course of action is to ignore these scumbags. Don't let them know they got your goat. It may take a while but they'll get the message."

"George," I said, starting in again, "how could he do this? He was always a little weird. Maybe he and I didn't get along all that well. But he did this to Rory, not just to me. Why? Even if he didn't love Rory, even if it was only for the pleasure, how could you turn on someone like that? Especially when they're dead."

"You want my personal opinion?" Leo asked.

"Yeah."

"I think there's a special place in hell for people who try to get rich and famous spreading lies about the dead."

"A place in hell, yes. Like in Dante's Inferno."

I sat down on Leo's sofa. The band looked relieved.

"A circle above the Inferno." I grabbed a legal pad and pen."Yes, a circling jet over the Inferno. On board is George, the flight attendant.

"The crew and the passengers are all evil spirits. 'Ladies and Gentlemen, this is your captain speaking. Our landing at Los Angeles International has been put off another hour due to factors beyond our control.'

"The men are drunk. The women are hysterical. The kids are running wild. The babies are wet and screaming. And you, George, you have no Pampers. You're out of vodka, vermouth, and mixed nuts. The fat man in Row 5 is going to punch you out unless he gets mixed nuts, now.

"The sinks and toilets are all clogged. A child attacks you with a water pistol. A rock star is screaming through the phone that she's going to have her sister boiled in salad oil. The people in her band are having a food fight. You, Carter." She pointed to the drummer. "You started it."

"'Ladies and Gentlemen, this is your captain speaking, we regret to inform you that our landing at Los Angeles International has been delayed another hour.'

"Not an hour, George. For all eternity. And this is what you chose, for what you did, to get your stupid face in the paper."

I started writing again. "I think this is a good sign," Roseann said.

"Yes," Leo agreed. "It looks like Longianna feels a *song* coming on. I hope it gets her mind off the suit. She's got better things to do than fool around with *Nightfall.*"

∗∗∗

Sister Agnes didn't remember much about Gertrude's funeral. For the most part, she felt as if she weren't in full contact with the ground.

The Requiem Mass was held in Saint Catherine's. The Church wasn't as crowded as it had been for Eddie's funeral. So many of those people had died in the past few years. Eddie's lawyer, Dave Wolfe. Monsignor Hayes. Biddy O'Toole. All in Good Shepherd Cemetery.

Rory's dead too.

The priest, whom Sister Agnes didn't know, spoke of her mother as "our sister, Gertrude, who often replenished her spirit at the Lord's table."

Sister Agnes found it difficult to concentrate during the prayers. "Eternal rest grant unto her, O Lord, and let perpetual light shine upon her. May the soul of our sister Gertrude and the souls of all the faithful departed rest in peace. Amen."

Sweeney was there. Sister Agnes had managed to avoid him all during the wake. She wondered if he remembered that she'd hauled off and belted him. Apparently not. His drinking problem was more than an idle rumor. It was quite possible that Sweeney had reached the stage of alcoholic blackouts. He had no idea how his car got wrecked, or why the tree in back of the convent had to be cut down.

What a splendid pillar of the community he was.

There was a brief service at the cemetery. After the service, there followed a brief get-together in the convent parlor. Sister Agnes was no longer able to give Sweeney the slip.

"I want to tell you how sorry I am about your mother," he said. "How very, very sorry. What a wonderful woman she was, so devoted to her family."

Aloysius, if you only knew.

"Yes," she said. "Ma will be missed."

"Sister, may I tell you something?"

What could it be? she wondered. *That I have a brilliant future in the ring?* Sister Agnes nodded.

"As you know, a man in my position has to keep up with things. Especially with the young people, to know what sort of influences they're under. Well, Sister, to make a long story short...."

Please do.

"...it has come to my attention, that you're not going to have your Las Vegas night this year? That you've invited Longianna Rae, here?"

"Aloysius, I'm very tired."

"I can't help but be concerned. I was reading an article about her, somewhere. And it seems she's not the exemplary Divine Compassion student she pretends to be. But I've taken steps—"

"Mr. Sweeney, can it wait?" Sister Edith said firmly. "Sister Agnes had been through so much strain during the past few days. Perhaps some other time."

"Yes. Quite right. I'll be in touch. Sister Agnes, my deepest sympathies. I'll remember your mother in my libations."

He meant to say orations. Freudian slip.

Sister Edith went with Sister Agnes back to her cell. "Isn't it just about time for your medications?" she asked.

"Yes," Sister Agnes said. She didn't know what it was, only that it was stronger than Valium. It silenced the voice that said, *You killed Ma.*

"Let me sit down for a while."

"Certainly. You have to take care of yourself. But, Sister, I was wondering...are you sure you want to go through with this rock concert? It's only two weeks away. After all you've been through, do you feel up to it?"

I have to, I must, if I can't see Longianna I'll die.

"I'm going to do it," she replied. "The students. I can't let them down."

"Of course," her Superior said, and had the decency to leave her alone.

Sister Agnes swallowed more pills. The students weren't calling her Agnes Agony of the Jungle any longer. Instead, she was the neatest principal who ever lived.

They don't know my motivation; they don't have to. I have to see Longianna.

She heard car doors being shut in the parking lot. The guests were leaving. Her eye fell on the headline on the obituary page. GERTRUDE MCCORMICK DIES; FORD DEALER'S WIDOW.

Nowhere did the article say, "beloved mother of the late Rory Michael McCormick."

Why, Lord? Why can't I do anything right? she thought. *If I had any decency, I'd have insisted on listing Rory's name in the obituary. Who cares what people think? And I almost had Sweeney right where I wanted him. But I gave in to Sister Edith and didn't report him to the police. Always, the scandal. How would it look? A convent, crawling with cops.*

As a drunk driver, Sweeney deserved to have the book thrown

at him. That would have gotten him off the Snappy board once and for all. *I didn't have the courage to go over my Superior's head*, she thought. *Sweeney will do it again and maybe next time, he'll kill someone.*

She leaned back in her chair. Among the objects she'd taken from Ma's room were the Infant of Prague and the First Communion picture of herself and Rory. She picked it up and held it in her lap.

"If only we could have stayed children. If only."

Never mind. Longianna was coming to her. Longianna would be here in "zero minus fourteen days and counting."

Only Longianna had the authority to forgive the sins she'd committed." In the back part of her mind, a choir of young nuns was singing Gregorian chant.

Agnus Dei, qui tollis peccata mundi, miserere nobis.
  Agnus Dei, qui tollis peccata mundi, miserere nobis.
  Agnus Dei, qui tollis peccata mundi, dona nobis pacem.

Sister Agnes fell into a fitful sleep, muttering about the Lamb of God whose blood washed away the sins of the world.

Chapter 19

AT ZERO MINUS EIGHT DAYS AND COUNTING, SISTER AGNES found herself in Archbishop Ricardo Montero's private study with Sweeney. He sounded almost funny, the way he tried to emphasize every point. He was like a stand-up comedian trying to do Aloysius Sweeney.

"Your Excellency, I feel I must object to Sister Agnes' sponsorship of this rock concert at Cardinal Corby High," he said. "Now, Sister Agnes and I've been good friends for many years."

Speak for yourself, Aloysius-Baby.

"Nevertheless, I feel that this Ms. Rae isn't a proper influence on innocent young girls. She may have been a fine student at Divine Compassion in Los Angeles, but since then she fell in with evil companions. I call to your attention this article in a publication known as *Circuit*."

Archbishop Montero put on his glasses and scanned "Longianna Rae Without Illusions." Sister Agnes looked around as he did so.

The Cuban-born Montero was Corby's successor. Whereas Corby would have blasted the notion of a rock concert at a Catholic school, Montero had confessed to being a fan of the Miami Sound Machine.

He certainly had improved the decor of this place. Sister Agnes remembered when it had been Corby's den and the last time she was in it. Thank God Montero had gotten rid of the picture of Rosalie riding her damn horse.

Why was it so hard to focus her thoughts? Sister Agnes kept recalling that Rosalie Corby had gone to Europe after it dawned on her that the engagement really was over. She'd met a widowed Italian prince who had a title but no money. She had money and was drooling over his title. It was a marriage made in a lawyer's office if not in heaven.

"I understand that this Ms. Rae is a most controversial figure," the Archbishop said. "But, Mr. Sweeney, I don't see where she's done anything *wrong.*"

"Your Excellency, permit me to call your attention to *this*. It may be distasteful, but sometimes the truth is hard to take."

Sweeney whipped out *Nightfall*. Just as quickly, Montero pushed it aside.

"I know of this paper," he said. "I've no faith in it."

"But—but—" Sweeney had to play his one ace. "You see, in this *Circuit* article, where Ms. Rae says she feels her life has changed? Perhaps she's trying to tell us something."

"Aloysius, just what are you implying?" Sister Agnes asked.

"I mean, " he said, "that Ms. Rae may be harboring this deadly virus *herself*. In which case, she's a threat to public health and ought to be quarantined."

"No! No," Montero said. "Let me explain this, Mr. Sweeney. I'm no authority on this disease. I'm only an archbishop, not a doctor. But I do know that it's very difficult to catch. And from what it says here, there's no way Ms. Rae could have caught it from the unfortunate Michael."

"But, Your Excellency, suppose these so-called authorities are wrong?"

"We're using common sense guidelines in Mercy Hospital. And we have had no problem with transmission of this sickness to our health care workers. Therefore, Mr. Sweeney, I must decide this matter in favor of Sister Agnes. She may have her concert and I wish her much success with it."

"Very well," Sweeney said, and was unduly quick to leave.

"Sister," the Archbishop said, "my sympathies on the recent death of your mother."

"Oh, thank you, Your Excellency."

At times, she forgot Gertrude was dead, or felt that Gertrude had died many years ago. The pills were affecting her sense of time.

I can get rid of them, once Longianna is here.

At zero minus one day and counting, Sister Agnes heard two of her students talking.

"My mom had to take the day off, because she had to go to the Snappy stockholders meeting," one said. "Well, anyhow, you know that Sweeney? He was raising this terrible fuss, that he was going to have Longianna's contract terminated because of this AIDS business. Then someone else on the Board said they'd never terminate Longianna, she was making Grimalkyn so much money. After all, they're running a profit-making business, not the Watch and Ward Society."

"So then what happened?"

"They tossed Sweeney off the Board. Said he was an embarrassment to the whole corporation. Mom says you should have seen it."

"Awesome."

Thank you, Jesus. Sister Agnes thought. Part of her mind tried to warn her: *Sweeney's not dead. He's wounded. Watch out.*

She didn't listen to it. Longianna's arrival was now less than twenty-four hours away. That was all that mattered.

A kid with a boom box strolled down Wheeler Avenue. A disk jockey was shouting that here was the Number One song in the U. S. A. "Forever."

***

There were no classes on the Feast of Saint Kristen. It would hardly be practical. Early in the morning, Sister Agnes went over to the school. The janitor, Mr. Murphy, was giving the corridors one last buffing. Never had the school looked better: WELCOME LONGIANNA and DIVINE COMPASSION IS #1 posters were everywhere.

Only the portrait of Benny Corby looked out of place. His scowl was firmly fixed. "Patricia, it's lucky for you that I didn't live to see this day," he seemed to say.

"Awful cold out, Sister," said Mr. Murphy. "Smells like snow's on the way."

"Nothing's going to stop this," she said, and went to her office just as the phone rang.

"Sister Agnes?'

"Longianna! You're in town?"

"No, I'm in Peoria. Aw, sure I am. I'm at the Ritz."

"When? When will you be here?"

"Later. I want to go over today's schedule with you."

"Oh, yes."

"First, I want to thank you for letting us use your office as my dressing room. I promise you, we'll not leave a mess behind. Now, as to the schedule: I'll be sending Carla over in an hour or so with the band and the road crew. They'll be setting up the equipment in your gym and running some sound checks."

"But...you?"

"I won't be over till way after lunch. I have to be at Mercy Hospital."

"Are you sick?"

"Never felt better. No, this is part of what I do. I'm going to be visiting the PWA's there."

"The...excuse me?"

"The Persons With AIDS, Sister."

"Oh." That certainly wasn't what Sweeney called them. "What do you do for them?"

"A lot of the same things I did for Rory. I sing for them. Quietly, you understand, which is why I don't have the band with me. After all, it's supposed to be a quiet zone. I talk to them. I make them laugh."

"What about those who aren't in their right minds?"

"It's even more important that I talk to them."

"I see."

"But I don't want this to get into the press. They have a tendency to make it look so *sappy*. Now, about security. You have a private firm?"

"Yes, we have Rent-a-Cops."

"Good. I'll be sending my bodyguards over at about two to coordinate with them."

"Not that I expect any incidents."

"We sure don't want any to spoil your students' fun. That's why my bodyguards are so unobtrusive. Oh, one other thing. There might be some messages coming in to your office for me. Don't worry about them. Carla will take care of everything."

"Messages?"

"Yes. I'm having a present delivered to someone else today. I have to make sure it gets there."

"I see. But I do want to get together with you."

"Tell you what. My flight doesn't leave till after noon tomorrow. We can have a fine chat in the morning, how will that be?"

"Oh, that would be wonderful. Perhaps I might even show you around."

"I'd love to see the places where Rory grew up. Lemon Tree Lane. Saint Catherine's Church and School. Padgett's Park."

"I know where they are. Very little has changed in that part of town."

"Wow, I'd love to see it. It's a date. Just a sec. Yes, Carla?"

There was a pause, and "Sister, the limo is here. I have to run. See you later. Keep an eye out for Carla."

Sister Agnes felt like she'd just run a long race. "Mother of God," she said. "After all these years...I have a date."

She leaned back in her swivel chair. The emotional wheel she was on turned faster.

Too fast.

She reached in her pocket for a pill, looked at it, and asked herself, "Who needs this? Longianna is here and she's going to make everything all right for me."

"Excuse me, Sister," a delivery man said. "Is there a Carla MacIvey here?"

"Not yet, but I'm expecting her."

"Can you sign here for these? Thanks."

There was an envelope and a small package. Sister Agnes noticed that they were both from the law office of Carstairs and Leveque, San Francisco, California.

"From Father Leveque, for Longianna," she told herself. "I wonder."

She tried rattling the package, but whatever was inside was too well wrapped.

In slightly over an hour, Sister Agnes met a pretty young woman with curly blonde hair. "Hello, Sister. I'm Carla MacIvey, Longianna's secretary."

"I'm most pleased to meet you. Yes, I've talked with you before, haven't I?"

"I remember. Here are the people who are going to help us set up. And here's Longianna's band. This is Carolyn, who is on rhythm guitar. Steve's on lead. Paul's on bass, Riley's on keyboards. These are her back-up singers: Cherie, Roseann and Flo."

"How do you do." She knew she'd never remember who all of these people were.

"Sister, if you could show us to your gym, we'll have the guys start moving our instruments in."

"Of course," she said. "Oh...wait. These came for Ms. Rae."

"My gosh, these are from Phillipe." Carla said. "Longianna has been expecting them. No, I'd better not open them. Best to wait till Gianna gets here. Thanks for signing for them. Hmm, I wish I knew what was in the box."

I'd give my back teeth to know.

They processed down the long corridor, passing empty classrooms and labs. "Longianna was saying something about giving someone a present?" Sister Agnes asked Carla.

"Yes, she has a gift for Phillipe Leveque that she hoped would give him the surprise of his life." Carla smiled. "She said he'd get a big bang out of it. The present was due to arrive last night."

"Oh." Sister Agnes put on her sweetest smile. "Ms. Rae used to speak to me about Mr. Leveque during Mr. McCormick's illness. I gather they were quite close."

"Yes, they still are," Carla said.

"This present...is it...."

"Sister, you must swear you won't tell anyone," said Carla. "Longianna wants this kept out of the papers."

"I promise."

"All right, I'll tell you. Phillipe has been a feeling a little down, and Longianna wanted to cheer him up. So," Carla whispered, "she had his mother flown over on Air France. Longianna picked up the tab and everything."

"Why, that's marvelous. How very thoughtful of her. Has Mr. Leveque been ill?"

"A bit."

"Does he have AIDS?" Longianna had never told her.

Carla stopped at the entrance to the gym. The expression on her face told Sister Agnes that she'd crossed a forbidden barrier.

"I'm sorry, Sister," she said. "We can't talk about who has AIDS. Gianna's so uncomfortable about it. It's one of our strictest rules; we're not supposed to give out that information to other people without her permission. You understand why: if word of it gets out, it can really hurt that person, human nature being what it is. So....*never.*"

"Forgive me," said Sister Agnes. She wished the ground would open and swallow her up.

Carla immediately went about directing the road crew. Sister Agnes stood alone in the gym.

I know the answer to my question is yes, she said to herself. *But, Lord, I really screwed up, didn't I? I should have known. I'm not part of Longianna's world, after all. I'm an outsider. I have no right to know.*

"Sister?" one of the Rent-a-Cops called. He looked like he was a hundred years old. Sister Agnes wondered what he was doing with a gun.

"Just a minute." *Dear Lord*, she thought, *don't let Carla tell Longianna I asked that question. I've never been so embarrassed.*

"Sister?"

"Yes?"

"There's a man out front who says he has to see you. Wouldn't give his name."

She turned away. They all looked so busy. Carter pounded on his drums.

"All right," she said. "It's probably someone else with a delivery."

She stopped when she saw who it was.

Sweeney! He was in a new car, looking balefully at the door.

"He says it's real important."

"Very well," she said, and pulled on her heavy shawl.

"Sister Agnes," Sweeney said. She got close enough to smell his breath. He was, at least, cold sober.

"Aloysius, we all have a lot of work to do."

"So, you're going ahead with this? You're inviting Miss Plague Carrier into your school?"

"Now, listen," she whispered. "I've warned you about that."

"They threw me off the Snappy Board. After seven years of faithful service, look at what I get in return. The bum's rush. And all because of that creature you're treating like a visiting head of state."

"I suggest you go home."

"This sure has shown me who my friends are. The archbishop stabbed me in the back. The corporation stabbed me in the back. And now, you. After all I've done. It was my money that paid for your gymnasium. I guess you'll be taking down the plaque with my name on it. Let me tell you something. Benedict Cardinal Corby would never treat a friend the way the whole pack of you've treated me."

Sister Agnes said, "Go home."

"I only saw Cardinal Corby one or two times. Let me tell you, he was a man. If he knew what was going on in a school named after him—"

"Go home."

"What?"

"Better yet, go to Danny's. Get soused."

"I ought to do just that. But you've not heard the last of me. Not by a long shot."

Sister Agnes strained to keep from striking him again, and said between clenched teeth, "Go to hell."

"Fuck you," he said, and his car took off down Wheeler Avenue.

The guard wasn't around. He was inside the warm school lobby, paying no attention, working on a crossword puzzle.

"You," she said.

"Eh? What say?"

"That man."

"Which one?"

"The one who was just here. The one in the car."

"Oh, him."

"Yes, him. *Under no circumstances whatsoever* is he to come back. Or even be around while Ms. Rae is on the premises. Do I make myself clear?"

"Sure."

"Do you know who I'm talking about? Did you see him?"

"Yeah, I got a good look at him. I think I saw him on TV. Who is he? One of those preachers?"

"Never mind. Just remember, if he comes back, I want him arrested. And watch for that car. It's an '89 Lincoln Continental, black, and here's the plate number which you didn't get."

"Right," he said. "Not to worry."

"Don't I wish. Don't I *hope*." Sister Agnes said, and went back down to the gym, where the noise was coming from.

※※※

When the sound system was set up, and the sky outside grew darker, Sister Agnes saw another long black car pull up.

"Can it be?" she wondered. Words from her childhood came back to her. She and Rory were going to Communion and Monsignor Hayes prayed: *"Domine, non sum dignus ut entres sub tectum meum, sed tantum dic verbo, et sanabitur anima mea."*

"I'm not worthy that you should come under my roof. Speak but the word...sing but the song...and my soul will be healed."

A man got out of the car, went to the other side, and opened the door. Longianna got out.

"Carla!" Sister Agnes emitted a most un-nunlike shout. "She's here."

Sister Agnes ran out the door, down the sidewalk, thinking of herself as an elderly, pregnant Elizabeth lumbering out to greet her cousin Mary.

"Longianna!

"Sister Agnes?"

The bodyguard looked alarmed but backed off when Longianna said, "Why, of course. Hey, it's great to finally see you."

Sister Agnes tried to hug her but it was difficult because of Longianna's heavy coat. "Let's go inside," Longianna suggested. "Guido, here, is used to this weather. He's a tough from North Jersey. I'm not. California sunshine is more my style."

"Such a soft coat," said Sister Agnes, feeling it. "Suede?"

"Yes. Would you believe, it was Rory's? He bought it to wear to Aspen and never got to go. Strange, how well it fits me, even if it does button up the wrong side."

The silent bodyguard held the door. "This is fantastic," Longianna said. "Your students want me to feel right at home. What a beautiful woodcut of Saint Kristen."

"One of my art students made it."

"Ah, there's Cardinal Corby. Most impressive. Hey, something smells good."

"Your secretary had dinner delivered. It's in my office."

"Great. I'm starved. But I feel funny, going to the principal's office. I remember those little visits I had to make to Sister Jude Thaddeus' office."

"Really, now!"

"Yes. They weren't social calls."

"I can hardly believe it."

"That I acted up? Oh, yes. Here I am, folks."

"Gianna," the others said.

"Now, recall, you're in the principal's office," she cautioned them. "No messes. What have we got here?"

"Pizza with black olives, just the way you like it," said Carla.

"I'm so starved it's pathetic. Have you all met my dear friend, Sister Agnes Mary McCormick?"

"Yeah."

"Sister, might I interest you in some pizza?"

"Well..one slice won't hurt."

Longianna cut it for her. "It's interesting that you told me your name was McCormick," she said. "You might be a distant cousin of Rory's. His Grandma McCormick had seventeen children."

"I suppose...I might be...."

"I tried to find Pat, but I guess that wasn't meant to be. Well, dig in. I tell you, I'm so starved...."

Longianna sat down at the desk, beside the telephone.

"How did your day at the hospital go?" Riley asked her.

"It was absolutely incredible. I got to visit everyone in the AIDS wing. Just being with them, it's mind-boggling. The things they tell me. Oh, Carla. Have you got all my stuff?"

"Your dress is hanging up in the bathroom."

"Great. When I was in school, we weren't even supposed to know that Sister Jude Thaddeus had a private bathroom attached to her office. There was only this closed door with PRIVATE on it."

"That's the way it used to be. We Sisters weren't supposed to have bodies."

"Somehow, we always figured out that you did. Speaking of bathrooms...should I, over dinner? Flo, you remember that song we used to sing?"

"Do I ever."

Longianna and her back-up singers went into an *a capella* version of a song about using the bathroom as an echo chamber, locking it up so no one else could get in. They all collapsed into giggles at the end.

"Sister Agnes must think we're all insane. Don't worry, Sister, that little number isn't on tonight's program."

"Ommigawd, Gianna!" Carla suddenly said.

"What?"

"This came. It looks top priority."

"Oh, wow! It's from Phillipe."

Carefully, Longianna wiped the tomato sauce from her fingers before handling the package. "Sister Agnes, have you got a letter opener?"

"In my top drawer."

"Yeah, I'll say this is important. It's about my lawsuit."

"Lawsuit?" Sister Agnes asked.

"Yes. I've decided to sue *Nightfall*. I don't know if you know why."

"I do know. I saw that—that—"

"That trashing."

"And I say, good for you."

Longianna, if you only knew what seeing it did to Ma.

"I'll have to see what Phillipe says. He was having his staff look into the matter before we go to court. Let's see what he has to say."

"Gianna, did he get the present?" Carla asked.

"We'll soon find out."

"Longianna, will you please tell us what it says?" Carter asked.

"I...had...no...idea," she gasped, took a drink of water, and turned to Sister Agnes.

"I really regret having to ask this, Sister, but would you mind stepping outside for a while? I'll explain later. This is...this is something I can't discuss outside of this group."

"I understand," she said.

Sister Agnes went next door, to Mr. Murphy's broom closet. Every word spoken in her office came through the heating vent.

"For pity's sake, Gianna, how bad can it be?" Carla asked.

"Worse that you think," she said, and started to read.

My dearest Longianna,

The matter of your wishing to file suit against the tabloid *Nightfall* has come to my attention. I promised you I'd have my staff thoroughly investigate this matter. I have the results of my study now and I ask that you consider them with care before you take any legal action.

I ask you to bear with me while I preach a bit. The lessons I learned in the seminary stay with me always. The topic of today's sermon is forgiveness. Instead of filing the suit, I'm asking you to forgive George Stephenson, and to forget those pitiful, small minds at *Nightfall*.

You say, is it always possible to forgive? I, of all people, know that it's not. If you ask me, do I forgive Adolph Hitler, I'll say, no, never. Sometimes you *can* forgive if you know all of the facts. And I trust, knowing what prompted this attack on you, you'll put this incident in the past.

Longianna, George is in San Francisco General Hospital. He ...."

Sister Agnes heard someone in the band say, "Oh, shit!" Longianna read on.

He has one of the worst AIDS cases you can imagine. It attacked his brain. That's what caused him to get in contact with *Nightfall*, tell those lies, and sell them that picture. He was jealous, especially of you, and angry at the whole world. The thing he feared the most has come to him.

I pray that he'll die soon and his terrible suffering will be over. Knowing this, perhaps you can forgive him, and join me in asking for an end to all of his useless pain. Please understand. You're Number One on the charts. You're a big target, easy to hit. George had to lash out at something. You were there."

"Jesus," Carla said. "What now?"

"There won't be any lawsuit. Call Sister Agnes back in."

Quickly, she emerged from the closet, considering the irony of being there. "You can come back in now," Carla told her.

"See what I've done?" Longianna asked. "I tossed the principal out of her own office. Sister Jude Thaddeus would have my head on a platter for that. With a baked apple in my mouth."

"You need not apologize," Sister Agnes said.

"Isn't there more?" Riley asked.

"Yes. Let's see, now."

"Longianna, I ask that some day you have the happiness I now have with *Maman* here. I wish to reciprocate. I'm sending you a present under separate cover. I'll love you always. Phillipe François Leveque, Attorney-at-Law, Alsatian Pretzel."

"A present?" Carla said. "That's what's in the box."

"Phillipe sent me a present." Longianna's eyes grew wet. "Can you imagine?"

"Well, let's see it," Flo demanded.

"All right. Somebody certainly did pack this well. Ah, yes, there it is—I can't believe this. I can't."

At first, Sister Agnes couldn't see what it was. The band members crowded around.

"Look at it," said Flo.

"That's the most gorgeous thing I've ever seen," said Roseann.

"Where on Earth could he have gotten it?" Cherie asked.

"Put it on," Carolyn demanded.

"Please help me put it on." Sister Agnes saw tears drop from Longianna's lashes as Cherie fastened the clasp in the back.

"Why, what is it?" Sister Agnes asked.

"A Saint Kristen medal," said Longianna. "This is the one that belonged to his cousin."

"The one who was in the concentration camp?" Carla asked.

"Yes. Jean-Pierre. He gave this to Phillipe just before the SS took him away."

"The way it shines!" Flo said. "It looks like it's alive."

"If the Nazis had gotten their hands on this they'd have melted it down for their death machine."

"Phillipe gave it to you," said Carla. "He must really love you."

"I can't believe he did that," said Longianna, dabbing her eyes. "What time is it in San Francisco now? I have to call him and thank him. Sister, may I use your phone? I'm going to use my card and have it charged to my home phone."

"Certainly." Sister Agnes perked up her ears to learn what that home number was.

Yes. I've seen that medal before. Father Leveque used to wear it back in the Sixties. I had no idea it was Jean-Pierre's.

The band maintained a reverent silence. "It's going through," Longianna said. "One ringy-dingy. Two. He ought to be home." Then, "Anne? Guess who this is? Yeah, right. Is Phillipe there?"

Sister Agnes wasn't sure of what happened next. She felt as if the ceiling caved in. Longianna turned stark white and said, *"When?"*

"When, Gianna?" a shaken Carla asked.

"Not fifteen minutes ago." Longianna's tears turned from joy to pain. "When we were singing about locking up the bathroom."

Sister Agnes made the Sign of the Cross and kissed the crucifix on her rosary. She remembered that someone from the band, she didn't know who, escorted her back to the corridor.

"We'll take care of her," he said. "Phillipe's mother was with him at the end. Longianna made that possible."

Don't shut me out now, she wanted to say. *I have to be with Longianna.*

Can't you people understand? I love her, too!

Chapter 20

He was so *funny*. That was what hurt. Phillipe was like an actor in a French farce. He left behind a trail of defused arrogance and shattered dentures. No, I couldn't face up to the fact that the world was now without him.

I depended on him, perhaps as much as Rory Michael did. Maybe more. And I loved him, too.

I talked to Anne, and to Madame Leveque. It was Madame Leveque for whom I was hurting the most. First Jean-Pierre. And now Phillipe.

Finally, I hung up and gave the phone over to Carla, to change my travel plans.

"Are you O.K., Gianna?" Carter asked.

"Yeah." My face was a shambles. I'd have to go into the bathroom and do some major improvements.

"Sister Agnes is outside."

"You threw her out *again?*"

"Yes. She wants to know if you're canceling the concert."

"Absolutely not. Ask Sister Agnes to come in."

"Yeah. Sure."

Carla told me of my new schedule.

"Do you remember those plans we had for tomorrow?" I asked Sister. "I must ask you to give me a rain check. The first flight to San Francisco leaves at seven A. M. I have to help Phillipe's family with the funeral."

"I understand," she said, but her eyes betrayed a bitter disappointment. "I was wondering if you really wish to go ahead with this concert."

"You know how it is. 'The show must go on.'"

"Yes."

"There will be one change in the program, Sister, which I have to go over with the band. We were going to do the Top Forty version of "Forever." But now, I think I'll do the extended mix."

"Is that different?"

"It's somewhat longer."

"Long and strong," Carter said. "Sister Agnes, it's a mind-blower. This is one evening you'll never forget."

"I have to go over the arrangement with the band," Longianna said. "I'm not getting rid of you. But this is all technical stuff."

"Fine. I'll...find myself something to do. I think some of the parent chaperons are waiting for me."

We heard more and more cars arriving in spite of the snow. "Sounds like the gym's just about packed," Carter said.

"And I'm going to give them the best performance of my life," I promised.

Carla was in the bathroom with me, helping with my makeup.

"Does Sister Agnes strike you as kind of odd?" she asked.

"No more so than Jude Thaddeus. Why?"

"Well, her eyes. They're kind of...off."

There was something strange about her eyes. Rory's eyes looked the same way after Randi gave him a shot of Dilaudid.

"I know what you're probably thinking," I said. "But nuns don't get stoned."

"Maybe not."

"Aw, it's not important. She must have knocked herself out to pull this off. She's just tired."

"No doubt."

I asked, "How do I look?"

"Terrific."

"Then, let's go."

I held the St. Kristen medal as I waited backstage for my cue.

***

"Is everybody *happy?*"

With the stage lights shining in my eyes, I couldn't see anything beyond the front row. The chorus of shrieks I got told me that the answer was "yes." I saw Sister Agnes, smiling sweetly, in the front row.

"All riiiight! Let's heat this joint up!" The band went right into the introduction of *Heat Wave*. "Come on, ladies, let's shake it," I reminded the backup singers. When we finished the number, I was dripping wet.

"Thank you!" I acknowledged the applause. "Before we go on, I'd like to introduce some pretty special people in the band." I went through the whole bunch.

"Thank you," I said. "And now, I want to acknowledge a terrific person I'm sure needs no introduction. Here's the one who thought this up in the first place: your principal, Sister Agnes. Let's hear it for Sister Agnes!"

Wild cheering filled the gym as Sister Agnes stood up and took a modest bow.

"We'd like to do some new material for you. Something a bit quieter, so we won't hear any complaints from the neighbors. Hey, neighbors, are you having fun? Great. Here's the title cut from my new album, *White Rose*."

Sister Agnes looked like she was devouring me with her strange, stoned eyes. She seemed not to move, nor even breathe throughout the entire concert. It was odd how I remembered that during Holy Week, if you listened to the entire Gospel of the Passion of Christ and stayed still, you were supposed to get some sort of indulgence.

I couldn't remember what. I never qualified.

"Thank you," I said. "Yes, you're Number One."

I let the applause die down. "And now, I'd like to do a special number in honor of one who couldn't be with us tonight. One who is always going to mean a lot to me. He gave me this. I wish all of you could see it. It's a Saint Kristen medal. And it's from one person I'm going to remember *Forever*."

The extended mix started slowly. Sister Agnes looked like she was holding her breath as Steve went through the opening chords.

Then, I really cut loose. At Rory's memorial I had done it like a hymn. This time, I wanted Phillipe to hear me.

When I came to the part that goes, "He Will Live Forever," Sister Agnes crumpled up. She looked up at me, shaking with sobs, turned, and dashed out of the gym.

I had never seen anyone so profoundly moved. I was feeling

for her, too. Her Superior, seated beside her, looked up the aisle but didn't go after her. Because of the darkness none of the students had seen her leave.

The president of the student council presented me with a bouquet of white roses tied in a gold ribbon. Backstage, I signed a pile of *Forever* albums and posed for pictures with the senior class.

But it wasn't over for me, yet. I had to find Sister Agnes.

"I've never seen anyone react like that," I said to her Superior. "Do you know where she is?"

"There's a little chapel on the lower level," Sister Edith said. "I believe that's where Sister Agnes went. We can get there down these stairs."

"Gianna," said Carla, "remember what time we have to leave in the morning."

"This won't take long."

"All right, I'll go with you. Shouldn't we have a guard along?"

"I'm going to a chapel. Nothing can go wrong. Guido has to get the car. Guido?"

"I don't believe it," he was muttering. "That guard was at his post, all right. Snoring."

Sister Edith led us down a darkened corridor. A light shone through the open chapel door at the end. I heard sobs.

"Oh, dear," said Sister Edith. "Sister Agnes has been under so much stress lately. She didn't want to tell you. She was afraid you'd cancel out. But her mother died."

"Do you mean recently?" I asked.

"Two weeks ago."

"And she didn't say anything about it? If only I'd known. I'd better talk with her."

I went in alone, and gently pushed the door shut. Sister Agnes knelt in front of the altar rail, as if deep in prayer.

"Sister Agnes?" I said softly.

"I confess to Almighty God, to Blessed Mary ever Virgin, to Blessed Michael the Archangel, to Blessed John the Baptist, to the Holy Apostles Peter and Paul, to Kristen and all the saints.."

She took a deep breath and continued. "...to Jean-Pierre and all the martyrs, and to you, Longianna Raimondi, that I've sinned exceedingly in thought, word and deed, *mea culpa, mea culpa, mea maxima culpa.*"

"Sister, you've been under too much strain. You should have told me your mother died. I could have sent something."

"Oh, no, I couldn't have told you that."

"Of course you could have."

"But if I did...I'd have to tell you her name...."

She was making little sense. "Sister, why don't you sit down here? I'll have Carla get Guido. He'll see you back across Wheeler Avenue. What you need is rest."

"No, I've had quite enough, thank you. More than I deserve. What I need is...forgiveness. And you're the only one who can give it to me."

"Sister Agnes...."

I reached out for her. She backed away as if fearful that I'd touch her. Her eyes darted to the chapel door. Suddenly, she got up and locked it.

"Nobody's coming in this time."

For the first time I was frightened. I knew how disturbed people are set off by celebrities. I had seen strange behavior before but not like this. Wasn't Sister Agnes the principal of Corby High?

Stay calm was the first rule. Sister Agnes was rooting around in the small Confessional for something. I was thinking of bolting for the door when she charged at me with the priest's stole.

"Here," she said, "put it on."

"Oh, no, Sister. No, I can't. It would be wrong."

"Yes, yes, you must."

"Sister, there are rules against that sort of thing."

"Please, Longianna. Don't talk to me about rules, not now. I need you to hear my Confession."

Oh, my God.

"Sister Agnes, listen to me, that's impossible. I'm no longer a member of your Church. I couldn't go on obeying the letter of your law in good faith. And even if I were still a member, I can't ever be ordained. Surely you know why."

"It doesn't matter. Only you can forgive me."

"Listen to me, please. I don't have the authority to forgive sins. Neither can I walk on water or cure AIDS. Sister Agnes, I'm just a small-time saloon singer who got a lucky break, and that's all I am."

"You stayed with Rory Michael. You gave him a tangerine."

I looked closely at her eyes. For the first time I saw what was really so strange about them. They were a rare shade of green. Rory was the only other person I had ever seen with that exact color.

"All right," I agreed. "I'll do this if it's what you want. But if something is troubling you, you should speak to your real confessor about it."

"No, I can't tell him...he'd never understand. He thinks I'm so great. He has no idea...."

"Calm down."

I put on the stole. I felt awful about doing this, and I had forgotten the formula. If only Phillipe were able to tell me.

"Where do I start?" I asked. "How long has it been since your last Confession?"

Sister Agnes had already started on how she'd sinned in thought, word and deed. Then she said to me, "I couldn't tell you that my mother died because I knew you would want to send something. And I'd have to tell you her name. My mother's name was Gertrude Mary Mulligan McCormick. And my father was Edward Vincent McCormick, president of McCormick Ford. I was born a twin on June twenty-first, nineteen-forty-six."

I felt a chill. "No," I said. "No, that cannot be."

"My name in the world was Patricia Marie McCormick. That night you called me, I lied to you, Longianna. I went on lying."

"I'm sorry. I can't accept this. I told you those names the night I first spoke with you. Look at you, look at the state you're in. Your mind is playing tricks on you. Stop trying to hurt yourself."

"Longianna, I knew Phillipe Leveque. *Father* Phillipe François Leveque of Saint Catherine's Church on Lemon Tree Lane in the year 1968."

There was no way she could have obtained that information from me.

"They were together, they were always together, Phillipe and Rory. I should have guessed they were lovers, but how could I? After that birth control business blew up, Phillipe became leader of the dissident priests' movement. The Tenth Avenue Six—that's what the papers called them. Cardinal Corby came down on Phillipe like a ton of bricks. Tried to make an example of him."

"You *are* Pat," I said.

"Yes."

"Why did you lie to me?"

"I was afraid. See all I've built up. All of this...this school...my life...my so-called example, it covers up the *scandal.*"

She bent over.

"Can you imagine what it was like, Longianna? I'd go into a room full of talking people and the instant they saw me, they'd clam up. The old ladies—they were the worst, there was so much *pity* in their glances. 'Oh, the poor dear,' they'd say behind my back. 'Imagine having someone like Rory Michael in your family, the *shame.*'"

"You were ashamed of Rory?"

"Yes, yes. Being...being queer was the worst thing you could possibly be. I spent my whole adult life trying to put Rory Michael behind me. When you called and said he had AIDS, it all came back. I couldn't admit that I was the one you were looking for. I wrote down your number...so I could talk to you...."

"So you could use me to *spy* on Rory."

"He was still my twin. But if I admitted it, that scandal would be out in the open again."

"Then you went on lying, to set a good example to your students, is that it?"

"Yes, and—"

"No. Please stop now."

"I can't stop. I need to say it all out loud."

"I don't want to hear any more."

"You must."

"Shut up!" The words were alien in this holy place. "I've just lost one of the most precious friends I've ever had. Tomorrow, I help his mother put him in the ground. You want to wallow in self-pity and your misguided notion of scandal. You're telling me you ran your life by what the Biddy O'Tooles of the world think."

"Times have changed. You weren't here twenty years ago, you don't know—"

"I said, shut up."

Sister Agnes backed away.

"Now, you listen, Pat. And compare this to your neurotic notion of scandal."

I stood up, took off the stole, and draped it over the altar rail.

"Rory's death took *three solid days.*"

Pat covered her ears. "No!"

"By Sunday morning, I wanted to run out of that house, screaming. I didn't leave him. I stayed, right there. And I wished—if he could have been crowned with thorns, scourged, forced to carry a cross up a small hill, and suffer on it for only three hours. If only he could have been *let off easy.*

"You let him suffer. *You let him.* You could have let him know you were there. But that doesn't go with your image, does it?"

"Forgive," she whined.

"Pat," I said, "I can no more forgive you than Phillipe can forgive Adolph Hitler."

I tried to leave, but Pat held on to me. I pushed her off. She darted ahead of me and put her hand over the lock.

"I love you," she whispered.

I saw no way out except to do what the SS did to Madame Leveque's front door. One good kick, and this door flew open.

"I'm lost!" Pat cried. "I'm going to hell."

She didn't follow me. "Carla! Guido!" I called.

Carla was down the corridor, looking at the February sports bulletin board. "What happened?" she asked.

"Tell you later. Come on, let's go. Gimme the flowers and let's get the hell out of here."

We went back up the stairs. "Where's Guido?" I asked.

"Here," he said.

"Didn't you get the car?"

"No, I was waiting for you."

"Go get it. Come on, Carla, we'll wait outside."

"Your coat," she was saying.

"Let's go." I pulled Rory's coat on, but left it unbuttoned.

"Is everything cleaned up?" I asked as we hurried through the corridors. At the other end of the main hall, I saw Cardinal Corby glaring at me.

"Everything's just as we found it. Gianna, what happened down there? I was getting worried."

We were outside. No one else was around and traffic on Wheeler Avenue was sparse. Snow fell steadily.

"You sure you don't want to come with me?" Guido asked.

"No, we'll wait. I have to talk to Carla."

"O. K. I won't be long," Guido promised.

When he was gone, I whispered, "I found Pat McCormick."

"Oh, no," Carla said. "Are you sure...."

I nodded. "No question. It was her."

"Pat was Sister Agnes all along?"

"Yeah," I said, "what a rotten thing to do."

Carla suddenly looked up. "Gianna, do you smell something?"

"Like what?"

"Like...skid row?"

There was a stench of alcohol in the cold air. A man came at us from behind the sign that said BENEDICT CARDINAL CORBY MEMORIAL HIGH SCHOOL.

"You!" he said to me.

I took a step back. In the distance, I saw Guido trying to get my limo around the corner. The car slid on ice, its wheels spinning.

"Who are you?" I said. Then I saw his face. He was the one on TV whom Rory had dismissed as a jerk-off artist.

"What do you want with me, Aloysius Sweeney?"

Don't panic!

Sweeney looked as if he'd written a speech for this occasion but couldn't remember a word of it. That's all I'm sure I saw.

Sometimes, I think I remember a metallic *zing*. My mind will not go any further.

Chapter 21

"*L*ORD, HEAR ME!" PAT MCCORMICK WAILED. "I've been denied absolution. There's no hope for me. And I didn't even get a chance to tell her how I murdered Ma."

Her tears came up from an infinite well. She thought they'd never cease.

"Dear God in heaven, how will I go on with this sin on my soul?"

She staggered out into the corridor, leaning on the wall. Never before had the school been so silent.

"I now know I can't go on. Tomorrow, I'll resign. I'll request to be released from my vows. I'll...what is that sound?"

Perhaps not all of the students had gone home quietly. She heard a series of firecrackers popping outside.

"Five of them. I suppose I must put a stop to that. My last act as principal."

She pulled her large body up the staircase, then heard a woman screaming.

"Help me! Quick, call the police!"

Oh, dear, she thought, *Somebody's gotten entirely out of hand*. She tried to reach the front door but someone blocked her way.

For an instant she thought the students' legend had come true. Benny Corby, and he'd come to life to punish her.

"Good evening, Sister Agnes," the apparition said.

"Aloysius, what are you doing here? Who let you in?"

"Don't I have the right to come in? Didn't I pay for all of this?"

"You're drunk," she said. "You smell like a distillery."

There was another odor coming from him, something hot and burning.

From outside the school there were more screams, clearer now. "Guido, quick! Get help! There's blood all over!" *It was Carla MacIvey.*

"Let me by, Aloysius," Sister Agnes said.

"Why? Nothing's wrong."

"A woman is screaming."

"I don't hear her."

"Get out of my way."

"Sister, nothing is wrong, I've made everything right. Have faith, Sister Agnes. Have faith in *me*."

She pushed him aside. Drunk, he lost his balance and fell. She ran to the open front door. There she froze.

Guido had the limo in the middle of Wheeler Avenue with the lights flashing. He was shouting into the car phone. Carla stood there, screaming. The sleeve of her coat was soaked with blood.

Longianna lay still in the snow.

Pat's scream mixed with Carla's. She tried to go outside, but Sweeney overtook her and pulled her back.

"Look, Sister Agnes. I must tell you—before it's too late. Look....Cardinal Corby. There he is. I did this for him. I destroyed a human life. For him. Because he was a real man."

"You can't get away with this, Aloysius. Listen—the police are coming." Already she could hear sirens and see flashing red lights down Wheeler Avenue.

"Corby was a real man," Sweeney said. "I never got near him while he was alive. Never got to tell him how much he meant to me. I'll tell him now."

He loosened his grip and Pat escaped. She thought she heard another explosion behind her but didn't look back. All she could see was Longianna, in the snow, as still as a statue of a martyred virgin.

***

"No, no, please don't take her away."

It was too late. A pair of paramedics placed Longianna in an ambulance. Blood ran from her nose and mouth. Pat heard them say, "female, late twenties, gun shot wound in right lung, unconscious and in shock."

Carla and Guido went with her. When Pat tried to join them, Guido gave her a firm "no" and shut the door.

They took Longianna away.

Police cars formed barriers on both ends of the block. A yellow tape marked CRIME SCENE DO NOT CROSS went up around Corby High. Crowds gathered behind the barricades. Flashbulbs popped. A van from Channel Two News appeared as if from nowhere. Across the street, the other Sisters watched in horror.

"Oh, please," Pat begged, "please, no scandal."

"Sister Agnes, come with me," a detective said. She knew him. He was Lieutenant Meehan, a sophomore's father, who had given the students a lecture on police procedures. He was with the homicide division.

"This is a serious matter," he said. "We can't have any evidence altered."

"Oh, well, I'll go back to my office and be out of your way." She couldn't go back to the convent and explain this to Sister Edith.

"Sister, I'm afraid I cannot allow you back inside the building."

"And, why not? I'm the principal."

"Sister...."

A policeman held open the door. Two men who had the word CORONER on their coats rolled out a gurney on which lay a covered body.

"Believe me, you don't want to look," Lieutenant Meehan said.

She did look inside and saw clumps of reddish matter clinging to the portrait of Benedict Cardinal Corby.

"Male, about sixty, gunshot wound to head, apparently self-inflicted," one of the paramedics reported. "No vital signs."

Only then did Pat realize what Sweeney had done. He'd placed the barrel of the gun in his mouth....

The slice of pizza Longianna had given her took a flying leap upward. She struggled to hold it down.

"Sister, I'm really sorry about this, but we'll be needing a statement from you," Meehan said.

"It was Sweeney," she said.

"Sweeney? Aloysius Sweeney? You're sure of that?"

"Yes, yes! He did this to her!" She broke down.

Meehan put his notebook back in his overcoat. "We can get the statement later," he said. "For now, you'd better get back to the convent."

"No—wait—Longianna! I must know...."

"Sister, Mercy has the best shock-trauma unit you can imagine. I know. My wife is a nurse there. Ms. Rae is going to get the best possible care—"

"Suppose it's not enough? What if she dies and it's my fault? What if she's already dead?"

She collapsed in the snow. Reporters were shouting in the distance.

"Is that Sister Agnes?"

"Is she the principal?"

"Sister Agnes, did you invite Ms. Rae here?"

"Were you aware of any threats against her?"

"Sister, do you know who shot her?"

She tried to block out what had happened. Yet beside her was a large bloodstain and an outline of how Longianna had fallen. Meehan helped her up.

"Come on, Sister Agnes. Ignore those vultures. I know how tough this is, believe me."

"It will be my fault if she dies. I've no right to ask for a miracle. Not after all I've done. And yet...and yet...look. There's one. This is the miracle which I don't deserve. Oh, thank you," she wept. "Reverend Mother Kristen, thank you for sending me this."

"She's hysterical," Meehan said to his assistants. "Help me get her back to the convent."

They didn't know. They couldn't see the miracle that had taken place right in front of them.

There were white rose petals everywhere. White roses, and they had fallen instead of snow.

***

Pat shook off the effects of a heavy dose of Valium. She looked at the familiar surroundings of the convent infirmary. A brilliant winter sun shone through the window.

Longianna. Is she dead? Was it my stupidity that killed her?

Pat rolled over in bed and turned on a small television. Before the picture formed, a voice said that, "We feel that 'miracle' isn't too strong a word."

A commentator was saying that "Ms. Rae would have been killed if she hadn't been wearing this."

The camera focused on Carla MacIvey's hand. In it, she held a medal with the words "Sancta Kristen Ora Pro Nobis" on it. She turned it over. There was a huge gash in the middle of the white rose.

Pat got out of bed. She opened the window to let in cold air to clear her mind. The commentator came back on the screen.

"The rock world is still reeling from the attempted murder last night of popular singer Longianna Rae. Ms. Rae, whose smash hit 'Forever' is Number One on the Billboard chart, was shot after giving a benefit concert at the Benedict Cardinal Corby High School."

A picture of Corby High, still surrounded by CRIME SCENE tape, filled the screen.

"Aloysius Sweeney, president of the Traditionalist League, an extreme right-wing organization, was charged with the crime. After shooting Ms. Rae, Sweeney apparently turned the weapon on himself and took his own life."

A film of Sweeney's body being carried out of Corby High was shown. Pat saw herself on the periphery.

"Oh, terrific," she said. "Tell me about Longianna, you fool."

"Ms. Rae remains at Mercy Hospital, where her condition has been upgraded from critical to serious."

"I must see her. Even if she still hates me...."

Pat heard footsteps outside the door. She dived back under the covers before the door opened.

"Who left that television on?" Sister Edith asked.

"Why, I wasn't aware," Sister Irene replied.

"I want it off. I'll not have Sister Agnes disturbed further. The doctor said she ought to sleep till at least noon. And who left that window open?" Sister Edith demanded.

"I...I don't know."

"Never have I seen such incompetence. The poor dear might catch her death of pneumonia. Hasn't she been through enough? Oh, why do they call it common sense when there's so little of it!"

Pat jumped out of bed when the sisters left.

There was a small closet here, full of used winter clothing donated for the poor. Even the poor had rejected these leftovers. Pat put on a threadbare coat and scarf and a pair of hideous sunglasses with rhinestones in the frames. She took twenty dollars from her pocket and stuffed it into a cracked plastic purse.

Perfect. No one would mistake her for the principal of Corby High in this ghastly outfit.

She arranged the bed to look as if she were still sleeping, opened the window Sister Irene had shut, and went down the fire escape to the parking lot.

Taking the convent's station wagon would be too risky. She ran out to Wheeler Avenue and hailed a passing cab.

"Where to, lady?" the cabbie asked.

"Mercy Hospital," she said.

"I don't know. Did you hear about that rock star getting shot last night? That's where they took her. They've got screaming teenagers and guards all over the joint. Tough to get in unless you're a doctor. Or you need an operation, quick."

"My daughter is there. She's having a baby."

"Oh, well. In that case."

A previous passenger had left a morning paper on the back seat. Pat read the headline story during the short ride.

"A police spokesman said that five shots were fired at Ms. Rae. The first entered Ms. Rae's right lung. The second ricocheted off her Saint Kristen medal. Another grazed the arm of her secretary, Carla MacIvey, who was treated at Mercy Hospital and released. The remaining two were fired into the air. Autopsy results are pending on Sweeney, but initial tests show a high content of alcohol in his blood."

He was drunk, Pat thought. *Suppose he'd been sober? Suppose Longianna didn't have that medal? That Phillipe hadn't sent it to her?*

Trembling, she looked back at the paper. "Deaths Elsewhere," she read. "San Francisco. Phillipe François Leveque, a former Catholic priest who gained fame in the Sixties as a civil rights activist—"

"Here you are, lady. Lots of luck getting in. Congratulations on your grandbaby."

She thanked him and paid him. The hospital grounds were full of people. There were no screaming teenagers. Instead, Corby students were carrying on an orderly rosary vigil.

Of course, they don't have school, Pat told herself. *They can't get back in the building. Even after the police are finished, we'll need a clean-up. I wonder if they can restore that portrait of Benny Corby. Maybe we can get rid of it and have a poster of Longianna instead. Just like the one in Sweet Daddy's.*

Pat walked beside the students. The disguise was so good that none of them recognized Agnes Agony of the Jungle.

So far, so good. How do I get inside?

There was the Channel Two van. A woman reporter was speaking into a microphone. "A hospital spokesman confirms that Ms. Rae is conscious and able to respond to questions but is still experiencing postoperative discomfort."

Pat bit her lip. She'd heard the term, "postoperative discomfort." Ma, with all her talk of sickness and surgery, had told her that it was one of the greatest understatements ever made.

Longianna is having pain. Dear Lord, help me. I must see her.

She edged her way towards the door. Two armed guards stood there, like angels at the gates of Eden. It didn't look at all promising.

Perhaps I ought to try the emergency entrance, she thought.. *What would I say? "Excuse me, I think my appendix just burst?"*

There was a sudden screech of brakes. An airport cab pulled up beside her and a pack of reporters and photographers ran over to it. An angry-looking woman wearing a full-length mink stormed out.

Longianna? Pat thought. No, this wasn't Longianna. Very much like her. But not Longianna.

Is this her sister? Is this Donna?

"Do you have any statement for us, Ms. Raimondi?" asked a reporter.

"I might have known something like this would happen, sooner or later." Donna snarled. "Always running off. Always taking stupid risks."

Pat was standing so close to Donna she could smell her perfume. She could also feel the rage. *Don't go,* she wanted to say. *Don't go near her till you've quieted down. She's in pain.*

All eyes were fixed on the elegant Donna, not on the female disaster in the background.

"This is just another typical Longiannaism. It's like the time she dropped everything to take care of that sick faggot. I used to call her up and beg her to leave his house. She was cleaning up his messes, spending all night in his room. Lord, have pity. But oh, no, there's no reasoning with Longianna when—"

"Now just a minute."

The voice that rang out was that of Sister Agnes Agony of the Jungle, restoring immediate order to a classroom gone wild.

"What?" the reporters asked. "Who is this? Some bag lady?"

Donna turned to Pat, like an opera singer interrupted in the middle of her greatest aria.

"Who are you?" she demanded.

Pat McCormick took off her scarf and glasses.

"It's Sister Agnes," one of the seniors said.

"Our principal."

"Principal of Corby High," the reporters muttered. Pat felt the hot lights in her face.

"Sister Agnes, would you care to give us a statement?" one asked.

"Well, I *never,*" said Donna.

"You stay and you listen, Ms. Raimondi," Pat said as if to a student who had been hauled into her office for a grave offense. "That so-called faggot you were disparaging was Rory Michael McCormick. My twin brother."

The cameras kept turning. The students passed word on. "Michael was her *twin.* She never said anything."

"My twin loved other men. I failed to accept this. He died, slowly, of AIDS. It was Longianna who stayed with him in my place. When I didn't have the courage or decency to go to him myself. When he needed me the most, I wasn't there. That's the thing I shall regret—forever. And if you call Rory a faggot again, I'm going to—punch you—in the nose!"

So saying, Pat turned away from the cameras, broke free of the crowd, and ran.

"Go after her!" the cameraman said.

"No," said a woman reporter. "Don't. Let her be."

She kept running through the snow drifts, into Good Shepherd Cemetery, to the willow tree. She pushed the snow off the grave where her father was and where her mother soon would be.

"I told them, Dad," she said. "I told the whole world."
Eddie had nothing to say.

***

There. It was done.

Not only had Pat McCormick told the world, she'd submitted her resignation as principal of Corby High and requested release from her vows of poverty, chastity and obedience. Alone now, in her cell, she organized her few possessions.

Tonight, she would go to the Divine Compassion motherhouse upstate, where she'd once suffered under the rule of Reverend Mother Maria Immaculata. This would isolate her from the media and give her time to think out her decision.

She'd have preferred to go to a motel, someplace secular. Not full of nuns. But she couldn't afford it.

From the television downstairs, she heard the anchorman say, "A bizarre new twist today, in the attempted murder of rock star Longianna Rae. The nun who invited Ms. Rae to sing at Benedict Cardinal Corby High School revealed herself to be the long-lost twin of the man who inspired the Number One hit, 'Forever.'"

She paused and listened.

"And if you call Rory a faggot again, I'm going to—punch you—in the nose!" she said aloud. That wasn't the local news, that was the national news.

"Nice going," she said to herself.

There was a tap at the door. "Sister Agnes? May I come in?" Sister Edith asked.

"Of course."

Sister Edith sat on the bed. "I understand your reasons for having to get away," she said.

"Yes," said Pat. "I'm afraid I'm something of a star now myself. And with all those reporters hanging around, my students won't learn a blessed thing. I have to go away from here."

"Well, the students certainly have learned a lot today," Sister Edith said. "A lesson I hope they'll remember."

She thought for a moment. "Sister Agnes, I've your written request to leave the Order of Divine Compassion. I ask that you reconsider. You've been through so much and this should not be done rashly."

"It's what I want," she said.

"Sister," she said, and stopped. "Yes, I know, you probably think of yourself now as Miss—no, *Ms.* McCormick."

"Ah, yes. So many changes in the past twenty years, so much to catch up on."

"I hope you don't mind if I call you Sister. I'd like to think of you that way. Sister...I wish you'd come to me last September and told me Rory had AIDS. I'd have given you permission to go to Los Angeles. In fact, I'd have insisted that you go."

"I'm sorry, Sister. It's too late now. I see how wrong I was. The thing is...I'm not the same person now I was back then."

"Of course," Sister Edith said. "Just let me know when you're ready to leave."

"I will. I want to make sure I haven't forgotten anything."

They both knew what that meant. *In case I never come back.*

As Sister Edith stepped out, the phone in the hall rang. She picked it up.

"Divine Compassion Convent," she said. "Yes? I'm sorry, you'll have to speak up...who? Sister Agnes? May I tell her who is calling? Longianna Rae?"

Pat flew out of her cell. "It's Ms. Rae," said Sister Edith.

"Yes, hello?"

"Sister Agnes?" said a small, weary voice. "Are you mad at me?"

"Mad at you? How can I be mad at you?"

"Last night...."

"Oh, please. You're alive and that's all that matters. But where are you now?"

"I'm out of intensive care. But I'm not supposed to be making calls. I wouldn't have this phone if Kevin hadn't smuggled it to me."

"Kevin?"

"Kevin is Allie's lover. Allie is one of the PWAs I met yesterday. Yesterday. Seems like a million years ago. If the head nurse finds Kevin in here, he's really going to get his fanny smacked. Right?"

"Right, Gianna," she heard a male voice say.

"Sister, I had to call you. First to say that I'm really sorry about the way I blew up at you last night."

"But it was wrong of me. I wasn't thinking—you'd just lost Phillipe—what a thing to tell you right then."

"There's something else I have to say. Before I wear out. I saw you on the news tonight. You were fantastic."

Pat felt her face redden.

"If only you'd seen the expression on Donna's face when you said you were going to punch her in the nose. I laughed so hard I almost broke my stitches. Let me tell you, that stuck a pin right in her ego."

"Why...thank you. But how are you feeling?"

"A bit better than I was this morning. Outside of having a hole in my side big enough to drive the limo through, I feel great. And Sweeney? Did I hear that he did himself in?"

"I'm afraid so."

Longianna paused and coughed.

"Are you all right?"

"Yeah. Sure. Ouch! Oh, ow. No, Kevin, I'm fine."

You're not fine. Pat wanted to say. *You're having pain. I feel it, too.*

"Listen. Do you know my address in Los Angeles?"

"Yes." It had been Rory's address.

"Do you have my home number there?"

"Why, no."

"Here it is." Pat wrote it down.

"As soon as I can get out of this place, I'm going back home to recuperate. I'd like you to come out and see me. I'll buy you a ticket if you need one. There's a lot we have to discuss, you and I."

"Yes, yes, we do."

"I think I hear somebody coming. It's about time to change my dressings. I'll be back in touch. 'Bye."

"Good-bye, Longianna, I love you."

Pat turned to Sister Edith. "I'm going to Los Angeles soon," she said. "There was a miracle. Longianna is going to live."

"I'm delighted," Sister Edith said. "I'll pray for her complete recovery."

Sister Edith took it upon herself to drive Pat to the Divine Compassion motherhouse. All during the trip, Pat spoke of nothing but her conversations with Longianna.

Chapter 22

I FINALLY GOT WHAT I WANTED. I got to be left in peace. And I need this time alone to do all the work I couldn't do after Rory died.

I feel how much I miss him. And Phillipe. And now, Gertrude McCormick.

Gertrude. I came to know her so well. I felt as if she were my own mother.

After I got back home, I had a long phone conversation with Pat about Gertrude. She told me how her mother died.

"Oh, Jesus," I said.

"And I feel as if it's all my fault, Longianna," Pat gulped. "As if I had...murdered her. My own mother."

I couldn't get a word in edgewise as Pat plunged on. "I did as you said. I gathered up all my tranquilizers. And I flushed them down the toilet. But now I have no way to turn off my mind. Nothing to do but to think about the mistakes I've made—all my regrets. If only there were a time machine. If only I could go back to the beginning of my life and undo all the mistakes I've made."

"Sister Ag—excuse me, Pat?"

"Yes?"

"If you did that, you'd be making an even bigger mistake. When you start heading backwards, you're going in the wrong direction."

"Do you really think so?" she asked.

"Of course I do."

"Then—do you think—am I guilty? By not telling Ma that Rory had AIDS...letting her find out by accident—did I murder her?"

"You think you have to face some sort of Kafkaesque trial?"

"Yes. And plead guilty."

"And have someone else pass sentence."

"Thank you. I deserve much more."

"Oh, come on, Pat. Look, it's not any one person's fault."

"Nobody's?"

"I suppose, if it's anyone's fault, it's mine, for getting famous in the first place. How can it be George's?"

"The terrible things George said to the reporter from that trashy paper."

"Pat, I think I'd better tell you. I went to San Francisco and saw George before he died."

"He's dead, too?" Pat asked.

"Yes. May he rest in peace, poor little Georgie. He told me to keep my seat belt fastened. We'd hit some turbulence. That was all he was able to say. I suspect that's all he told that sleezebag reporter, who made up the rest."

"Lord, have mercy," said Pat. "Did George recognize you?"

"I don't know. I had to assume that some part of him did, and I told him I was sorry for all the times I snapped back at him. You know what the hardest part of all is, Pat? The ones I can't reach."

"That you can't—" Pat stammered.

"Not just the ones like George who aren't in their right minds. The ones who *are*. They know exactly what's going to happen to them, Pat, and it hurts them so much they'll take it out on anyone, especially me."

"But—"

"Ah, yes. You're thinking: Longianna the glamorous rock star, she has no problems. The opposite is true. When I have to deal with those who are so full of denial and anger they have to throw it at me...that's tough, Pat. That's really tough."

"Why on earth would anyone take it out on you?" Pat asked.

"Because it hurts too damn much. Phillipe said it best. I'm a big target. Don't go feeling sorry for me, though. This is what I have chosen to do. This is my path. Now, what about your path? What are you doing now?"

"Now?"

"Yes, now."

"I am at the Divine Compassion motherhouse, waiting till all the brouhaha blows over."

"You're not at Corby High any longer? Not teaching any classes?"

"Oh, mercy, no. I'm too controversial."

"What do they have you doing all day?"

"I pray. I reflect. I do the Sisters' laundry. You know, I have requested to be released from my vows, but I don't think any action has been taken on my request."

"Not good, Pat," I said. "What you're doing is stagnating in your past. You have to get on with your life."

"Yes, but how?"

"I wanted to save this till you got to L. A., but I think I'd better tell you now. I've been getting letters from former students of yours who saw you on the news."

"Oh, mercy."

"*Fan* letters, Pat. For *you*."

"For...me?"

"Here's one. 'I had Sister Agnes for science. When I started at Corby High, I was a teenage airhead. I was the one who gave her the nickname Agnes Agony of the Jungle. Sister Agnes didn't take any lip off me. In addition to science, she taught me the meaning of long-term goals and self-discipline. Today I'm training to be an astronaut.' Pat, she says she owes that to *you*. And that's not the only letter I have."

"I think I know who sent that letter," Pat said. "Diane. The girl had the talent; she just needed the motivation."

"Which you provided. If you hadn't, all that talent would have gone down the drain. Here are some other letters. One of your students became a state senator. Another is a Federal judge. Here's a letter from a surgeon. Consider the irony: in a school named after a man who believed that women are created for housework and self-sacrifice, you did so much."

"Longianna, at this point, I hardly feel I deserve a standing ovation."

"Pat, did it occur to you that we were both put into this world for reasons? Mine is to sing. And yours is to teach."

There was a brief silence. Pat said, "I suppose that's what I missed about being a principal...not being in the classroom. Not seeing their minds reaching out. But what can I do now?"

"There's a lot you can do, Pat. That's why I want you to come to Los Angeles, because I'm into an AIDS education project and I need a good teacher."

"You want me?"

I tried not to start coughing again, but it was inevitable. "Excuse me," I said.

"Are you...are you all right?"

"Fine. Fine. I sometimes forget how much that encounter with Sweeney took out of me."

"Oh, dear. I feel...I feel...."

"Don't start wallowing in the past. Besides—you want to hear something really gross?"

"Oh, yes."

"My manager has a wonderful way of expressing himself. He says my being shot is the biggest thing since Michael Jackson set fire to his hair. Believe me, there are a lot of other career moves I would prefer to make."

"If you need me, I'll be there," Pat said. "Just give me two weeks to wrap things up here."

***

Pat didn't look forward to saying goodbye. Yet how different this was from the way it had been twenty years ago. Back then, she would have had to sneak out the kitchen door. This time, although there were tears, there was a sense of a new life beginning.

"Goodbye, Sister Agnes," the students said. "Good luck. We'll remember you forever. Michael, too."

Sister Edith drove her to the airport. As Pat's flight was announced, there was one final embrace, which would have been forbidden under Maria Immaculata's rule.

"There are times I wonder if you'd change your mind," her former Superior said. "You really are the best principal we ever had."

"But, Sister, a plague has broken out and our brothers and sisters are dying. What would Saint Kristen have done?"

"Yes. Of course. Go to them and God be with you."

Pat memorized the details of the airport as the plane picked up speed and took off. It made a slow ascent over the city. Far below, Pat saw Mary Queen of Martyrs Cathedral.

"Good-bye, Benny Old Boyo," she said to the real man, entombed in one of its walls, whose red hat still hung over the altar. "I'm rid of you at last."

There were miniatures of Mercy Hospital and Good Shepherd Cemetery. "'Bye, Dad. 'Bye, Ma."

Before going up through a cloud bank, Pat saw the neat suburban squares of Lemon Tree. Then there was nothing but the tops of clouds and her own reflection in the glass.

Am I...is it possible...that I love Longianna? Suppose I do? I guess the question is: is it so terrible?

She looked in her worn copy of *Circuit*. Strange, she'd never taken time to read the entire article till now. There, under the picture of Longianna cracking up, was:

I guess it's time for me to *come out* and admit it. I really am straight. Naturally, Michael turned me on. Good-looking men have that effect on me. As I said, I know a lot of Lesbians, I respect them, I depend on them, my tax consultant is a Lesbian and I'd be in a fine mess without her, however...."

Sometimes, you can't always have what you want. You have to tell yourself, no. This is off-limits.

Pat closed *Circuit*. "If I love her," she asked herself, "am I like Rory? Have I been like him all along?"

There was a program from Rory's memorial which Longianna had sent to her. She opened it up and read:

"'If I speak with human tongues and angelic as well, but do not have love, I am a noisy gong, a clanging cymbal. If I have the gift of prophecy and, with full knowledge, comprehend all mysteries, if I have faith great enough to move mountains, but have not love, I am nothing."

Pat closed her eyes. It was 1968 again and Rory was reading that passage at a Students for Peace in Vietnam Mass in the chapel at Saint Ignatius College.

"'If I give everything I have to feed the poor and hand over my body to be burned, but have not love, I gain nothing. Love is patient, love is kind....'"

Yes, Rory. You always knew. The worst thing is when you don't love anyone. Nothing else really matters. And you did love Father Leveque.

Rory continued, looking so serious under his long yellow hair.

"'When I was a child, I used to talk like a child, think like a child, reason like a child. When I became a man I put childish ways aside. There are in the end three things that last: faith, hope, and love, and the greatest of these is love.'"

"Yes," Pat said. "And I get crushes on rock stars like a child."

Pat had to think about that. By the time the plane was over the desert, the sky was clear and so were her thoughts.

No. What I feel for Longianna Rae is not what Rory came to feel for Phillipe Leveque. I have a teenage crush, left over from my own teenage years when I thought I was beyond that sort of thing. If it's my nature to love other women...is it so bad? And isn't it about time to find out if I do?

A voice came over the loudspeaker. "Ladies and Gentlemen, this is your captain speaking. We are preparing to land at Los Angeles International Airport."

Free from you, Benedict Cardinal Corby, old boyo. Released from the vow of silence I was forced to give you. Free to be the person God made when he made Pat McCormick. It's a pity He made only one of her. She's wasted enough precious time while the plague wasted none.

Pat leaned back and closed her eyes. A fullness in both ears told her that the descent had started. Soon enough, she would be back on the ground, where Longianna Rae was waiting.